FOREVER, CEDAR KEY

MICHAEL PRESLEY BOBBITT

APHRODITOIS BOOKS

Contents

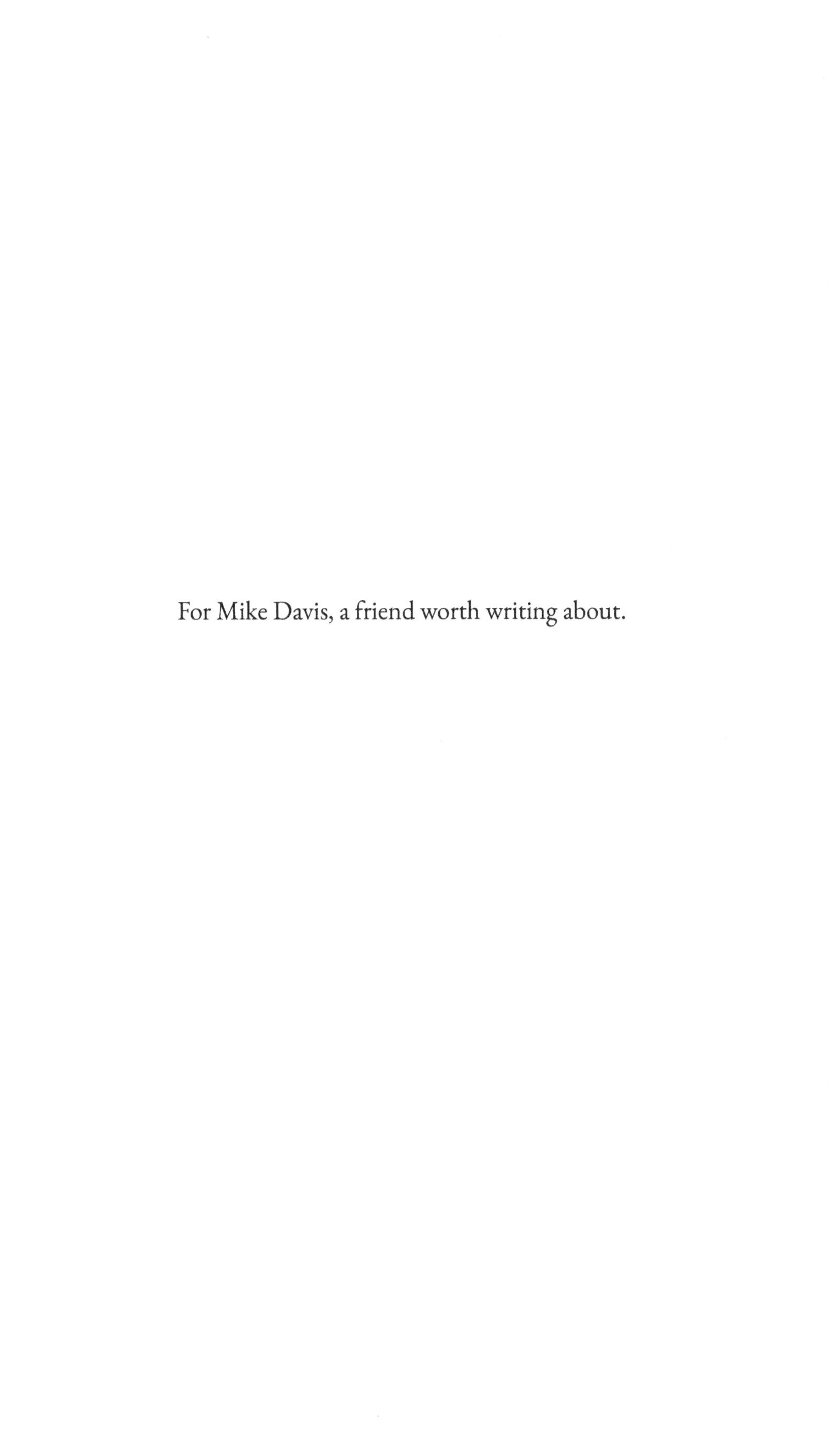

For Mike Davis, a friend worth writing about.

Praise for "Godspeed, Cedar Key"

"... a propulsive, character-driven post-apocalyptic ride... a brutal tale of survival with a refreshingly kaleidoscopic perspective."
Kirkus Reviews

"A touching end of the world story filled with hope and community."
Independent Book Reviews

"The straightforward prose is deceptively rich, drawing readers into a world where adversity is met with unwavering strength and unity."
LiteraryTitan

"Despite the theme of a nuclear tragedy, it's not a dystopian novel, but an excellent piece of literary fiction with rich prose and deeply developed characters."
SA Examiner

2024 Medalist for Literary Fiction
Florida Writers Association Royal Palm Literary Awards

"A few years after a forest has been burned another generation of bright and happy trees arises, in purest, freshest vigor; only the old trees, wholly or half dead, bear marks of the calamity. So with the people of this war-field. Happy, unscarred, and unclouded youth is growing up around the aged, half-consumed, and fallen parents, who bear in sad measure the ineffaceable marks of the farthest-reaching and most infernal of all civilized calamities."

John Muir

PROLOGUE

On the 15th of February in the second year of the new world, a battered Piper Archer burst through low-hanging clouds, sputtering and wild, missing the water tower by a nose hair and plunging, more or less uncontrolled, into the Daughtry Bayou a hundred yards short and wide of the George T. Lewis Airport runway.

An old man emerged from the wreckage, laughing, and began the short swim for home.

1

EVERYTHING OLD IS NEW AGAIN

With no other reasonable thing to do, Cedar Key kept on living.

Luke and Kinsey were married on the one-year anniversary of the flash across the bay when Cedar Key's horizon, like so many around the world, became an instant irradiated blur.

Death had swept across the Wacassassa Bay, taking first the clam boat captains and crews working on the water that cold February morning, then casting her gaze upon the elderly and infirm all around the island. For most of that first year, she was never far away, waiting always to pull others into her embrace. She had stoked the fire of conflict between the islanders and the mainland community of Sumner just across the Number Four Bridge, grinned as she spun up the once-a-millennia hurricane that took Jonah and so many others, warmed herself by the great fire that came for the Baptist Church and a third of the buildings in town, then grew bored and drifted away.

There were two hundred and fifty islanders left, down from an old-world population of just under eight hundred. Almost all of them were on the little beach in the city park, blanketed in the soft pastels of an approaching Gulf of Mexico sunset, to witness the young couple exchange their vows. The lukewarm entanglement of marriage in the modern age seemed as far away from them now as the Civil War. When they promised to love, honor, and protect each other, they were committing to action in a dangerous world. There would be sickness, and care would be required. Forsaking all others would be the easy part; they were wild in love.

Hayes David had been the mayor of Cedar Key for most of his adult life, running the ship of state for the island town in the same hyper-competent, squared-away manner as his obsessively tidy clam boat. He was fussy, fit, discerning, a tireless advocate for the island, and a respected waterman with a deep knowledge of the Gulf. His best friend Thomas Buck was his opposite in almost all ways—an impractical, grandiose-thinking writer and clam farmer who had only avoided the same fate as the other captains because his boat's poorly maintained motor had failed to start on the morning of the flash. Both men were delighted to witness Luke marrying the girl from Sumner, but even in the midst of the celebration, they were preoccupied with the Colonel's return from the sky.

"He barely looks like the same man," Hayes said.

"It is him, though," Thomas replied. "There's that same cockeyed twinkle in his eye he had waving from the plane before he took off."

"How did he survive that long out there?"

Thomas grinned. "Because we sent the right man. I learned a long time ago not to bet against him. That guy's a killer."

"What did he see?" Hayes asked impatiently. "And what took him so long to get back?"

"He'll tell us soon enough. He's only been back a few hours. Geoff and Melinda Beth deserve a little time with him first."

Hayes and Thomas had stayed with the McClouds after the Colonel disappeared into the gray sky those many mornings ago, heading south on a mission to see what remained of the outside world. The islanders had heard almost nothing from the mainland in the weeks since the smokestacks across the Waccasassa Bay were enveloped in a microsecond of piercing light and then simply vanished. While they cared for the clam boat captains and crews caught on the water and overwhelmed with radiation, they could only assume the worst. With so many more strategic targets at the military bases around the state, a bomb for the civilian power plant fifty miles south in Crystal River almost certainly meant an all-out attack—the nightmare total war scenario that had seemed so unthinkable until it hadn't.

The plant's twin hyperbolic cooling towers were never torn down or imploded after its nuclear reactor was taken offline in 2009. It was water vapor, not smoke, that rose from them and blended into the clouds each day, but even when told this fact, people still called them smokestacks. They had dominated Cedar Key's view across the water for more than a half-century. When they disappeared, more than a thousand people living and working near the plant seared into instant inexistence along with them. Slower processes of dying began with the watermen and women working on the clam leases and then, eventually, all across the island and everywhere else.

A year later, the empty stretch of water past the barrier island of Atsena Otie remained a grim reminder of the day the world's forward progress, heretofore undeterred for several hundred years, began its backward march.

There had been enough fuel in the Colonel's Piper Archer that day for a 5-hour reconnaissance flight. By hour six, the quiet, empty sky begot panic. A few hours more brought resignation and sorrow. Most of the crowd that was assembled to watch his return gave up and returned to their homes. When the sun set at the end of the little runway, little hope remained that the Colonel would ever return. He had understood the possibility of encountering deadly radiation if the big cities had fallen, but he hadn't hesitated to accept the mission. He knew that without some information about the wider world, the island could not hope to make the best decisions for its survival. The Marine Corps pilot, now in his seventies, had flown a Sea Knight helicopter throughout his time in-country during the Vietnam War, distinguishing himself with valor in one firefight after another during the Tet Offensive. His island needed the military pilot to fly into harm's way once more, and he had answered a call that seemed, until just hours before the wedding on the beach, to have killed him.

"Hey, Dad, you gonna dance or just stand there yapping?"

Thomas smiled at his son. "Sorry, Luke... be right there."

"Best listen to the boy," Hayes said.

"Alright, Mr. Mayor, you too. The Colonel can wait till morning. My son just got married!"

Hayes and Thomas shifted their focus and joined the party on the beach. Jim Walcox played his old Gibson archtop while Mark David, the mayor's dad, fried shrimp in a giant pot over a fire made from cedar and driftwood.

It was here in the park, many months prior, that the islanders had met for the first joyful gathering since the smokestacks fell. Nearby off Dog Island, Luke Buck discovered the annual arrival of the white shrimp in the waters around Cedar Key. They came every year in huge numbers, but months of gray had cast the Gulf in such a pallor that it hardly seemed to be alive at all. The flits and swirls disturbing the surface of the water had sent a charge through Luke, who used his cast net to fill a kayak full of the enormous, nearly translucent shrimp. When he pushed it across the bay, wading through chest-deep water back to the shore, he was met on the beach by an excited crowd. Word spread across the island, and by sundown, everyone arrived ready to celebrate, dressed in their Sunday best.

So much of the energy and effort those first several months had been required just to stay alive. The shrimp fry in the park was the first bit of real living the islanders had enjoyed since the old world ended. Rogue beams of moonlight found their way through the gray sky for momentary illumination of dancers on the beach. They danced in defiance of a world set against them. They danced because their bellies were full, and their hearts unburdened. They danced for people they lost and those who were saved.

They danced for each other.

A year into the new world, they were dancing again for the lanky, wild-eyed Luke, a few weeks removed from his twenty-third birthday, and the girl from Sumner he had first met hunting in the scrub across the channel with his buddy Ryland. Her avalanche of red hair had given her away in the woods moments after she killed a deer the boys had been stalking. Luke was smitten even before the pools of dark buck blood had cooled in the sugar sand and crisp October air.

Kinsey was related in a distant way to Little Don Meade, the Sumner outlaw who ordered the pre-dawn raid that killed Folksy, the island's Episcopal minister. The islanders had put down the invaders with no additional losses on their side, then mounted a retaliatory strike on the mainland that left Little Don in a pile of bodies and a sickness in their own hearts that time had tempered but not healed. That whole first year was shrouded in difficulty and death.

The wedding on the beach was a reason to hope that maybe this year would be better than the last.

"Just a little while longer." Melinda Beth's tone was loving and instructive in equal measure.

The Colonel smiled warmly at his wife, whose youthful face belied her years. To him, she would always be the girl who cheered for him on the basketball court in high school. The Cedar Key School was the smallest public school in Florida, with senior classes that regularly contained a handful more or less than ten students. With so few kids from which to field sports teams, and despite a rowdy island fan base that packed the school's gym to cheer on their hometown *Sharks*, there were few victories to celebrate. Robert McCloud had an above-average jump shot and stellar hand-eye coordination that would serve him later in life as a Marine Corps pilot, but it wasn't enough to make up for the numbers advantage of the always larger schools they faced. Even when the other team was running up the score, there was always Melinda Beth, smiling at him from the stands.

She was smiling at him again, overcome with the joy of his unexpected return, unwilling to turn loose of him even in service of the island they loved so much, even to let him deliver the message to Hayes that was filling him with such urgency and unease.

The Colonel indulged the warmth of her arms and the smell of her hair on his face for a few minutes more before pulling himself from her and onto his feet. "I'll be right back, I promise."

"The last time you told me that, I lost you for nearly a year. What could be so important, Robert? Tell me."

The old pilot rubbed his face in his hands and looked away. "By my figuring, we've got a day or two before they get here, but we should start making plans now."

"Plans for what?" his bride asked worriedly.

"Maybe you and Geoff should come with me. Everyone should hear it together."

Cedar Key is a southern town. It lies at the western terminus of State Road 24, at its confluence with the Gulf of Mexico in rural Levy County, sixty miles due west from Gainesville and the University of Florida. Until the islanders blew it up to hamper invaders from across the channel, the Number Four Bridge spanned from the mainland to the thirteen-island archipelago first described by Spanish cartographers in 1542 as *Las Isla Sabines* or *Cedar Islands*. Most of the actual town of Cedar Key is situated on Way Key, with the remaining barrier islands like Atsena Otie, North Key, Snake Key, and Seahorse Key having no meaningful development.

When a 1994 constitutional amendment banned the most common type of commercial net fishing in Florida waters, a generational way of life in Cedar Key abruptly ended. Displaced commercial fishermen, keen to keep working on the water, turned to a new government-funded program to develop clam farming in the area. In the thirty-odd years between the net ban and the fall of the smokestacks, Cedar Key became one of the largest producers of farm-raised clams in North America. Most days of the year, a fleet of distinctive bird dog boats could be seen planting and harvesting out on the clam leases.

So it was that awful February morning when first the shockwave, then the heat, and finally the haunted wind overwhelmed the boats on the water. In all, 27 men and two women were cut down together that first day. Dozens more on the island would follow over the coming months, for reasons mundane and tragic, until a grim equilibrium was reached and a difficult but predictable rhythm of life in the new world set in.

They reopened the school and held a candlelit prom. There was a 4th of July parade, and gardens were planted in front yards all around the island. Wood gasifiers, solar panels, and a water tower brought miraculously back to life created a tenuous foothold of stability that would have seemed impossible to the Colonel on the day of his fateful flight. So agitated was he by the information he now carried for Hayes and the others, Melinda Beth's excited stories about all they had accomplished while he was away had failed to make an impression. The McClouds now walked briskly toward the celebration on the beach, the Colonel moving with remarkable fluidity for a septuagenarian who just hours before had crashed a plane into the bay.

"Colonel!" Luke called across the beach when he saw the McClouds approaching. He let go of his bride's hand and ran to meet them. "I heard you were back and was hoping you'd come. Did you bring your mandolin?"

"Sorry, Luke, not this time. But we'll play together soon. The piano at your dad's house still in good shape?"

"Yes, sir. I have to tune it by ear, and my ear's not that good. Maybe we could look at it together."

The Colonel smiled at his young friend, wanting to lean into the comforts of the home he had fought so hard to get back to—knowing he would never tell them everything he had seen and done—then grabbed Luke by the shirt and pulled him close, the hug lingering long enough that even the dancers took notice. The music faded. The Colonel let go.

"Soon, Luke. I promise."

For the next half hour, he did lean in—deciding he was unwilling to ruin Luke and Kinsey's day—though in the revelry, his mind raced with calculations about distance, speed, and time.

Cedar Key sunsets seldom disappoint. The western horizon between Deadman's Key and North Key features unobstructed open water all the way to Playa Escondido on the eastern shore of Mexico. In the old world, weekenders and locals alike would line G Street in front of the Beachfront Motel to watch the sun boil down into the Gulf each evening, hoping to catch a glimpse of the elusive green flash of light so loaded with lore and mystery. The flash is so rare and difficult to see that many dismiss it as legend, but NASA has confirmed it to be a real occurrence, explaining away the mystery by noting that two optical phenomena converge—a mirage and the dispersion of sunlight through the Earth's atmosphere like a prism. Folklore has assigned the green flash a variety of meanings, from a good omen about matters of love to a soul returning back to this world from the dead.

There was no green flash on the horizon that day as the Colonel danced close to Melinda Beth, but in the waning twilight came an even more fantastic sight; enormous, unfurled sails began to fill the Wacassassa Bay.

The Colonel's calculations were wrong.

2

WHAT THE COLONEL SAW

When the wheels of the Piper Archer first cleared the runway, on that thirty-fourth day after the smokestacks fell, the Colonel felt a rush of power he had not experienced since his last firefight during the Tet Offensive in 1968. So energized was he by heroic purpose, the risks associated with the flight were entirely out of mind.

The altimeter showed a steady rate of climb as the Colonel banked hard over Seahorse Key on a heading of 180 degrees—due south toward Tampa Bay. Off his left wing, he caught a final glimpse of his family and neighbors still lining both sides of the runway, then turned his focus to the mission. By the time the relatively slow-climbing little plane reached its cruising altitude of five thousand feet, the town of Weeki Wachee was passing beneath it. When the Colonel and Melinda Beth were still in high school, they skipped school and drove an hour and a half south to see the underwater mermaids at Weeki Wachee Springs State Park. It was the early 1960s, at the height of the attraction's popularity, and the young lovers were mesmerized by the whole experience. Melinda Beth had shushed him when he tried to explain the details of how the performers were able to seemingly breathe underwater. The science was meaningless to her; she was there to soak up the magic.

During his time learning to fly in the Marine Corps, first fixed-wing aircraft and then helicopters, the Colonel grew to intellectually grasp the mechanics of flight, but even when the science was thoroughly ingrained in his thinking, an element of magic remained each time he left the surface of the Earth. To be sure, there had been adventure on the stone crab boat he used to make a living when his military service was completed, usually the result of the Gulf's temper tantrums or motor problems, but nothing that carried him away like the miracle of flight.

It was such a state of dreamy thought that overtook the Colonel as he passed Spring Hill, flying along the coast parallel to US-19, enjoying the tactile sensation of the controls. He could have lingered in that moment forever, when all that mattered was the feeling of weightless freedom, when the stretch of barren nothing ahead of him had not yet registered in his brain as out of place.

Several full minutes passed as the Archer cut a placid 115 knots per hour through smooth, crisp air toward a horror beyond anything the Colonel had seen in southeast Asia. There, at least, the destruction had been incremental, targeted. Approaching what should have been Tarpon Springs, he finally processed the scene before him. He had flown this route more times than he could remember; by now, the undeveloped stretches of North Florida should be behind him, and the unending sprawl of the greater Bay area should be filling his field of view—Dunedin, Clearwater, Tampa, Saint Petersburg.

For a moment, the Colonel felt like a new pilot again, disoriented by the scenery outside his plane that did not square with the instruments inside. He remembered his first flight instructor's frequent admonition: *whatever happens, just keep flying the aircraft.* So he kept flying, south from the relative verdancy of the Nature Coast, south into a near total absence of manmade landmarks, south a thousand years into the past.

If the actual bay of Tampa Bay and the Hillsborough River were not still clearly discernable, the Colonel could easily have misjudged his position to be above a foreign planet. Dumbstruck, he just kept flying the aircraft, past the enormous gray cavern that had been the U.S. Central Command at MacDill Air Force Base, past a stretch of water that had once been spanned by the imposing Sunshine Skyway Bridge, south past his intended turnaround point, south past Sarasota until, at last, stretches of roadway could be seen again.

Little remained of Sarasota proper, but the orientation of Tamiami Trail across the Intracoastal from Siesta Key and bits of Interstate-75 beyond that helped to reorient his general thinking. The information he had come for was obtained, and already he was further south than intended, but just as he began an aileron roll that would turn the Archer northward again, the Colonel caught a speck of movement ahead of him. It was then, against the juxtaposition of the movement, that he could appreciate the horrifying stillness that had punctuated his entire flight that day. Before the quick burst of movement that was too far away to be identified, all below him was stillness, somber as a hymn.

Rolling back toward the movement, south again away from home, the Colonel strained to make out the details of an object that blurred into the sky one moment and the water the next. By then, the old military pilot had regained full situational awareness, so the decision to pursue the object was made with a clear understanding of its consequences. If he didn't turn for home within the next half hour, the Archer would lack the fuel to make it back to Cedar Key. The universe of stillness thus far in the trip and in the weeks since the smokestacks fell, however, made the moving object an irresistible target.

The Colonel continued south.

For seventeen minutes, he saw no additional movement. Stump Pass and Don Pedro Island were easy to identify off the left wing, as was the distinctive round shape of the Rotunda West area of Englewood. Few buildings remained, but the unnatural circle of roads was unmistakable from the air. A light rain started falling along the Gulf coast, and sporadic, higher-level clouds thickened and moved lower as the Archer continued south. As he neared the decision point for turning back, VFR flight conditions remained, but visibility was diminishing.

Approaching the northern edge of Boca Grande and the Gasparilla Sound, the Colonel tried to process the grim demography of the missing cities and the likely millions of dead Floridians beneath him. He indulged the bleak calculus a few seconds longer before a flash of movement returned to the water ahead of him, much closer now than before. The plane and the object had been moving in the same general direction, but the aircraft's faster speed was closing the distance between them. The next flash of movement solved the mystery. Rounding the back side of North Captiva Island, whose land mass had hidden it for a time from the approaching airplane, came the 87-foot United States Coast Guard Cutter *Sawfish*, a marine-protector class patrol boat.

In the old world, these types of cutters were used to combat drug smuggling, illegal immigration, and commercial fishing violations, along with search and rescue support. Boarding operations were conducted from the cutter's stern launching platform that housed two fast-moving rigid-hull inflatable boats. A pair of 50-caliber machine guns were mounted near the bow. The cutter is normally powered by diesel engines that can push it to a maximum speed of 26 knots while consuming 26 gallons of fuel per hour.

The sight of the Sawfish nearly took the breath from the Colonel, who felt a rush of elation at the thought of the U.S. military continuing to operate. A vessel this size implied the existence of infrastructure sufficient to run it— a government and a nation that yet endured. The feeling and the implication ended instantly when the Colonel made out sprawling sails fastened to the cutter with makeshift rigging. In such a configuration, the Sawfish was dreadful to behold, a hulking anachronism sailing against its place in time. Still, the Colonel flew south toward it, hoping against his better judgment that good news was somehow still possible.

The likelihood of an airplane's VHF radio being able to contact a civilian boat was near zero, as aircraft and marine radios use different frequency bands, but the Colonel knew that Coast Guard stations and vessels monitored the international aeronautical emergency frequency.

He switched his radio to 121.5 MHz, clicked the mic with his thumb, and began a frantic broadcast, "Coast Guard vessel abeam North Captiva Island, this is Piper Archer November 82083, approximately 10 miles north of your position. Do you read?"

No response.

"Coast Guard Vessel abeam Captiva Island, do you read?"

Still no response.

The Colonel grabbed a small, printed binder from a compartment on his left, flipped through an index of nearby airports, and began broadcasting his call on their various Common Traffic Advisory frequencies, hoping, irrationally, that the cutter might be listening. When he was met with only more silence, he pulled back on the throttle and began a controlled descent toward the water.

It took some time, miles, and a hard slip maneuver to burn off four thousand feet of altitude by the time he neared the cutter that seemed to now be actively tracking toward his position. Leveling off at five hundred feet, the Colonel put the Archer into slow flight just above its stall speed and made a pass near the cutter, rocking the wings back and forth as he flew by. There was an immediate response from the Sawfish, a flurry of moving bodies, and a lowering of sails to slow its forward progress. The Colonel, delighted, made a wide turn and lined up for another pass, his eyes peeled for some signal or acknowledgment from the slowing craft. The pace of the movement on the deck of the Sawfish increased as the Archer flew by again. On the Colonel's third such pass, a few hundred yards out, he noticed two men, not in uniform, running toward the bow. Before he had time to process the positions they took at the mounted 50-cals, they were already firing upon him.

An icy calm descended on the Colonel, who pushed the throttle hard full and made an immediate evasive roll, staying just ahead of the reflexes of the gunners. He began a turning climb away from the bow of the boat, but the 180-horsepower Lycoming engine of the Piper Archer made only 667 feet per minute on its best day, so there was little hope to outclimb the rounds chasing after him. The Colonel's evasive maneuvers continued, placing his aircraft at a difficult angle for the mounted guns to effectively engage him. This strategy might have won the day and effected his escape were it not for the half dozen men on the stern of the boat now firing 5.56 mm rounds at him from rifles. Two rounds cut through the thin aluminum of the cockpit and out the other side, a third lodged in the dash, disabling the attitude indicator, and a fourth, fifth, sixth, and seventh punched holes in the wings.

Fuel began to stream from the tanks in both wings, but the Colonel still had control of the Archer. Calmly, methodically, he kept flying the aircraft, continuing to gain as much altitude as possible and eventually putting a safe distance between himself and the Sawfish as the building rain and clouds obscured his position.

Twelve hundred feet above the Gulf, the last of the fuel in the porous tanks streamed out into the sky. The Archer's motor sputtered, surged briefly again, and then fell silent. The Colonel, cool and sharp as ever, put his aircraft into a controlled glide toward the long, white-sand beach of Cayo Costa Island, seen only in brief glimpses as it peeked through small breaks in the cloud bank.

"Mayday, mayday, mayday," the Colonel announced reflexively over the radio before remembering that no one was left to hear the call.

The dancing stopped suddenly.

"Oh no," whispered the Colonel to Melinda Beth.

The wedding attendees crowded shoulder to shoulder along the water's edge, straining to get a better look at the boats beneath the wall of sails. They seemed to be piling one upon the other in the main channel just beyond Atsena Otie. By the time the flotilla—or armada, depending on intentions that hadn't yet become clear—stopped in formation abeam the fishing pier at the end of Dock Street, it blended more by the minute into the gray evening.

Hayes called out, "Captains, muster your crews. Get to your boats!"

The Colonel shouted back, "I know these people. They're not friends."

"Colonel, you're with me," the mayor replied.

Luke kissed his new bride quickly and followed after Hayes and his father. All around, men and women sprinted from the shore, through the city park, and toward the docks along the back canal off 3rd Street, where the bulk of the makeshift island navy was moored.

After his flagship was destroyed in the opening salvo of a Sumner War that never fully materialized, Hayes' bay boat, the Cogency, was fitted with a wood gasifier that fueled its Suzuki outboard motor and electric generator, rigged with rifle mounts on the bow and stern, and put into service. There was a steampunk aesthetic to the island navy, its modern boats piled high with scrub oak and pine logs to feed bulky contraptions that fueled their motors.

In the years between the First and Second World Wars, many European nations began to perfect a device that could turn wood into a combustible compound known as wood gas. It could be built with ordinary components, and the basic design was remarkably simple. Wood was burned in a low oxygen environment that prevents combustion, resulting in gases that are then burned at high temperatures in a separate container to produce a substance that can power internal combustion engines.

Mr. Johan, a 94-year-old Swedish transplant to the island, had grown up with the now mostly forgotten technology and shared its design with Hayes and Thomas before he was taken by the great hurricane. Along with rooftop solar panels scavenged from vacant second homes or the homes of the dead, gasifiers were responsible for the island's rapid advancement from the pre-industrial circumstances facing it during the early months after the smokestacks fell.

It took some time for the crews to make it to their boats, the fires to be started, and the wood gas to start flowing. As they worked to ready the Cogency for departure, the Colonel told a jumbled, bullet-point version of what he knew about the vessels they had all just seen, but in the frenzy of the moment, it was nearly indecipherable. By the time Hayes led a formation out of the back channel and into the bay, a dark night was stretching out in front of them. The temperature dropped quickly toward the dew point, and a light fog rolled gently across the water. Visibility was impeded to some degree but not enough to explain what they encountered as they reached the fishing pier. Where there had been sails stretched from Dock Street to Atsena Otie was now just open water and channel markers.

"Where'd they go, Dad?"

Thomas replied, "I don't know, son."

Hayes relayed orders over the radio, sending boats around the backside of the barrier island while the Cogency motored into the channel on a heading toward Seahorse Key.

"They didn't just disappear," Mark David yelled from the bow. "If we gotta cover every inch of the bay, we'll get 'em."

From Snake Key all the way to Gulf Jackson, the patrol pushed into the night, finding only darkness and a building chop from an offshore front moving toward them. After hours with no success, Hayes recalled the fleet to the back channel, frustrated and confused. A crowd of captains gathered on his clam dock, looking for answers.

The husky, belligerent Joey Bannon paced the dock in a huff. "I don't like feeling crazy, Hayes. I know what I saw."

"We all saw them."

Geoff McCloud had overseen the island's chicken breeding program in the early days of the new world, becoming something of an expert in the field. He was less skillful on the water but had managed to convert his father's pontoon boat into a capable, if lumbering, gunboat in the new navy. "Maybe some kinda mirage," he said.

Joey replied, "There ain't no goddamn mirage makes a dozen sailing ships appear and then disappear. No disrespect, but let's get serious here."

"No... no, I don't guess there is," Geoff said meekly.

The Colonel stepped to the middle of the gathering and ended the speculation. "Those ships are real. I thought we had a day or two more before they got here. The wind must have been with them."

"How do you know all this?" Hayes asked.

"Bad luck, I reckon... luck too bad to even believe," the Colonel replied. "But what you need to know now is these people are here on purpose and we likely didn't find them out there because they're being led by a man who knows these waters as well as us."

"How?" asked the mayor. "Who could that be?"

"Buddy Skipjack's boy."

The name hung in the air, and the men on the dock fell silent.

"Dammit," said Mark David at last, looking toward Allen Mikes, who stared quietly into the distance.

3

STOLEN CLAMS

The commercial fishermen in Cedar Key are not a delicate bunch. When a single persuasively worded paragraph on a 1994 ballot took away their nets, removing them from the work of their fathers and grandfathers, heavy resentment hung over the island for several years. Boxes of roofing nails were routinely thrown into the water at the two main boat ramps in town, targeting the recreational fishermen who were the perceived instigators of the net ban. Even after the Harbor Branch Oceanographic Institute utilized grant money to retrain many of the fishermen as the first new clam farmers in the state, hard feelings remained.

Net fishermen were islands unto themselves, spending the majority of their lives in the solitude of the Gulf, chasing mullet and chasing away from the cares of the world. Clam farming grew to be a reliable living and even a path to prosperity for some, but while the nets were a way of life, the clams were in many ways just another job.

It was against the backdrop of this discontentment, in the early spring of 1998, that clams began to go missing from several farmers' leases.

Mark David saw the other captains on the dock at the outside boat ramp as he returned from his leases, his insides boiling from what he had just discovered.

Robby Witt, one of the first fishermen to complete the retraining course and get clams in the ground after the net ban, called out, "You too, Mark?"

"A hundred damn bags. How bout you?"

"Just fifty for me, but they got Allen for three hundred."

Allen Mikes was a bruising trunk of a man, hardened from a life fighting crab traps in bad weather, and any man that crossed him for any reason at all. There was a terrifying calm about his demeanor; even in the midst of a fight, his fury was calculated and purposeful. When he said a thing, it was taken by all who knew him as gospel. As he considered his stolen clams and those of his friends, Allen picked at a back tooth, spit something into the water, and said, "I'm gonna find the sumbitch, and I'm gonna cut his nuts off. You can count on that."

The stolen clams were reported to Florida Fish and Wildlife Conservation Commission officers—game wardens to anyone that was ever caught with an undersized redfish in the cooler—but they were little help. In their defense, the clam leases were spread across a large area of the Gulf and the thief was almost certainly operating at night. The odds of catching them in the act, even with a dedicated surveillance operation, were long.

For several months, clams continued to disappear. Because the net ban had driven so many of the island's men to the brink of bankruptcy, the foothold of stability provided by the new business of clams remained a tenuous one. Every lost bag of clams would have brought the farmers around a hundred dollars at market, but their disappearance cost them something more. Each day that passed without a thief in custody pushed the watermen toward a collective rage that ate away at their guts. A sign-up sheet was created, and two boats began patrolling every night from dusk until dawn, one at the Gulf Jackson leases on the western side of the island, and the other at the Dog Island leases to the east.

The stories that comprise the folklore of a place, true or apocryphal, tend to grow in scope and consequence over time and from one retelling to the next. It's the big events that get most of the attention, but most legends begin small—a quiet decision or a mundane action that builds into something of consequence. So it was in the small hours of a Wednesday morning in the early years of the Cedar Key clam industry, a quarter mile north of Gomez Key on a lease farmed by the cantankerous Hodge Hals, that a tiny flicker of light tore apart the stillness and raced toward infamy.

"Did you see that?"

"Yeah... I mean, maybe," Mark David replied.

Allen Mikes squinted in the direction of the flicker. "I definitely saw a light."

Mark said, "I'm afraid if I start the big motor, they'll take off, and we won't be able to catch 'em."

"Let's creep that way with the trolling motor and see what we can see."

The old friends sat on the edge of their seats in the 19-foot skiff as it quietly knifed through the dark water.

Another flicker.

"Shhh..." Allen whispered.

The skiff pushed on. The new moon had left a night so dark the entirety of the Milky Way seemed to be enveloping them. Stars and planets crackled with light and energy overhead, but near the water, they could not see their hands in front of their faces. A northerly wind pushed the sound of the electric trolling motor and the moving boat behind them as they moved, cloaking their advance in the sounds of the Gulf.

Then a crash of wood and fiberglass, a rush of movement and yelling, a chain reaction begun that would change the island and these men forever, as the skiff ran broadside into another boat.

Mark David flipped the switch on a handheld spotlight, blinding a man atop bags of clams in the other boat and backlighting a crazed Allen Mikes as he leaped from the skiff toward him.

The clams in the other boat had definitely been planted by Hodge Hals, but the bloody man atop them now was definitely not Hodge Hals.

"Alright, Allen, that's enough. You're gonna kill him."

"Isn't that what we came here to do... find the sumbitch and kill him?"

Mark David let the blows continue a few moments more. "Not like this. We got to take him to the others. They need to see his face."

"What in hell for?" asked Allen. "Let's dump him at the wreck out past the reef."

"We aren't the only ones that was stolen from. This decision ain't just ours to make."

"Aww hell," Allen replied, throwing the thief down onto the stolen clams, his body landing still and heavy. "Toss me that line, and let's pull the boat back with us. At least ol' Hodge will get some of his clams back."

The other patrol boat was radioed with the news. It had a shorter ride back to shore, so by the time Mark and Allen reached the outside ramp, word had already raced across the island. Nearly every clammer from the fleet was at the dock to meet them.

"Who is it?" Robby Witt asked as Allen secured the skiff and pulled the line attached to the other boat, bringing it alongside the dock as well.

Allen replied, "I didn't recognize him right off, but it was pretty dark, and I wasn't in a thinking state."

"By the time I got a good look at him," Mark added, "He was worked over pretty good."

Just then, the man in the boat began to stir, pulling himself up to a seated position. Multiple flashlights illuminated his face such that his battered features were clear to the gathered crowd.

"Please...," he said. "I'm sorry."

In the frenzy of the moment, his words were an incitement.

"Piece of shit," Joey Bannon said, lunging toward the boat, failing to reach the thief only when three of the other captains held him back.

From the back of the crowd came a muted voice. Twenty-three-year-old Hayes David, a few weeks away from his election as the youngest mayor in the history of Florida, knew that the bad business before him was best left to the older captains. Still, a moment of recognition had hit him, and without thinking, he said, "Mr. Buddy!"

In Cedar Key, as in many southern towns, there existed an unwritten protocol for cross-generational interactions. It would be unthinkable for a person Hayes' age to call an elder by their first name alone. Unless they knew one another well, the required salutation included a Mr. or Ms. paired with a last name. If they were friends, the Mr. or Ms. could be paired with the older person's first name. The fact that Hayes had called him Mr. Buddy and not Mr. Skipjack was due to the friendly interactions they had always shared when Buddy Skipjack brought mullet and blue crabs to his family's fish house to sell. From time to time, they would also pass each other on the water, always with a little wave and a smile.

"That boy of yours is gonna run everything one day," Hayes had overheard Mr. Buddy telling his father when he was younger. As he surveyed the disgraced man now in the boat, he could remember how happy those words had made him feel, and this nostalgia overtook him.

"There's gotta be some mistake," Hayes yelled above the agitated voices.

Mark David cast a withering glance toward his boy. "Best head on back home, son."

There is a moment in most young men's lives when first they push back against the absolute authority of their fathers. It had taken Hayes longer than others, owing mostly to Mark David's impenetrable demeanor. It was as surprising to Hayes as it was to everyone else at the dock that this moment would happen in such a public way.

"No sir," Hayes replied sharply. "I've got clams out there, too... and I know Mr. Buddy good as any of you. What are you gonna do with him?"

The younger David's ascendancy ended as quickly as it began.

"I wasn't asking, Hayes."

As he turned to walk away from the crowd, Hayes managed meekly, "Whatever Mr. Buddy did, he's still one of us."

None of the men on the dock were swayed. Buddy Skipjack's crime was stealing clams, but they meant to punish him for a good deal more— the months of worry leading up to the vote to ban the nets, the years of struggle and listlessness that followed, the persistent hum of loss that did not quiet even when clam money surpassed their earnings from the mullet boats. There would have been no outcome but brutality in store for the thief, save for the intervention of the Chief of Police.

"Step aside, gentlemen."

Chief Vernon had lived his whole life on the island but was relatively new to the job, having spent most of his career as a Florida Highway Patrol officer. He knew the momentum of the evening was pushing toward a thing he could only stop with decisive action. When none of the captains gave way, the Chief turned quietly but quickly back to his truck, producing a 12 gauge from behind the seat and firing it over the crowd.

Among lesser men, such a blast might have caused panic; on the dock this night it served only to open a narrow path between Vernon and Buddy, the captains murmuring curses as they took begrudging half steps to one side or another. With the shotgun under one arm, the Chief pulled Buddy from the skiff and onto the dock.

"This doesn't concern you, Vernon," shouted Robby Witt.

"Go home... all of you," replied the Chief. "You'll be glad I showed up once you've had time to think it through. No amount of clams is worth killing for."

Allen Mikes, expressionless, seethed, "It ain't about the clams."

"All the same, nobody's getting killed tonight."

The Chief knew his life thereafter on the island would be more difficult, but he was, despite moral failings as myriad as any other man on the dock, committed to his work and to the law. Buddy stumbled along beside him, relieved to be under arrest.

On the way to the county jail, Buddy and the Chief chatted as amicably as they could, given the circumstances. Buddy was just beginning to explain his actions, seeking some kind of forgiveness, if not absolution, when a tight spasm clenched the muscles in his chest. He took two hard breaths and let out a faint whimper.

"What's that?" asked the Chief.

Buddy did not reply, slumping over quietly in his seat, graveyard dead.

Buddy Skipjack's death was a problem.

The coroner's report listed heart failure as the official cause, but the beating from Allen Mikes had left a body so bruised and cut up that controversy was unavoidable. Despite a wall of silence from the clam farmers and even Chief Vernon, few believed the official account. Controversy gave way to scandal when the Skipjack family held an open-casket funeral.

Abraham *Buddy* Skipjack was survived by a brother in north Georgia, two elderly uncles in the panhandle of Florida, a handful of cousins in mainland Levy County, and a single child that lived with him on the island, a sixteen-year-old boy he named Isaac because his wife told him to. The Old Testament symbolism was lost on Buddy, but had he known the story of Abraham's absolute obedience to God—the perverse willingness to sacrifice his only son on Mount Moriah to prove his devotion— he would have objected to the name. Despite a record of failures in most other areas of life, Buddy was a devoted father with dreams that skipped past his own life and focused squarely on Isaac and his well-being.

Upon seeing the condition of his brother's corpse, Jacob Skipjack vowed to solve what he viewed as a murder, plain and simple. Several well whiskeys deep at the Island Hotel's Trident Lounge, he swore vengeance on the whole island to anyone that would listen. Johnny Beacham, a short-tempered blue crabber, got tired of listening and "Popped him in the snoot," as Mark David tells the story. When it became clear after the funeral that Buddy was leaving behind no money or property to speak of, Jacob Skipjack skipped out of town, taking home a crooked nose and leaving a too-young nephew behind to mostly fend for himself.

Jacob Skipjack's righteous indignation may have been less than sincere, but young Isaac was genuinely tormented by his father's death. When the older cousin that was put in charge of the boy began to disappear for weeks at a time, various islanders did what they could to look after him. Modest social security benefits kept the wolves at bay, but Isaac's struggles only increased over time. The weight of his father's death, especially the mystery that surrounded it, pushed in on the boy's chest each night as he lay in bed fighting sleep.

One morning in that spring of 1998, a few weeks after Buddy's death, Mark David noticed Isaac Skipjack sitting on a bench near the boat ramp as he launched his bird dog full of clam bags that needed planting. The boy sat quietly, staring into the Gulf. He possessed a striking calmness for a person his age, to the point that adults were often unsettled by it.

Mark David, unsettled by nothing on Earth, called out to him, "You okay, son?"

"Yes, sir, Mr. Mark. Thanks for asking, but I ain't nobody's son anymore."

Mark stared for a moment at the throttle of his 28-foot Trembly bird dog, trying to will himself into pushing it forward and leaving the trouble of the boy behind. He couldn't help but fixate on the mental picture of Isaac's father atop the stolen clams, withering beneath the blows from Allen Mikes. He grasped the throttle hard but could not move it forward. Finally, too much time had passed, and Mark had to say something.

"Aren't you supposed to be in school?"

"I am," Isaac replied.

"So why aren't you?"

"What's it to you?"

"Look here, you little shit," Mark shot back. "I don't guess I care whether you're in school or not... but it's too nice a day to waste sittin' on a bench like a damn hobo. You hurt or disabled somehow?"

"No, sir."

"Well, you got two choices then, son. I can call Chief Vernon down here, and he'll haul your lazy ass back to class... or you can come with me and learn how to plant clams."

"I know how to plant clams," Isaac replied, a tepid defiance rising in his voice. "My daddy taught me."

"Well, come on then."

Isaac made his way onto the boat without protest, wrapped his arms around the power roller at the stern, and held on tight as Mark David threw the coals to the motor and sped away. In a few minutes, they had made the short ride to the Dog Island clam leases.

In New England, wild clams are harvested from the mud with rakes and tongs, a back-breaking and tedious endeavor. Clam farming in Cedar Key was conducted at scale, with clams grown in bags of twelve hundred each, staked to the floor of the Gulf on submerged land leased from the State of Florida.

"How many bags you planting today?" Isaac asked as Mark throttled the motor to an idle and glided onto lease L-802.

"Just a hundred."

"That's a lot to do by yourself," Isaac replied.

"Hayes was supposed to be helping, but he's got some kind of stomach bug."

"My dad wouldn't have let me out of work just for being sick."

Mark chuckled. "Well, I didn't need him shittin' on my boat. And I don't mind being out here by myself. It's peaceful."

"Sometimes I'd plant 40 or 50 bags by myself but never a hundred."

"Then it should be easy work for the two of us."

Mark threw Isaac a pair of rubber work gloves and hopped overboard into the waist deep water. Isaac put them on and followed. The late morning sun reflected off the glassy water, blending Gulf and sky into an infinite loop. Just beyond the boundary of the clam lease, two dozen white pelicans floated aimless as clouds, stupid and regal, their eyes still pale blue from the breeding season but fading into the dull hazel of summer.

Isaac proved his worth, needing little instruction from the more experienced waterman. They soon found a rhythm in the work, Mark dipping briefly underwater to set the corner stakes of the first bag into the soft bottom of the Gulf while Isaac walked backward, unrolling the belt—five clam bags fastened together—following directions so that a straight line was made between the first bag and the last. When Mark gave the thumbs up, Isaac would sink down to set his corner stakes; then, each man would work down one side of the belt, setting a stake at each junction of bags.

In a little less than an hour, Isaac pulled the last belt of clams off the back of the boat, shouting, "Last belt!" at the top of his lungs.

"What are you yelling for?" Mark asked.

"Oh, sorry," Isaac said, embarrassed. "It's dumb."

Mark pressed, "I'm the captain here. The captain decides what's dumb and what ain't."

"It's just a thing my dad and I did. I don't remember how it got started, but whenever we got down to the last belt, whoever pulled it off the boat, usually me, would yell *last belt* and anybody else working that day, usually just him, would yell it back and then we'd laugh about it."

Mark felt a sting in his belly but made no outward showing of it. "I don't guess that's too dumb. Why don't we give it a shot."

Before he had time to feel much about it, Isaac belted, "Last belt!"

When Mark boomed the enthusiastic reply of, "Last belt!" long and low like the sound of an oncoming train, a wave of complicated feelings overtook them both and they finished the rest of their work contemplative for reasons that were different but fundamentally connected.

Back at the dock, Isaac sat on the same bench where Mark had found him earlier, reasoning that his labor had purchased amnesty from returning to school that day, and the business between them was over. Before heading to get his truck and trailer, Mark pulled a fifty from his wallet and handed it to the boy.

"You don't have to do that," Isaac said.

"Goddamnit, son. You don't get to tell me anything, you understand?"

"Yes sir, I just…"

"It's a hundred for a full day's work, so this is more than you deserve, but I ain't got no change, so just take it."

Isaac was a quick study; he took the money with no additional protest.

"Thank you, Mr. Mark."

"You won't thank me tomorrow. It's a Saturday, so be here at the dock at 6 AM, ready to put in a day's work and then some. We'll harvest in the morning and plant just after lunch. You get your full hundred, but I aim to work a little extra out of you for overpaying today."

"Wait... huh? Just like that, we're working together now?"

"Shit no, we ain't working *together*. You'll be working for me. And don't even think about being late."

That's how it all started—the complicated relationship between a boy who had questions about his father's death and the elder waterman who had answers he could never share.

4

— · —

THE BATTLE OF DEER ISLAND

By Hayes' count, there had been at least ten vessels under sail in the channel. It was inconceivable to him that none were seen again during their search. As he lay in bed, sleep eluded him as he fixated on the missing boats and the unbelievable stories the Colonel began to share with him in private after the other captains left the dock.

While he stared toward the ceiling, a detailed map of every island, cove, creek, and bay ran through his mind. His earliest memories were in those waters with his dad and Uncle Allen. As a teenager, he had captained his own net boat from the lost shore of the Wacasassa to the reef past Seahorse Key and even north into the Suwannee River, bringing his catch to his family's fish house in the canal between Fannie's Café and the marina. The longer he searched these memories for an idea of where the mysterious vessels could be, the more his temper—quick and destructive in his youth but tempered now by the punishment of age— welled up within him.

At the Wabi-Sabi cottage on E Street, the abandoned former vacation rental where they made their home, Luke and Kinsey Buck spent their first night together as a married couple. When Luke returned from the unsuccessful search, he called to his bride from the front porch. She came out to meet him, and he swept her up into his arms and carried her across the threshold because his dad had told him it was a thing he was supposed to do. Kinsey leaned down and kissed her husband as he continued carrying her across the modest living room and into the one small bedroom of the cottage. There were questions to be asked and fears to be assuaged about the sailing vessels that had interrupted their wedding celebration, but not before the last of the wedding day rituals was finished.

Afterward, staring quietly at one another in the low light of a small candle, Luke was content to let the outside world stay outside the walls of the Wabi Sabi, but he could tell Kinsey wanted to talk.

"You okay, honey?" Luke asked.

"I'm always okay when I'm with you," she replied, meaning it, of course, but not answering the question he was actually asking.

"The sooner you tell me, the sooner we can talk about it," he said.

"It's just," Kinsey began, pausing for a moment, almost changing her mind, then continuing, "I remember how stirred up everybody got when they thought the people from Sumner were about to attack again."

"Me too," Luke said.

"And the kid from Sumner they caught planting that stupid flag on the beach... you said if Mr. Hayes hadn't intervened, they might have really hurt him."

"I don't think it would have really come to that," Luke replied.

Kinsey pulled gently away from Luke and sat up on the bed. "I was in Sumner when the islanders came after Little Don for what he did to your minister."

"He had it coming," Luke said, the first stirrings of defensiveness finding their way through the lingering glow of the sex.

"He did, Luke. I believe you. But all the others, the ones that got caught up in it—"

"I know," Luke said, interrupting her but not meaning to. "I know it got out of hand. But we didn't start any of it."

"I had to help them bury the bodies, Luke. It took three days."

"I know how awful that must have been," Luke said looking away.

Kinsey had the upper hand now, but she would wield it gently. Even in his naiveté, Luke so pleased her heart that she sought only to find understanding between them.

"I'm just worried things might get out of hand again if you find the sailing ships."

"We're gonna find them," Luke said confidently.

"Then what?"

"I'm not sure," Luke replied. "The Colonel says they're not friends."

"Does that make them enemies?" Kinsey asked.

"I guess we have to treat them that way until they prove otherwise. We've got too much to lose to let our guard down, " Luke answered reflexively.

"That seems backward to me," Kinsey said. "And a way to always be fighting somebody."

Luke could not think of a good response, because he could see the obvious wisdom in her point of view, but the memory of the men attacking his grandfather's house on the day of the flash, just hours after the first bombs fell, was still fresh in his mind. When his dad arrived there to take him home to the safety of the island, already a mob was throwing bricks and waving guns. Only an overwhelming use of force had kept his grandfather's big house from being overrun. In that instance, any delay in meeting the threat head on would have ended badly for himself and the people he loved most. Luke could still see the face of the man that tried to chop into the house with an axe, laying still and gray on the concrete walkway after he and his cousin Haden shot him through the door. He would maybe always see that face so Luke knew the cost of aggression, but in his personal experience—he had not been on the raid in Sumner to see the bodies piled around the one man the islanders had come to kill—the cost of inaction was the heavier toll.

A few more moments of silence passed and Luke never thought of a good response. Thankfully, he didn't need one. Kinsey slid back down beside her new husband and put her arms around him.

"I love you," she said, feeling a little better by having said it all out loud.

"I love you too," Luke replied, pulling Kinsey close and holding her until they both drifted off to sleep.

As the morning sun began to peek above the Dog Island clam leases, wood was already smoldering in the fleet's gasifiers. The search for the missing sailing ships commenced at first light with boats fanning out across the bay and backwaters, but a heavy fog made the going slow. The air was frigid with the kind of wet Florida cold that used to surprise snowbird tourists in the old world. One of the state's great sleight-of-hand tricks had been to convince would-be visitors that it was always temperate in the Sunshine State. In reality, North Florida was often unbearably cold, especially on February mornings like the one unfurling before the fleet.

The search dragged on. One by one, frustrated captains called over the radio to report seeing nothing but fog and water, an occasional pelican, or schools of dolphins going about their exuberant dolphin business.

"Let's call it," Hayes announced over the radio. "This weather's set in. All we're doing is wasting wood."

Jud Bollins called through the speaker, fast and elevated, "Hold up, hold up... Deer Island. Back side. Hurry!"

Hayes called back, "That's a ways up there. You okay, Jud? What's happening?"

"I don't know. I think it's a boat. Get here."

Hayes replied, "Roger. All hands, all boats. You heard him. Deer Island on the quick," then turned the Cogency to the north and pushed the throttle down hard to the helm.

Jud Bollins had softened some with age, both in disposition and belly. Over time, his wife Jonya's home cooking and steady guidance had helped to grow his waistline and stature in the community, but in his youth, Jud was as wild as the Gulf. In his early twenties, he managed to talk his way onto a Greek sponge-diving crew and spent years adventuring from the west coast of Florida all the way to Central America, fighting storms, smoking pounds of high-power weed, striking it rich and going broke, sometimes all in the same week.

From the deck of his 32-foot stone crab boat, the Miss Jonya, 56-year-old Jud idled through the fog, impatiently waiting on the rest of the navy. He was sure the faint outline ahead of him was some kind of vessel, but the angles were all wrong. When Hayes and a few of the other boats began to arrive, Jud led them closer to the shore.

"That's my boat!" yelled the Colonel.

"Are you sure?" asked Thomas.

In the heap of twisted aluminum and fiberglass, two discernable pontoons were pushed in on themselves, forming an exaggerated V-shape, the words Melinda Beth upside down but legible on both.

"I'm sure," the Colonel replied with worry in his voice.

They could not know then the extent of the violence that had transpired there, but as they landed on the sand, the islanders were on alert. In all, the Cedar Key Navy comprised as many as thirty boats, but only twenty or so were actually ready to operate at any one time. With a small contingent left to guard the home island, fourteen boats of various sizes had been on patrol in the fog when Jud's call came in. Nine had found their way to Deer

Island and made landings along the shore, their crews fanning out in all directions.

"Keep your heads on a swivel," Hayes announced loudly.

The Colonel examined his mangled boat closely, remembering the autumn sunsets he and his wife had enjoyed on it in the channel past Deadman's Key.

"How big do you think the other boat had to be that did this?" Thomas asked.

The Colonel answered knowingly, "Not a boat. A ship."

"If so, they were lucky not to get stuck in this skinny water."

"We've got to find my son and his crew," the Colonel announced sharply. "Who was with him?"

Hayes said, "Normally just Randal Solaro but he's down with the flu so we lent him the Angel of Death from our crew."

Rolf Alvarez, III, had worked on Thomas' clam boat in the old world. Along with Hayes, the three men formed a trio of friends whose devotion to one another was absolute. Despite his small stature, Rolf had been a perennial U.S. Army combat fighting champion in his life before Cedar Key. When the Meade clan from Sumner launched the raid that killed Folksy, Rolf had personally killed four of the ten invaders, one with an old rotary telephone in hand-to-hand combat, one with a model 1911 at close range, the others with an overpowered big game rifle. Since that day, Hayes and Thomas often referred to him as the Angel of Death, though he was never sure whether it was meant as an honorific or the kind of thinly veiled derision that only close friends could deliver.

A trail led from the beachhead into the wooded interior of the island.

"This way," Hayes said, starting along the path.

Deer Island contained a single house near its center, modest but professionally constructed, with a long dock Hayes had helped to build many years prior. The house had been unoccupied since just before the flash when its yankee owner and seasonal occupant had returned north for good. Luke Buck and Mark David stayed behind to guard the boats while everyone else headed toward the house.

Shortly into the woods, Thomas stopped suddenly. "Blood! Here on the tree and in the palmettos."

"More up ahead," Jud said, pointing along the path.

"Shit," said Hayes.

The pace and the unease quickened. The Colonel sprinted to the front of the formation, consumed with worry for his boy.

A better plan might have involved a flanking maneuver or some cautious reconnaissance of the situation ahead to lessen the odds of being caught in an ambush, but the sight of the blood and the image of the mangled pontoons overtook them as they charged headlong toward the house. When they emerged into the clearing near the dock, Hayes spotted Rolf immediately, sitting against the front wall of the little house, waving one arm wildly. The other arm held firm to Geoff McCloud, whose face was drained of color such that it blended into the gray fog more with each labored breath. Blood seemed to be swallowing them both, a dark crimson pool collecting in Geoff's lap and running over onto the ground.

"Help him!" Rolf cried out.

The Colonel took control in a flurry of movement as his Marine Corps training took over. He applied pressure to the wound in Geoff's belly, then directed others to help prepare for the long carry back to the boats. He knew his son's best chance of survival rested with getting him back to Nurse Toni's clinic as quickly as possible. Before they started for the path, Hayes caught Jud's glance as he helped lift Geoff off the ground, noticed the sad resignation in it, and then turned to Rolf.

"How many?"

"Hard to say exactly," Rolf replied. "Maybe a dozen at first. Two less now. You'll find them in the house."

"Y'all shoot it out here?"

"Those two got the drop on us while we took fire from the tree line. Just dumb luck, I guess... but they both opened up on Geoff through the window. They probably didn't mean for it to work out that way."

"Looks like you made 'em pay at least."

"Some good it did Geoff," he said.

"We'll get him fixed up," Hayes replied, attempting optimism both men knew was misplaced.

"We held our own after they rammed us. I know he's a dipshit most of the time, but when they hit his daddy's boat, Geoff went apeshit. I was trying to get us off the beach and hidden, but we couldn't shake them. Geoff fought like a lion in the woods. He gave 'em hell the whole way."

"Neither of you were hit until you got here?" Hayes asked.

"No. Not till they flanked us. There were just so many of them."

"There was blood everywhere on the trail," Hayes said.

"Good," Rolf replied, squinting hard and gritting his teeth. "Then Geoff must have got the motherfuckers."

"How did you hold off the rest of them until we got here?"

"I didn't. When I came back out of the house, everything was quiet. They could have overrun us easy."

"Guess they didn't think so," Hayes said.

"None of it makes sense," Rolf said. "Since when is the Coast Guard the bad guys?"

Hayes furrowed his brow. "It's a different world now, I guess."

"They were armed more like Marines than Coasties," Rolf replied.

Hayes looked through the shattered window of the house, noticing the bodies on the floor, and replied, "Jesus. They're just kids."

"They didn't fight like kids. This is bullshit," Rolf said, trying but failing to push back against a wave of emotions. "He hasn't even been back a full day… and now Geoff is—"

"He's nothing yet," Hayes interrupted. "Nothing's happened until it has."

Hayes searched the bodies in the house, taking their weapons but finding nothing else of consequence, then called to Rolf, "Square yourself away, buddy… we gotta move. We didn't leave enough boats back home to do much good if they got past us somehow."

"They were heading that way when we tried to intercept them in that damn pontoon boat," Rolf said. "We were stupid. You should have seen the size of that thing, Hayes."

"Maybe you slowed them down enough to give us a chance to catch 'em. Motors against sails give us the advantage. Let's go!"

Rolf pulled himself to his feet, slung a splatter of Geoff's blood off his hands and arms, holstered the Sig Sauer that had put down the men in the house, and then followed the mayor running back into the woods toward the beach.

Geoff McCloud was an average-sized man, but something about a limp body adds extra weight and difficulty to anyone trying to carry it. Even with several islanders helping, the going was slow on the way back to the boats. Hayes and Rolf had started well after the main group but made up time running full speed through the woods. When they burst onto the beach, flush with adrenaline and breathing hard, they heard it: the low, mournful bellow of a father in agony— the singular agony possible in no other circumstance but the darkest of all parental fears realized.

The Colonel knelt in the sand beside his boy, keeping useless pressure on a wound that had never stopped bleeding, delirious for any gaze he could catch, searching for hope in hopeless eyes and calling for help he knew could be no help.

His son was dead.

Hayes led his navy home from Deer Island. The fog was too heavy to run full throttle, but each of the captains knew the waters well, so they made solid time. The Colonel held tight to his son's body on the deck of the Cogency, struck silent with grief and guilt.

Hayes looked toward Thomas. The friends were accustomed to filling in the gaps for one another—when calculated leadership was needed, Hayes took charge; when words were required, Thomas would answer the call. As he sat on the deck next to the Colonel, Thomas saw the thousand-yard stare in the old man's eyes, the kind mythologized in war movies, and knew intuitively that the right words were none at all. Instead, he grasped one of Geoff's hands and stared quietly ahead with the Colonel, the fog and rushing wind composing the kind of dirge that words could only spoil.

As the navy passed the end of the airport runway, the fog began to break. By the time they rounded Piney Point, the water tower and a few houses on the home island were visible. Four friendly boats floated in the main channel. No sails could be seen in any direction.

"Doesn't look like they're here," Mark David yelled to Hayes from the bow of the Cogency.

"I guess that's a good thing," Hayes replied. "But we can't keep chasing ghosts around in this damn fog. I'd rather just get it over with."

"Maybe they're lost somewhere out in that soup," Thomas said.

The Colonel looked up from his boy. "No," he said sharply. "They're not lost. We just didn't find them."

"We will... and we'll settle up with 'em for what they did to your boy," Mark said in a fiery tone.

The Colonel looked away.

Hayes called over the radio to the fleet, "Joey, Jud... how bout you join the four boats in the channel and set up a patrol around the island? We'll send six boats to relieve you in two hours. Until we get a handle on all this, we'll need to keep these patrols going constantly. Everyone else... secure your boats in the back channel and go check on your families while we plan our next move. I'll alert the council."

A smattering of acknowledgments came across the radio, and a defeated navy headed for home.

During the Colonel's stone crabbing years, Melinda Beth made a habit of meeting his boat at the dock when he returned home from a trip on the water. Sometimes, he and his crew might be gone for three or four days at a stretch; even after technology made it possible to stay in touch the whole time, she enjoyed the ritual of meeting her returning waterman, usually in a summer dress and a dramatic hat to block the sun from her ageless face. The Colonel had not let go of his son on the ride in. He held out hope Melinda Beth would not be waiting when they rounded the bend in the back channel and approached Hayes' clam dock.

Of course, she was waiting.

Having been apart from the Colonel for so long and then separated so suddenly again by the ordeal of the mysterious ships, Melinda Beth had been waiting at the dock all morning, resplendent as ever, smiling with her whole body and energized with girlish excitement to see the imposing black outline of the Cogency coming into view.

She knew something was off when only the top of her husband's head was visible above the gunnels of the boat. His long gray hair was as thick as it ever was, whipping with the wind into a silver blur. For nearly thirty years during his military service, he had worn it buzzed short and tight. When he became a civilian again, he simply stopped cutting it. Occasionally, Melinda Beth could coerce him into letting her trim it up a little, but never enough to dampen the feral aesthetic.

There was no way to soften the blow the old mother was about to receive. The joyful energy from just moments before drained away as the boat drew closer to the dock.

Then there was her son, still and hollow in his father's embrace, cradled in the arms of death.

Melinda Beth leaped wild from the dock into the boat, crashing hard onto its fiberglass deck, fracturing her left wrist and bruising the side of her face, completely oblivious to the injury or pain, as she scrambled to her only child, violent and lost, pressed her battered face against his and screamed into the stillness.

The Colonel could only weep and look away. All of this was his fault.

5

— · —

Cayo Costa

The Piper Archer the Colonel borrowed from Bob Corliss' widow had a typical glide ratio of about ten to one, which means that for every thousand feet of altitude, it could glide without power for roughly ten thousand feet, or just under two miles, before hitting the ground. When new pilots are taking their initial flight training, they are often required to practice power-off drills, where their instructor will cut the power to the aircraft, and the student will have to set up for a controlled glide to a nearby airport, road, or field. Once the instructor is satisfied with the student's execution of the proper procedures, power would be restored before actually landing.

The Colonel had certainly done his share of power-off drills, and he crashed two helicopters in Vietnam, but he had never landed an airplane anywhere besides an airport runway. His first attempt at an off-airport landing would be complicated by low visibility but aided by the remarkable geography of a barrier island a little over a mile directly in front of him.

Cayo Costa Island comprises 2,506 acres with an oblong area of uplands near its northern frontage along the Boca Grande Pass and a narrow stretch of flat sand beach along its western boundary on the open Gulf that runs fairly straight for roughly five miles. Aside from a few minor improvements associated with the State Park on its northern end, the island looks mostly as it did when the Calusa Indians occupied it for more than four thousand years. Beginning in the early 1700s, Cuban fishermen utilized the island to construct *ranchos*— fishing stations for processing and salting fish caught in the waters of southwest Florida prior to shipment back to Cuba. In the late 1800s, a prominent fisherman named *Captain Pappy* Padilla settled permanently on the island, operating a large rancho until he and his family and workers were killed there in the 1910 Cuban Hurricane, or *Cyclone of the Five Days.* The island was never reinhabited for any length of time thereafter.

For the Colonel, the most important feature of the island now was the long beach, which would have to serve as his emergency runway. His relatively low altitude made it the only plausible place he could reach to land his disabled aircraft before it ran out of glide ratio. The George T. Lewis Airport on Cedar Key had the shortest public runway in Florida, measuring just 2,355 feet, with water off both ends. Landing routinely on such a short field made the more than 26,000 feet of Cayo Costa's beach seem to go on forever for the Colonel. If he could safely maneuver his way through the cloud bank, the actual landing would be relatively straightforward.

The Colonel spotted a break in the clouds, barely larger than the Archer, forming a cylindrical tunnel of clear sky all the way to the water and sand below. He banked down into it, careful not to reach the VNE—*Velocity Never Exceed*—which is the maximum speed the aircraft can sustain without risking structural damage. This steep dive burned off 600 feet of altitude in seconds. When the Archer broke through the bottom of the cloud bank, it had less than 500 feet of altitude remaining but still plenty to reach the beach.

The palm trees along the marsh side of the island gave a good indication of the wind direction, so the Colonel was able to set his aircraft up for a soft field landing generally into the wind, with only a marginal cross-wind component. He initiated a full 40 degrees of flaps and floated the Archer along the beach near its junction with the water. The firmer, flatter sand near the edge of the water would be less treacherous than the deeper white sand further up the beach. Landing in the soft stuff risked the tires digging in and flipping the aircraft upside down. Such a landing would still be completely survivable, but the old pilot's instinct was to save his aircraft if possible.

As the Archer neared the beach, the Colonel began an aggressive flare of the nose of his aircraft, pulling back on the yoke to hold it off the sand for as long as possible. A few feet off the ground, the stall warning began its loud buzzing, but the Colonel continued to gently caress the yoke further back, knowing that ground effect would distort the airflow below the wings, creating a cushion of air that would float the plane a little further along as it continued to slow, slow, slow. When all the lift had finally drained away, the Archer touched down so gently that the exact moment when flight became rolling could not be identified.

The Colonel caught a fantastic break as his airplane continued to roll out along the flat sand near the water. For reasons he could not discern, the heavier white sand to his right grew suddenly firmer along a hundred-yard or so stretch, allowing for a gradual right rutter veer away from the water and toward a patch of seagrass separating the beach from the marsh. The Colonel slowly applied the brakes, and the Archer came to rest in that fortuitous middle ground, out of reach of the tides and even partially concealed.

With the same military bearing exhibited in the war zones of his youth, the Colonel got to work gathering what supplies he could and exiting the aircraft. Using a knife from his flight bag, he frantically cut seagrass from the surrounding area and used it to further obscure the outline of the Archer. The work was grueling, but the Colonel was up to the task, bolstered by the unique adrenaline that only combat can create. He took measure of the damage to his aircraft, noting the four small holes in the wings and already thinking of how he might find materials for their repair. With a small rucksack of gear packed the night before for just such an outcome, the Colonel set out into the rain, putting distance between himself and the aircraft. He held out hope that the clouds and rain had obscured his heading from the Sawfish but worried those firing at him had been able to hear his engine dying and would be searching the area for the downed Archer.

He was determined that even if they found his plane, they would not find him.

Mark and Hayes David were already on the boat when Isaac arrived, on time but just barely.

"5:58 is cuttin' it close," Mark said.

"You said to be here by 6. It's ain't 6 yet," Isaac replied, intending less petulance than he conveyed.

Mark scowled. "Fair enough, but if something had delayed you a minute and a half or so, you'd be out of a job. Now, maybe you don't need the work, but if that's the case, why'd you come at all?"

"Dad, cut him a little slack. He's new," Hayes said.

"I do need the work," Isaac interjected. "I'll be more mindful from now on."

"Fine," Mark said, triumphant, as Hayes shook his head. "You know my boy?"

"I know of him," Isaac replied.

"Nice to meet you, Isaac," Hayes said.

"Same to you. I heard you're the new mayor now?"

"I guess so," Hayes replied.

Isaac, risking a joke he had not yet earned the right to make, asked, "Will you have enough time to do that job and still keep up with your homework?"

"I'm 23, you little shit."

Mark David let out a deep belly laugh. "I think he's gonna do just fine."

Clam farming is often a serene, meditative affair. When the bay is glassy calm, and the tide is low, it's easy for the farmer to think big thoughts about what everything means, to find allegory in a diving cormorant, metaphor in the interplay of light and water. These were not the conditions as Isaac and the David men sped away from the dock. The flat-bottomed bird dog boat beat hard against a heavy chop in the water, and a 25-knot wind from the southwest kept the tide from moving out. Planting clams in chest-deep water is easily five times more physically taxing than it is when the water is below the waist, but the clams have no preference one way or the other— when they need planting, they need planting.

By the time they reached the clam lease, rain was blowing sideways, and the June air had turned surprisingly cold.

"How bout it, boys?" Mark yelled, gleefully, as Hayes set the anchor.

"Good day for it," Hayes shouted back.

Isaac was already in the water.

The three of them worked without protest in the harsh conditions. Hayes and Isaac learned each other's movements quickly and in short order could plant a belt of clams with little need for words. They were so efficient that Mark returned to the boat, handing new belts overboard when needed but leaving the water work to the younger men. The rain eventually let up but not the biting wind and rough seas.

Two hundred bags into the three hundred they came to plant, with no motive or forethought, Hayes said, "I was really sorry to hear about your dad."

"Yeah," Isaac replied, deploying the instant, involuntary stoicism that always seemed to accompany the mention of his father.

"Mr. Buddy was good to me," Hayes continued. "I had a net boat like him when I was your age. We used to see each other on the water and back at the fish house. One time, he pulled me in all the way from Shell Mound when my motor quit on me."

"That sounds like him," Isaac replied.

"He was sure good with a net," Hayes said.

"Less good with clams," Isaac replied coldly. "But I guess everybody knows that."

They were far enough away from the boat that Mark David could not hear their conversation. From his perspective, the work continued until Isaac began howling across the water.

Hayes saw the boy convulse, freeze, writhe again, then sink under the water, arms and legs thrashing in a panic.

"Dad!" Hayes called out.

Mark David pulled the anchor and sped toward them as Hayes pulled Isaac to the surface.

"It's got me... It's got me!"

"What in the hell?" Hayes asked. "What has you?"

Isaac only screamed louder as the bird dog pulled up, and Hayes dragged the boy onto its deck. Isaac squirmed wildly as he struggled to remove his shorts. Mark expected to see a gaping wound, a wash of blood, or, at a minimum, a dreaded stingray barb protruding from the boy.

"Get it, get it, get it!" Isaac pleaded.

"Oh, hell no," Hayes said, trying his best not to laugh as he finally made sense of what he was seeing.

"Please!"

"Help him, son," Mark said, straight-faced and earnest.

And so he did. Thankful he was wearing rubber work gloves, Hayes reached down and grabbed the tiniest baby catfish he had ever seen, snatching its sharp barb from the business end of Isaac's pecker.

Isaac wailed, tears running in streams down both cheeks. "Did you get it?"

"Not as bad as you got it," Hayes said, no longer able to forestall the laughter.

"It ain't funny, Hayes," Mark admonished. "A dong-fish attack is serious business. We need to get him to the hospital right away."

Isaac caught his breath. "Wait, seriously? I think I'm okay."

"Shit no, not seriously," Mark said, laughing. "We got another hundred bags to plant. You'll be fine. This is why we wear pants."

Isaac grimaced through the pain in his swollen crotch, then pulled his shorts back up and headed for the water.

"Hang on," Mark said. "Hayes and I will finish up in the water. You stay here and collect yourself. Spray some WD-40 in the hole, and it'll help with the burning. The barb hole, not your pee hole."

"I got it," Isaac said, embarrassed but in on the joke now and laughing.

When he first broke through the clouds, the Colonel had seen a small roofline near the northeastern end of the island, on the marsh side, so it was this direction he now headed. The March air was colder than normal, especially for this part of the state. As he made his way up the island's long, narrow shoreline, the light rain intensified. By the time he had traveled a mile on foot, the rain was blowing sideways and bitter cold. There was nothing for the Colonel to do but continue toward the roofline. It took the better part of an hour to reach the building, a drab brown ranger's station for the Cayo Costa State Park. The door was unlocked, and the interior was strangely undisturbed. A small lobby with wooden chairs and a large check-in desk were just inside the door. Behind the desk was a small living area where rangers would sometimes overnight in the old world.

Getting dry was the Colonel's first order of business. A small stone fireplace on the back wall looked as though it hadn't been used in decades, but he headed right for it. Heavy drops of rain were slowly dripping down the chimney, and a low light emanated from it. With a Ferro rod retrieved from his rucksack, the Colonel got a fire going quickly. A stack of dusty park brochures made for good kindling to help ignite pieces of a small circular table he smashed apart against the concrete floor. It was definitely a risk to send smoke from a fire up the chimney and into the sky, but the need to dry his clothes and push away the chill made it one the Colonel would have to take. The rain and clouds would, at least, make the smoke less visible than it would otherwise be.

Once the fire was going in earnest, the Colonel stripped naked, wrung his clothes of water as best he could, and laid them near the fireplace. As he stoked the fire and waited for the cold to slowly leave him, he was suddenly aware of his naked body and how different in all ways it was from the one that had carried him through the war and years of stone crabbing in the Gulf. His legs looked wholly unsuited to the task of holding up the rest of his body, and his skin drooped sad and low now from thin arms that had once held a seemingly limitless store of power. He could not help but snicker at the sight of his penis, cowering inward from the cold, juxtaposed with the languid hang of testicles that had grown longer by the minute each year of his seventies. In the firelight, his fingers seemed cartoonishly long, extending from the veiny hands of an old man he would not recognize were he to meet himself on the street.

The Colonel was not normally given to self-pity but the thought of Melinda Beth, no doubt still waiting at the end of the runway for a husband that would not be returning home that day, laid him low with despair. The importance of the mission had overshadowed any concerns he had about its possible danger. In his zeal to answer the call of duty, he had indulged no worry for his wife, but now, by the fire, confronted with his own frailty and doubt, it began to overwhelm him.

The rain never let up that first day on Cayo Costa. The Colonel stayed inside the ranger's station, burning four chairs and several planks of tongue and groove pine wallboards in the fireplace. He slept fitfully but warmly on a small couch with a belly full of canned ravioli Melinda Beth had packed in the rucksack.

Morning broke dry but overcast in gray. The Colonel dressed and ventured out, following a path from the ranger station to a small lagoon on the eastern shore. All around him, the island was as beautiful as it was dormant. There was scarce wood for burning and no plants that looked edible. At the water's edge, the top of an old-fashioned wooden water tower could be seen on another island a few miles to the southeast. If he could figure a way to get there, the Colonel reasoned, it was as good a next step toward home as any other. The water between his present position and the other island was placid and shallow, with several sandbars visible along the path.

As he stared across the small bay, the Colonel resolved that even if he had to swim the damn thing, this stretch of easy water would not slow his progress.

6

THE HOME FRONT

Geoff McCloud was buried in the island cemetery, a few feet away from Confederate Lieutenant W.A. Crawford's above-ground sepulcher. It was in this tomb, broken open by a falling tree in the great hurricane four months after the flash across the bay, that a mama hen sat on four precious eggs until they hatched. The storm had killed or blown away all of the island's roosters, so the fate of Cedar Key's chicken breeding program rested on these delicate little birds. Without at least one new rooster to fertilize eggs from the hens in the flock, no new chickens could be grown.

While everyone waited to learn the sex of the new chicks, Geoff cared for them as though they were his own. He kept them separate from the rest of the flock, tended to their every need, and closely managed the public's access to them. A variety of homespun methods were posited for determining the sex of young chickens, but none inspired any real confidence that a savior rooster was among them. Weeks later, when the scientist Mike Allenby made the statistically improbable determination that all four of the chicks were hens, Geoff was inconsolable. While Hayes and Thomas and so many others had found their places in the new world, each contributing in varied and meaningful ways to the collective survival of the island, Geoff had, until the ordeal of the missing roosters and the new chicks, felt more useless by the day.

When all hope seemed lost, a tiny, half-beaked, one-eyed, limping rooster hobbled out of the sea grass on Atsena Otie. The mighty winds of Hurricane Jonah had snatched it from the flock in the back of the cemetery and carried it two miles away to the barrier island. Most of the other chickens that were caught up in the maelstrom had failed to navigate their way safely back to the earth; this lone, runty cock had somehow survived. When he left the ground on that fearsome updraft, he had been the lowliest of roosters in the pecking order. When fate returned him alive—battered and hard to look at but still packing working rooster parts under the hood—he was king.

Geoff undertook the care of King Arthur, as he became known, with the evangelical zeal of a newly saved sinner. His devotion to the messiah rooster was unfailing, and so impressed Hayes and the other members of the town council that Geoff was officially put in charge of the entire chicken-breeding operation. It was important if unglamorous work and transformative for a man who had lived always in the shadow of a war-hero father.

Almost every able-bodied person on the island attended the funeral service in the cemetery. Thomas delivered a stirring elegy for his friend that extolled the virtues of the man and the exigency of the work Geoff had done on the island's behalf. Though he had never served in the military before the smokestacks fell, Geoff's naval gallantry at the Battle of Deer Island earned him full military burial honors. Rolf, Thomas, Jenny Alverez, Tabby Lauer, and several other veterans wore the uniforms of their respective old-world services and held honorary salutes to the chicken man as Luke Buck played taps on a borrowed trumpet.

The Marine Corps Colonel made a show of strength for Melinda Beth's sake, but the first three haunting notes from the trumpet buckled his knees with the weight of uncontrollable grief.

When the service was complete, the Colonel refused any help filling in the hole that held his son.

Isaac Skipjack turned seventeen on the first day of autumn in 1998, five months after his father's death. Throughout that previous summer, he worked nearly every day on the boat with Mark David. Sometimes Hayes would join them as well, but increasingly, as the summer went along and Isaac's skills increased, Mark and Isaac became a regular two-man crew. It was during this time that the David family landed a contract to supply a large statewide grocery store with fresh clams weekly. They bought a second and third bird dog to help meet the demand, so the addition of Isaac to the team was as beneficial to the Davids as it was to the boy.

The Cedar Key School had a program for its seniors who wanted to enter the workforce early. For these students, depending on the number of core classes they needed to meet the state requirements for graduation, a large portion of the school day could be spent working in the community. Despite social difficulties and a troubled home life, Isaac had been an above-average student, such that by the time he was a senior, he had only an algebra class to complete to be eligible to graduate. Luckily for Isaac and the David family, this class was offered as the first of the day, which meant Isaac was free to do clam work beginning at 9:30 every morning.

Clam farmers are notoriously early risers, with most captains aiming to have their boats on the water just after daybreak, so it was a testament to Mark David's increasing affection for and reliance on working with Isaac that he was willing to delay the start of his work day for Isaac to finish his math class. Each weekday morning, Mark would be waiting at the dock, watching to see Isaac rounding the corner of 1st Street on his 1970s ten speed. Once, the chain on his bike broke halfway to the dock, and Isaac had to sprint the better part of a mile to make the boat on time, remembering Mr. Mark's admonition that *early is on time and on time is late*. When he arrived, flush and panting at 9:29 AM, Mark stared at his watch with feigned outrage before bursting into a self-satisfied laugh.

"Nick of time, young fella," Mark said.

"The chain on my bike," Isaac said, gasping. "It broke in front of the Faraway Inn."

"Sounds like you need to brush up on proper bike maintenance. Sure be a shame to lose a job 'cause you ain't oiled the chain."

Isaac shook his head, smiling. "Yes sir, Mr. Mark. I'm on it."

Demand for clams increases around most holidays, but especially for Thanksgiving. Some clam shops would make as much as thirty percent of their annual sales in the two weeks leading up to Thanksgiving. This fact turns late November into a mad dash gold rush for Cedar Key clammers. It's not uncommon for boat crews to go out as many as three times a day to harvest. During this time, the fleet's bird dogs could be seen ambling back to the dock loaded down so heavy with clam bags that only the gunnels of the boat would be above the waterline, and just barely. A normal day's work on the water might include a harvest of twenty to forty bags of clams, but during the Thanksgiving rush, it was common for boat crews to be hauling in as many as eighty per trip. That amount of weight made the ride back to the dock especially precarious, as even the gentlest of turns risked the boat rolling over and capsizing.

It was on such a day, on the 20th of November in Isaac's senior year, that Mark and the boy were returning to the dock with their third load of clams for the day, bone weary and haggard. Another exhausted captain nearly broadsided their bird dog as they approached the floating dock near the outside boat ramp. Reflexively, Mark turned his boat hard to port to avoid the collision. When he did, water rushed over the gunnels, and the overloaded boat rolled over as gently as a sleeping baby. The transition from right side up to upside down was so smooth that neither Mark nor Isaac registered that it was happening quickly enough to jump away from the boat as they went down. Mark was at the helm, away from the clam bags midship and at the stern where Isaac had been hanging onto the power roller, so he was able to swim out easily from under the overturned bird dog. As he caught his breath at the surface, he realized in short order that he could not see Isaac. Mark pulled himself onto the underside of the boat to get a vantage from which to see all around it. Several unnerving seconds passed, but Isaac did not return to the surface.

Mark screamed at the other captain and crew, "Get your asses in and help me. The boy's down there," before diving into the murky water.

The visibility was so poor that everything beyond a foot or so in front of Mark's face was a blur. He worked his way around the area under the boat, dragging himself along the tops of clam bags for a full minute before surfacing for a frantic, worried breath.

Still no Isaac.

On his second dive, Mark saw bubbles rising just in front of his face and followed them down to where he could make out only a pair of feet under a pile of clam bags. He worked at the giant pile, pulling bag after bag off the boy until, lungs burning and weak, he had to surface for another breath.

"Down here... he's pinned under the bags," Mark shouted at the other watermen before going under again. It took so long to free Isaac from the bottom, even with four men working together on the bottom, that he was limp and blue as they pulled him from the water and onto the other bird dog.

Mark's Coast Guard training kicked in immediately, and he began a wild effort to resuscitate the boy, using the palm of his hands to deliver thirty firm chest compressions, then pinching Isaac's nose and breathing hard into the boy's mouth. Isaac's chest rose slightly, so Mark breathed into him once more. The chest rose again, but the boy did not. Mark began the cycle over as the other watermen stood helplessly nearby. So much time had passed since the bird dog first rolled over—too much time for the men to believe that Isaac was coming back to them. When the last of the hope had left the most optimistic among them, Isaac's body lurched as water came spewing from him.

The boy, blue as deep water and shaking, coughed hard and long as he returned, miraculously, to the living world.

Mark David was overcome, grabbing him and rambling, "Isaac, Isaac... you're okay, son... you're okay."

Isaac, spectral and calm, looked into the face of the older man with strangeness in his eyes. "No," he said. "I saw my father in the water."

Mark stared quietly back at him until the silence lingered into unease.

"You're a lucky kid," the other captain said at last.

"Maybe so," Isaac replied, pulling himself to his feet and surveying the overturned boat. "But it's gonna be a long day getting all those bags off the bottom."

Mark David let out a cathartic laugh. "They ain't going anywhere. Let's get you to the clinic to get checked out."

The other captain, acutely aware that his negligence had pushed the day to its crisis, said, "The boys and I will get some ropes and get your boat pulled right side up while you're gone."

"Seems like the least you could do," Mark said, smiling small but sufficient for the other captain to know he was already forgiven.

The Colonel threw the last shovel of dirt onto his son's grave and found his way back to Melinda Beth. They had to hold one another up on the slow walk back to their house near the runway.

Hayes and Thomas walked a distance behind them so their conversation was not overheard.

"Man, that was tough," Thomas said.

"Yeah," Hayes replied. "It's so heavy I don't know how to even start to make sense of it. I'm gonna let the Colonel and his wife sit with it all overnight, but tomorrow, we have to get a full accounting of every detail he can remember about his time off the island. He may know something that can help us in the fight ahead."

"You feel sure there's gonna be a fight?" Thomas asked, knowing the answer but asking anyway just to move the conversation along.

"Seems like the Skipjack boy is here to settle a score, and I don't guess he's gonna think we're square trading Geoff for two of theirs."

"No, I don't guess he will," Thomas replied. "I've heard stories about how his daddy died, but no one seems to really know what happened."

"It was just before I became mayor, so... dang... twenty-five years ago."

"I had just met Luke's mama in Gainesville right after I got out of the Navy," Thomas replied. "That seems like ten lifetimes ago."

Hayes laughed. "At least."

"The story I heard was Buddy Skipjack got roughed up pretty good for stealing clams... and maybe it was that beating that killed him."

Hayes became visibly upset. "He was fine when Chief Vernon put him in the back seat of his car. The only thing we know for sure is that his heart gave out on the way to the jail. Anything else is pure speculation."

Thomas put his hands up. "Hang on, buddy, I'm on your side here, whatever happened. I'm just telling you what I heard."

"Well, you heard wrong," Hayes snapped. "I liked Mr. Buddy a whole lot, and I'm sure he had his reasons for what he did... but he was lucky Uncle Allen didn't gut him open and leave him for the crabs. Everybody was still hurting from the net ban. Clamming wasn't what it was when you got to the island. It was still a barebones, barely getting by kind of deal. Stolen clams meant farmers might literally go hungry. Back in my grandaddy's day, Mr. Buddy would have never made it back to the dock."

"What happened between Isaac and your dad? Again, I only know secondhand stories, but I heard he worked on the boat with you guys for a while before he left town."

"That part's true," Hayes said. "My dad took him in after Mr. Buddy died. They worked on the boat together for more than a year. I even remember being a little jealous at what a fuss my dad made about him. Seemed like every day he had some new story about Isaac this, or Isaac that. They were close."

"What changed?" Thomas asked.

Hayes stared ahead as he walked. "You know as much about that as I do. My dad never would talk about it. And when he doesn't want to talk about a thing, he don't."

"I believe that," Thomas said, forcing a muted laugh in a useless attempt to lighten the mood.

"It's strange he wasn't at the funeral just now," Hayes said.

"I thought so, too," Thomas replied.

"Strange ain't the right word," Hayes continued. "It's worrying. For all the grief he gave Geoff about the chickens, he had a soft spot for him. Let's stop by his house and see what's going on."

The friends walked on, waving at the Colonel and Melinda Beth when they reached Whidden Avenue and headed in a different direction. A few blocks before reaching the house on 4th Street, they saw Bette David, Hayes' mother, heading toward them at a brisk pace.

"Hayes!" she called out.

Hayes and Thomas ran to meet her.

"Mom, what's wrong?"

"Your damn fool father, like usual."

"I thought he was with you," Hayes said.

"He was," Miss Bette replied, out of breath.

Thomas said, "Take your time, Miss Bette. Here, lean on me for a minute to catch your breath."

"There ain't time," she replied. "Hayes, you got to catch him. He says he knows where Isaac might be, and he's gonna go settle this thing before it gets out of hand."

"Aw hell," Hayes said. "Did he say where? Did you see which way he was headed?"

"He wouldn't tell me anything because he knew you would come after him. But when he and your Uncle Allen were gathering gear out in the shed, I snuck over and tried to eavesdrop."

"Well?" Hayes asked, impatient and worried.

"He caught me almost as soon as I got to the window of the shed, madder than hell... but I did hear him say something about a gator, I think."

"Did he say gator or Alligator... do you remember?"

"Yeah, I think it might have been Alligator. Why?"

Hayes was furious with himself. "Of course. That's why we haven't been able to find them."

"What, man... what is it?" Thomas asked.

"They're in the river," Hayes said.

"Oh no," Miss Bette moaned, tears beginning to stream down her pretty face.

"Get Rolf and meet me at the dock as fast as you can, Thomas. I'll get the fire going."

"Go, son, you have to catch him... go!"

7

FROM CABBAGE KEY TO THE SUWANNEE

The wooden water tower the Colonel had seen from the eastern shore of Cayo Costa sat on a small hill on Cabbage Key, a roughly 100-acre private island that was deserted in the weeks leading up to the flash.

Like Cayo Costa, it had also been occupied by the Calusa Indians, housed Cuban ranchos, and faced the wrath of generational hurricanes. It passed through a variety of ownership hands until the Rinehart family, buoyed by Gratia Buell Houghton Rinehart's share of the Corning Glass Works fortune, purchased the island and constructed a large estate there in 1937. The water tower that had beckoned the Colonel, complete with a 41-step wooden dog-leg stair system and a six-thousand-gallon capacity, was completed that same year.

Over the intervening decades, Cabbage Key went through various iterations, eventually becoming a vacation rental destination with a large inn, restaurant, and bar created from the Rinehart's main house, and several rental cottages, a boathouse, and docks spread from one end of the small island to the other. Luminaries from Ernest Hemingway to Katherine Hepburn and Jimmy Buffet spent time on Cabbage Key, and the island remained, until the global economic collapse preceding the falling of the bombs, a popular destination for well-heeled travelers with a boat and money to spend.

The Colonel knew none of this history or that the island contained anything but a water tower. The relative desolation of Cayo Costa, however, and his own dwindling water supply from the two bottles packed in his rucksack, made the tower more than ample incentive for him to get there.

The getting there would be the issue.

For most of that first morning after waking in the ranger station, the Colonel searched for a kayak or canoe or anything even closely resembling a floating vessel. Finding nothing and nearing a decision to pull apart the walls of the station for wood in support of a preposterous momentary delusion that he could build a boat from scratch, the Colonel saw it—a giant white cooler hiding in the marsh grass on the eastern shore of the island, more than three feet long and about a foot and a half wide. The lid was open, so it was partially filled with salt water and mud, but otherwise, the cooler seemed nearly new. There was a sticker still affixed to its front advertising its 120-gallon capacity, dual snap-fit latches, and the ability to hold 188 cans. He emptied the cooler and pulled it to the edge of the lagoon, leaving it there while he returned to the ranger station for his rucksack.

When he returned, the Colonel put his rucksack and shoes into the cooler and prepared to start his trek across the shallow bay toward the water tower, hoping to be able to wade most of the way and hang onto the cooler for flotation in any places where the water was over his head. Just before entering the water, he remembered the ordeal of getting dry by the fire the night before and made the decision to strip naked and place his clothes inside the cooler as well.

Something about being naked again, imagining the ridiculous image of an old man paddling a cooler across the bay, made the Colonel laugh out loud. *It's the end of the world... gotta do what you gotta do,* he thought, feeling the rush of cool on his feet as he stepped into the water.

The tide was dead low, so the Colonel spent a great deal more time wading with the cooler than hanging onto it as he floated. It took the better part of an hour for him to reach a small spit of sand and mangroves called Primo Island. He rested on the sand there for several minutes, finishing one of the bottles of water from his rucksack. Continuing on, a gentle current pushed him through deeper water to a larger patch of land known as Middle Key. As he pulled the cooler to its eastern shore, the Colonel could make out the entirety of the water tower and a portion of the Cabbage Key Inn, formerly the old Rinehart home, less than a mile across what looked to be knee-deep water. The sight of these structures sent a charge through him as he imagined what supplies he might find there, hopefully, gasoline and maybe JB-Weld to patch the holes in the Archer's fuel tanks.

Surprisingly, there were no surprises between Middle Key and the shore of Cabbage Key, and besides a fifty-yard stretch of seven-foot water, the Colonel was able to walk easily alongside the cooler that held his gear. His clothes had managed to stay dry on the trip, and he was relieved to be putting them on again. All the way back to childhood, he had felt great trepidation being in the water naked; even in swimming pools that held nothing but clear water, he could not escape the pervasive thought that some creature in the deep would snatch the dangling bits clean off his body as easily as a bluegill swallowing a worm. Sitting on the shore tying his boots, he laughed again at the absurdity of it all, at his brain's ability to worry about such triviality when his present circumstances were so clearly steeped in legitimate peril.

In the old world, especially on the weekends, boats would fill every slip at the main dock extending from Cabbage Key's boat house. A relatively narrow but deep cut ran from the boat house to the main channel east of the island, a channel that extended out to Captiva Pass and the open Gulf of Mexico. This cut made it possible for extraordinarily large yachts to dock there, though only one such vessel at a time.

The Colonel donned his rucksack and took in the surroundings. The exquisite order of the island before him was disorienting. Aside from the lack of boats and people, so far as he could tell from the shore, everything seemed perfectly in place. Given all he had seen beneath the wings of the Archer the day before, the featureless gray tombs of Tampa, Saint Petersburg, and Sarasota, Cabbage Key's photogenic quaintness was a kind of intractable depravity that felt wrong to the Colonel as he headed for the front door of the inn.

Unlike the ranger station, the inn was locked up tight. The Colonel tried windows and doors at the front and back of the building to no avail. The owners had closed the island down in the way a northern sleepaway camp might winterize when the summer season ends. It was clear by the care they had taken all around the island that they had every hope of returning when the turmoil was over. Knowing now that the turmoil had blown the world over, the Colonel felt little guilt when he used a rock to break a small glass panel near the deadbolt in a French door leading into the back of the Inn's bar.

A quiet bar is normally a disquieting place, but never more so than when it is likely to never open again. Dollar bills, personalized with names and written messages, hung from the ceiling, walls, and support pillars throughout the bar. For reasons unknown, an insurance guy from Fort Lauderdale tacked the first dollar to the wall in 1971, and others quickly followed. There was now, according to a plaque hanging near the bar, more than 70,000 of them. It was this feature that gave The Dollar Bill Bar its name and cemented its place in local folklore.

The Colonel passed an old upright piano sitting quietly in a corner as he headed through the bar to explore the rest of the inn and restaurant. The refrigerators were predictably empty, but the back room held a storehouse of treasure—floor-to-ceiling shelves full of restaurant staples. There were at least fifty cans of yellow corn, enough green beans to choke an ox, okra aplenty, stewed tomatoes by the flat, fifty-pound bags of rice, flour, and corn meal, and strangely, multiple 5-pound jars of Big John's pickled eggs. These were not the fancy yellow pickled eggs Hayes David had once foisted upon him during an airboat fishing trip in the Wacassassa creeks; these were the neon pink variety seen often at convenience stores and truck stops.

Having eaten only a can of ravioli the day before, the Colonel opened a jar of the eggs and ate five in two minutes, soaking up the briny joy and feeling instantly rejuvenated.

"Alligator Pass," Hayes announced to Thomas and Rolf when they arrived at the dock.

"Huh?" Thomas replied.

Hayes moved about the dock with characteristic efficiency, putting more wood into the gasifier as he replied, "If Dad said alligator, he's heading for Alligator Pass."

"At the mouth of the Suwannee?" asked Rolf.

"Yeah. I always take the back way to the river, through the creeks, but Dad likes to stay in the open water. He runs the Suwannee Sound all the way to Alligator Pass."

"I've been that way with him before," Thomas replied. "We pulled a big cypress log off the bottom of the river near Salt Creek and brought it back to Mr. Herms' sawmill. We were gonna make a table out of it but never did."

"He's obsessed with those logs," Hayes said while making small adjustments to the gasifier. "We've been diving for them since I was a kid. He always says he's gonna make furniture with the wood, but he only ever did once."

"Oh yeah," Thomas replied. "The table in his dining room, right? It's incredible. You helped him make it?"

"Not me," Hayes answered.

"Who then?" Rolf asked.

Hayes strained his face into the forced smile of a person who's in on a joke about himself and said with spritely disdain, "Isaac damn Skipjack."

"Oh," Thomas said sheepishly. "Guess they really were close."

Hayes did not reply, turning his attention to untying the lines at the bow and stern of his boat.

Even with the slight performance reduction associated with the gasifier's inefficiencies, the Cogency still made 25 knots. Hayes was hesitant to take the direct route to the Suwannee, fearing a waiting fleet of sailing ships in the wide mouth of the river's opening, but he could not risk the extra time it would take to snake through the back creeks. Already, he would have to go the long way around the island because the tide was too high for the Cogency to make it under the little bridge in front of Fannies.

As they sped away from Hayes' clam dock on the 3rd Street canal, Luke Buck and Ryland Beecham stepped out of the mangroves where they had been crouching while the older men loaded the boat.

"I told you," Luke said. "I knew when I saw my dad and Rolf running toward the dock that something was going down."

"Why didn't they just tell us about it?" Ryland asked.

"He does this. Especially after the day everything went to hell, and we had to shoot it out with those fellas in Gainesville. He wouldn't let me go on the Sumner raid after the Meade boys killed Folksy, either. It's bullshit."

Ryland, who had not heard from his father since the day of the flash and who had, more than a year on, resigned himself to the fact that he probably never would, pushed back. "Yeah, man. It must be a real pain in the ass... your dad caring about you and shit."

Luke and Ryland had become close hunting together in the Sumner scrub over the past several months, so the weight of Ryland's response landed heavily.

Luke grit his teeth because he knew, in his belly if not his head, that he was wrong. "I don't mean it like that. It's just... I mean... obviously he's just trying to keep me safe. But newsflash, the whole world's unsafe, and if Mr. Mark's in trouble, it's stupid for them not to have more help."

"That last part's true," Ryland said. "Your little Outlaw skiff is still tied up at my dock. Fast as that thing is, we could run the backwater out to Gulf Jackson and make up some of the time we're behind."

"You got guns there, or do we need to stop at my house?"

"If we stop, we definitely won't catch 'em before they get to the river. I've got my deer rifle and a hunting bow there," Ryland replied.

"That'll have to do."

The young men mounted the bikes they had arrived on and pedaled for all they were worth toward Ryland's dock on the other side of the island.

Out in the Wacassassa Bay, the Cogency rounded Piney Point and turned north. From there, it was a little over 12 miles to Alligator Pass. Hayes kept the throttle pushed wide open. The big high tide meant they could take the most direct course possible without fear of running aground on the many oyster beds, sandbars, and mud flats that would have hindered them at low tide.

The Suwannee River's headwaters begin in the Okefenokee Swamp near the town of Fargo, Georgia. As it flows south into north Florida, the river is narrow, winding, and unremarkable. A large elevation drop near the town of White Springs breathes energetic life into the river, creating the Big Shoals, the only Class III whitewater rapids in the state. Just south of there, the upper Withlacoochee and Alapaha rivers flow into the Suwannee, joined by the Santa Fe River a little further south near the town of Branford. The river gradually widens along its 246-mile march to the Gulf such that by the time it reaches Alligator Pass, toward which three Cedar Key boat crews were now racing, the meandering Suwannee was a third of a mile wide and placid as a summer breeze most of the time.

Alligator Pass is the largest but not the only union between the Suwannee and the Gulf. Smaller junctions like the East Pass and Wadley Pass, along with a serpentine network of tiny creeks, give the Lower Suwannee a multi-headed hydra appearance from the sky.

Mark David and Allen Mikes, in a lumbering 28-foot Trembly bird dog with an under-powered Mercury kicker, had created, by virtue of their much earlier start, a bigger lead on the sleeker Cogency than Hayes, Thomas, and Rolf had on Luke and Ryland in the 16-foot flats boat the younger Buck had puckishly named the *Big Skiff Energy*. A Johnson 90-horse outboard pushed Luke's low-slung skiff more than fifty miles per hour on old-world gasoline and still well above forty on wood gas.

Ryland's plan had been a good one. When the Big Skiff Energy emerged from the back bay into the Suwannee Sound, a little black dot in the distance began to resemble the Cogency more by the minute as Luke pinned the throttle full to the helm.

"There they are!" Ryland yelled above the motor's wide-open growl.

"Nobody outruns the B.S.E!" Luke yelled back before both boys settled into triumphant, whooping yowls that echoed the rebel attackers from the

Battle of Station Four, two miles and a hundred and sixty years, give or take, off the starboard side of the skiff.

"What is that?" Rolf yelled to Hayes and Thomas as he pointed toward an aquamarine blur in the distance behind them.

Hayes took a quick look back, then returned to pushing the Cogency hard ahead. "Keep an eye on it and keep me posted," he said.

Thomas moved to the stern, straining to make out the details of the speck of color growing larger by the moment.

"A bunch of pelicans, maybe?" Rolf mused.

"Never seen a blue-green pelican before," Thomas replied, laughing, before a series of neurons fired in his brain in such a way that a spark of recognition halted the laughter in a snap. "That little shit!"

Two of the three boat crews in the multigenerational armada were now aware of each other. Hayes was crazed with worry when the B.S.E. had closed enough of the distance between it and the Cogency for him to recognize both of its occupants.

Hayes asked, "How do you want to handle this, Thomas... stop and send 'em back or keep going?"

It took Thomas a few seconds to process the question. In all their years of friendship, he had never seen Hayes relinquish the authority of his boat captaincy, even momentarily, to anyone but Mark David. In other areas of life—navigating divorces, real estate, anything to do with the written word—Hayes was often content to follow Thomas' lead, but on the water, his ascendancy was absolute. Later, when there was time to reflect on the events of the day, Thomas would come to understand the grace of Hayes' instant abdication. Luke was his best friend's boy, and he would defer to a father's judgment.

Thomas stared quietly ahead, paralyzed by the impossible choice before him. Any delay hazarded the lives of Mark David, a man he loved as a surrogate for his own missing father, and Allen Mikes, a man he feared and liked in unequal measure, but continuing on would lead his own son into the dangers ahead. Before he had settled on something to say, the B.S.E. jumped across the Cogency's wake and pulled alongside her.

The sight of his son at the helm of the little skiff was a revelation. There comes a time in every father's life when they can no longer protect their sons from the dangers of the world, when they have to let them become the men they will become. There in the midafternoon sun, as Luke's wild blonde hair blew away from his angular face, as he confidently steered his boat with one hand and waved carefree at his father with the other, the same smirk and swagger that had passed through a hundred years of Buck men commandeered the moment.

In his magnificence, foolhardy and exuberant, Luke Buck, captain of the Big Skiff Energy, accepted a knowing smile from this father and maneuvered into formation with the larger vessel—onward to the river, together.

8

— · —

ONE OF US

Christmas morning of 1998 was crisp but comfortable in Cedar Key. The temperature had hovered near eighty degrees most afternoons of the previous week, but by Christmas Eve night, a cold front had moved in, bringing sweater weather that made Christmas morning as much of a winter wonderland as Florida had any right to expect.

Isaac Skipjack walked the quarter mile from his government-subsidized duplex to the David house for a midday Christmas meal with Mr. Mark, Miss Bette, Hayes and his sister Lida Maria, and Samantha Maye, cousin to the Davids and seemingly everyone else in town. It had been almost nine months since Mark David caught Isaac skipping school and invited him to work on the clam boat for the first time. From that day on, Isaac was a regular member of the David crew, growing over time into a squared-away waterman on whom they increasingly relied.

Even away from the clam farm, the elder David was seldom seen around town without his young protégé in tow. When they weren't clamming, they began spending a fair amount of time running a now outlawed gill net, catching mullet to smoke and bring to Miss Bette for use in her famous smoked mullet dip. FWC officers had a devil of a time enforcing the net ban in the months and early years after a constitutional amendment essentially ended commercial fishing in the nearshore waters of the Gulf.

Over time, as fines and jail time began to accrue for repeat offenders, the net boats stopped running around Cedar Key. As much for pure defiance as anything else, Mark and Isaac began heading up into the Suwannee River to net mullet.

The town of Suwannee sits along the Salt Creek at its confluence with the river. It is often referred to as the white trash Venice—Italy, not Florida—due to it being situated on a network of canals that all run to the river and, a few miles downstream, into the Gulf. Nearly every parcel of land in the town is on a canal, and these are developed with mostly older mobile homes, some elevated as high as fifteen feet on concrete blocks, others right on the ground at the mercy of the oft-flooding river. Nicer houses and a few mediocre condominium developments were interspersed here and there but in insufficient numbers to dampen the low-rent charm of the place.

Suwannee is located twenty-five miles down a two-lane road from Old Town, the next municipality with any infrastructure or services. Because it had no police force of its own, a call to the authorities would mean a thirty to forty-five-minute response time for Dixie County sheriff's deputies to arrive. For this reason, there was a lawlessness about the river town that evoked the Wild West or, at least, the untamed Florida of generations past. This was exactly the kind of place to catch bootleg mullet with an illegal net, and Mark David enjoyed spending time there with Isaac Skipjack.

Hayes and Mark were in the backyard when Isaac arrived for Christmas, frying a turkey in a propane-fired pot of oil.

Hayes met him with a warm handshake. "Merry Christmas, Skipper."

Isaac had only ever been given hurtful schoolyard nicknames in the past, so he took extra pride in this derivation of his last name and how it tied him to the David family maritime culture of which he was increasingly a part. "Merry Christmas, Mr. Hayes."

"Damnit it, dude," Hayes replied. "It's just Hayes. I ain't enough older than you for a Mister."

"But you're the mayor," Isaac replied.

Mark David, who had been the mayor prior to his son's ascension to the job, laughed heartily. "Being mayor sure don't earn you any extra honors. It just means you're the biggest sucker in town. A measly four hundred bucks a month, and half the town hates you all the time."

"He's right about that," Hayes affirmed.

"Then why do y'all do it?"

"So some damn yankee transplant can't," Mark answered.

Isaac looked toward Hayes.

"I mean, there's also a sense of duty... community service... a desire to pay the island back for everything it's given us. Right, Dad?"

Mark rolled his eyes. "Uh..."

"Yeah, mostly to keep the yankees out," Hayes relented, laughing. "I've got some ideas about how to improve some of our services and modernize how we do the town's business... but really, all we want is for people who aren't from here to stop telling us how everything ought to be."

In this last response, Mark David was exceedingly pleased. The minute smile that signified his approval quietly exhilarated his son, who returned the gesture with a stoic half-nod.

"If things were so good in Michigan or New York," Mark mused, "Then why'd those bastards leave to come here?"

Isaac replied, "The warmer weather, I guess. And no state income tax. The cost of living is so high in the northeast they can bring big city money down here and live like kings."

"That was a rhetorical question," Mark shot back. "And what do you know about it anyway? What's the furthest you've ever been away from Cedar Key?"

"Tallahassee, once," Isaac replied. "But I read."

Mark laughed. "You hear that, son... we got ourselves an academic here for Christmas. 'Ol professor Skipjack gonna learn us up good."

"Back off, Dad. He thought he was helping."

"But yeah, obviously," Isaac interjected in an attempt to redeem himself, "Yankees suck."

"I'll drink a Christmas beer to that," Mark replied, tossing Hayes and Isaac a Coors Banquet from a cooler near the turkey fryer.

"Dad, he's 17."

"You ain't gonna tell the mayor on him, are you?"

The three men laughed together and cracked their beers along with the crackling of the turkey in the oil.

"You boys are gonna cook that bird to death if you're not careful," Miss Bette called through the open kitchen window. "The fixins are ready... just waiting on you."

"It's about done," Mark called back.

Hayes said, "Be right in, mom. Don't let Lida Maria eat all the mullet dip before we get there."

"Got a surprise for you fellas," Mark said. "Help me get this turkey in the house."

They had, in fact, overcooked the bird, but it was fried, so it would still be good. As they carried it through the kitchen, Hayes saw the new table in the dining room.

"Whoa. That's beautiful, Dad. You finally did something with all that cypress from the river."

"Yes sir."

"You finished it!" Isaac said excitedly. "Did you end up going with the polyurethane or the varnish?"

"Mr. Herms talked me out of the poly since we'd be eating off it. Look how good the varnish shows the grain."

Isaac examined the table with pride. "I didn't think we were ever gonna figure out these dovetail joints. The table could've been twice as long if I didn't keep messing up the cuts."

"I screwed up plenty, too," Mark replied.

Hayes had nothing further to say about the table; he took his seat quietly next to his sister.

The meal was lavish, southern, and refined, like Miss Bette. The conversation was irreverent, sharp, and loud, like Mr. Mark. Isaac held his own well enough in a family so steeped in traditions, inside jokes, and love. It was the first formal Christmas meal he could remember since before his grandmother died when he was little.

As Lida Maria and Cousin Samantha began to clear away the dishes, Miss Bette announced, "We did our family gift exchange this morning, but we got a little something for you, Isaac."

Hayes retrieved a thin, wrapped rectangle from the living room and handed it to Isaac. "This is from all of us."

"I didn't know we were doing presents," Isaac replied, embarrassed. "I didn't get you all anything."

"Hush with that," Mark said. "It's just a little something from us to thank you for everything you're doing with the clam farm and at the shop."

Eagerly, Lida Maria said, "Open it, open it."

Isaac tore away the wrapping paper, revealing an aluminum vanity license plate with the white *David Sea Farms* logo on a field of light blue.

"Cool," Isaac said with a note of hesitancy he tried to hide. "I think I can rig this up to fit the back of my bike."

The Davids exploded in laughter.

"Can you imagine?" Cousin snorted.

"Oh, Isaac," Lida Maria said. "That's funny."

The color drained from Isaac's face as he struggled for the right response to the laughter.

Was this another family joke he wasn't in on? Was he the joke... were they making fun of him?

"Somebody let the poor boy off the hook," Miss Bette admonished.

"Here," Hayes said, smiling, as he tossed a set of keys to Isaac.

The gift was so unfathomable to him that Isaac simply could not work out what it all meant. "I'm sorry, but I don't understand."

"These are the keys to one of the trucks from the shop. We had it cleaned up for you. Me and Hayes will teach you to drive it so you can get your license. But it belongs to you now."

Isaac Skipjack lit up as brightly as the tree in the adjoining room. "For real?"

"Merry Christmas, Skipper," Hayes said, giving in to the moment. "Your truck's out front. The tag is so folks will know you're one of us. Let's go put it on."

Isaac leaped from his seat and raced for the door, then turned back to quickly hug everyone in the room. Mr. Mark held on a few extra seconds so the boy would not see him wiping at his eyes.

Before the calendar rolled over into 1999, Isaac had fairly well learned to drive, and by February, he had his license.

Before the end of March, he'd be gone.

Cabbage Key was about as ideal a place to be stranded after a nuclear holocaust as a person could hope for. The fact that it remained undisturbed more than a month after the bombs fell was, the Colonel decided, a discouraging sign for the mainland's prospects. His home island had dealt with looters and raiders within the first week. Its isolated location in a rural part of the state had likely saved it from the total destruction he had witnessed beneath the wings of the Archer as he approached the greater Tampa Bay area.

Cabbage Key seemed to be in the unlikely Goldilocks Zone of being far enough into the Gulf to avoid the heat and shockwaves of the bombs but close enough to devastation so widespread that few survivors remained to seek out the island's resources. As the Colonel commenced a full reconnoiter of the island, however, he could not escape the knowledge that a hostile boat crew was operating in nearby waters. It was possible that the rain and clouds had fully shielded his escape, but it was equally likely that the sound of his dying engine had given him away, and the Sawfish was, even then, scouring the Gulf for the downed Archer.

The Colonel searched more than half of the rental cottages that first day on Cabbage Key, finding little of use beyond linens and a few straggler cans of condensed milk and green peas. The sight of the peas made him laugh. He said out loud, "Oh hell no. I'd rather starve." The mouth mush of green peas had made him gag as a boy, and his palate never evolved to find them anything other than unpalatable. The sound of his voice had a raspy and thin timbre that was jarring to him. He had been alone for a day and a half, and other than a few calls over the Archer's radio, there had been no cause for speaking. The weakness of the sound was so worrying that he began to sing a little while exploring to keep the pipes working and to quiet the pragmatism of his internal monologue that always wanted to calculate the long odds of ever making it back to Geoff and Melinda Beth.

As the sun began to set, the Colonel ended the day's exploration and returned to the inn. He ate his fill of canned corn and pickled eggs, deciding he would wait until the next day to build a fire to cook some of the abundant rice in the dry storage room. On the tables of the restaurant and in three large boxes near the rice, he found tea-light candles that had been used to create a soft glow ambiance for guests in the old world. According to writing on the outside of the boxes, each candle had a burn time of 6 hours, and there were 520 candles in each box. Out of boredom, the Colonel tried to do the math to determine the number of lighting hours he would have by burning one candle at a time. He was able to work out pretty easily that the three boxes contained 1,560 candles, but multiplying that number by six meant carrying a three, then maybe another three, and by then, he had lost count of what the bottom number should be—maybe it was still another three, but he couldn't be sure—so that by the end, discounting the candles on the tables altogether, he either had 936 or 9,600 or 4 years of available light. Whatever the correct figure turned out to be didn't matter much to him. If he had his way, he would find gasoline and the materials he needed to repair the Archer the next day and then make a plan to return home to Cedar Key.

For the rest of his life, the Colonel often thought of that first night on Cabbage Key, when his belly was full, and his heart emboldened with optimism as he settled in for a good night's sleep in a warm bed in the inn. Surely, he thought, the morning would bring him everything he needed to get home.

The Cogency and the Big Skiff Energy pushed ahead toward Alligator Pass as fast as the mix of old and new technologies powering them would allow. The Suwannee Sound was empty and calm as the East Pass appeared off their starboard sides. From this pass, a boater could run hard at high tide all the way to its intersection with the main river, a mile upriver from the town of Suwannee, and three miles from its intersection with the Gulf at Alligator Pass. In a few more minutes, the boats passed the entrance to Raulerson Creek, from which branched innumerable smaller creeks and cuts that a captain with local knowledge, like Hayes David, could use to dive in and out of the river from multiple points.

Shortly, they could see Alligator Pass ahead, but there was still no sign of Mark David and Allen Mikes. As they neared the mouth of the river, Hayes was unnerved to see nothing at all. No bird dog, no sailing ships, no evidence that anyone had been there recently. He had been so sure that the intel his mother overheard meant they were heading for the river. If they hadn't, there's no telling where they might be, and Hayes and the others had no prospects for figuring it out. Worse, two of the navy's vessels were away from Cedar Key if it were to be attacked. Weighing the risk of missing a potential battle against the possibility that his dad and uncle might just be further up the river, Hayes made a command decision, waving back at Luke and Ryland to follow him into the Suwannee.

The two boats covered the two miles from Alligator Pass to the town of Suwannee quickly, seeing nothing of note along the way. As they neared the first of the many canals that run into and throughout the town, Hayes waved Luke to pull alongside.

"I was sure hoping we catch 'em before they got here. Now I'm not sure if they're here at all."

"What's the plan?" Luke asked.

"We came all this way... I think we ought to ease through the canals to see if there's any sign of them," Hayes replied.

"If we split up, we could get it done quicker," Luke suggested.

Thomas disagreed, "I don't know how much good two boats could do if we run into their whole fleet, but one boat has got no chance."

"I agree," Hayes said. "We stay together."

The decision turned out to be a good one. A quarter mile in, the canal made a ninety-degree turn to starboard. The crew of the Cogency, in the lead, saw it first, but within seconds, the B.S.E. had rounded the bend as well. In the water against the marsh, abandoned, was Mark David's bird dog. In the distance, above the roofs of the covered boat slips that lined the channel peeked the top of a sailing mast.

Hayes wasted no time with sentiments or indecision.

"Luke, you know the way back, right?"

"Yes sir," he replied.

"Good," Hayes said sharply. "Ryland, hop over to our boat with your rifle and that bow. Luke, fast as you can push it, get home and rally the fleet. Tell Joey Bannon to take a half dozen boats up the East Pass toward the Suwannee Marina. Everyone else, come to this canal through Alligator Pass."

"What are you guys gonna do until we get back?" Luke asked worriedly.

Thomas intervened. "Go, son!"

Ryland leaped onto the Cogency with the rifle and bow. Luke spun the B.S.E. hard around, nodded once to his father, then pushed the throttle down.

9

LITTLE JUKEBOXES

In 1555, Nostradamus predicted a global calamity would descend from the sky in 1999, maybe an antichrist; in 1982, the artist formerly and again later known as Prince suggested that our defense for this terror was simply to party, though he was dreaming when he wrote it. When the year finally arrived, much of the world was consumed with fear that the Y2K glitch would lead to a computer-induced apocalypse. While a pedant would point out that the 20th century actually ran from 1901 through the end of 2000, making 1999 a year of no technical consequence at all, the less didactic, which is to say practically everybody on Earth, viewed it with a sense of wistful finality, an end of the era when humanity leapt from horseback to rocket ship, from an old world naivete to an information age that cast away ignorance the more it unfurled itself.

Isaac Skipjack would have been better off with ignorance.

That March had the characteristic bipolar weather of late winter bleeding into an island spring. The chill of evenings would swing almost forty degrees warmer in the afternoons. For Isaac, the cold was manic, thrilling; the indifference of a warm day weighed him down in the opposite fashion from most other people. Even now, driving his gifted pick-up to neighboring Chiefland for a final follow-up appointment at the dentist—the last his father had made for him—Isaac waved at passing cars, like people do in the South, and felt a stinging *otherness* with the world. He was a new driver, and he loved everything about it, save for the way being on the road seemed to always push his thoughts inward—past the goings-on of the day, deep toward the fundamental, to the core ingredients of himself, always to his father.

The squat, balding dentist greeted Isaac warmly when he walked into the exam room.

"How's it going with the new tooth? Any trouble?"

"I've pretty much got used to it," Isaac replied. "I went so long without one that it still feels weird sometimes."

"No pain, though?" the dentist asked.

"No sir, not really. I was sore for a long time after that last part, but not anymore."

"Terrific. An implant like this is a long process. I know you're tired of all these appointments, but this should be the last one. Let's have a look."

The dentist was especially proud of his work. "Very nice, very nice," he said as he felt and examined the implanted front tooth under the bright overhead light. "Everything looks just like it should. I think your dad would be real pleased with how it all turned out."

Isaac gripped the side of the exam chair, squeezing until his knuckles burned, fighting uselessly against tears that ran fast and heavy from both eyes, down his face, and onto the polished terrazzo floor.

"Oh gosh, I'm sorry," the dentist said, upset with himself to have elicited such a response from the boy. "Of course I didn't mean to... it's just... well I knew him a long time is all. I know what this meant to him."

"Anything else you need from me?" Isaac asked coldly as he collected himself.

"No sir," the dentist replied, "I just wanted to see how you were doing."

"I'm fine," Isaac replied, harsher than he intended. "What do I owe you for the visit?"

"Nothing. It was all paid upfront."

"Okay," Isaac said, rising from the chair and starting for the door, his embarrassment at the show of emotion manifesting as a lack of courtesy that served only to amplify the embarrassment.

With the moment heightened as it was, the dentist knew the risk of pressing, but something in his belly wouldn't let him keep quiet.

"Isaac, wait. I know there's nothing to say to make up for what you lost, but I can tell you Buddy sure loved you."

It was just then, as his temper flared again, that Isaac became aware of his backwards response to sentiment about his father—not just with the dentist but with everyone since Chief Vernon had first stopped by to tell him about the death. Even so, this understanding wasn't enough, yet, to change his behavior.

"What do you know about it?" Isaac asked sharply.

"Plenty," replied the dentist. "And anytime you need proof, go smile as big as you can in the mirror and take a look right at it."

"Huh?" Isaac replied.

"Everybody knows how tough it's been out there since they took the nets away. Buddy didn't want you to know what all this costs, but I think you ought to."

Isaac softened immediately, unexpectedly. "I never thought about it," he said. "Was it a lot?"

"I guess the actual number doesn't matter... but for the kind of work you needed, it'd be a lot for anybody."

"Then how?" Isaac asked. "How'd he pay for it?"

The dentist smiled, venturing a hand on the boy's shoulder. "See, that part doesn't matter at all. What matters is that he did."

Isaac, bereft, ashamed, searched for something to say, for some grown-up thing that would overtype his childishness with the dentist. When nothing came, he extended his hand, which the dentist shook warmly, then walked quietly out of the office.

Chiefland was the largest town in Levy County but not the county seat. Its development spread mostly along a two-mile stretch of US-19, its main artery. The southern end of town featured the original old-style storefronts from the 1950s, many shuttered or in disrepair, while the northern end comprised the cut-and-paste car lots, drive-through restaurants, gas stations, and strip malls ubiquitous in highway towns across the southern states.

Of course, there was a Walmart.

Most folks in Cedar Key went to Chiefland at least once a week for essentials, groceries that were cheaper than the island's mom-and-pop market, haircuts, car repairs, and dentist appointments. Isaac didn't care much about any of that. Only one thing about Chiefland would ever matter to him—Linette's Big-T Restaurant. For most of his childhood, it was Linette's Big-T Truck Stop, but I-75 slowly drained most of the traffic away from US-19 until the big trucks stopped going that way. Only the restaurant portion survived.

Thinking so intently about his father on the way over from the dentist's office, Isaac gave into the memories as he walked into the Big-T and picked a seat in a booth by the windows. As a child, he loved sitting in the wooden booths because each of them had its own miniature jukebox that would play a song for a dime. Buddy Skipjack would trade the waitress a dollar for ten of them for his boy as soon as they sat down.

"I know it's pointless to ask," Buddy was saying again, so crisp and clear in Isaac's mind that any second he seemed sure to materialize across the Formica table, "Since you're gonna get damn chicken fingers like always...

but be thinking about what you want so you can order when the girl comes back."

The rest of the memory now spread out across the restaurant. The long-closed salad bar was open again, and Isaac could see the big-haired old ladies at the table by the door to the kitchen, smoking and holding court. The green chalkboard on the wall displayed the specials—country fried steak or fried catfish with three sides for $4.99, salad bar included. Giant glasses of sweet tea sat on paper placemats at almost every table where hard, unkempt men, fresh from the road, ate fast, messy, and joyfully.

Isaac was putting the first dime in the little jukebox now, selecting A7 first, as always, to play his favorite song. The jangly up-tempo music began, bright and fun, as Mel McDaniel crooned the opening verse of his only hit:

> *Down on the corner*
> *by the traffic light*
> *everybody's lookin'*
> *as she goes by.*
> *They turn their heads,*
> *and they watch her 'til she's gone.*

On cue—this is a performance they have done countless times before—Buddy Skipjack drops his voice down low to sing, with surprisingly perfect pitch, the payoff line:

> *Lord have mercy*
> *Baby's got her blue jeans on.*

Seven year old Isaac laughs free and easy, so hard and loud that his seventeen year old self can hear it across the years, can feel his father's spirit bristling along his spine and the hair on the back of his neck, the two of them together again in the wooden booth, if only in recollection, in the mystic chords of his father's memory, in their deep and painful union.

There was no song playing when the real-time waitress arrived; the little jukeboxes were long gone.

"What can I get you, honey?"

Isaac did not look at her, staring ahead still, waiting for his father to appear.

"Chicken fingers, please."

"Be right up."

They were ten dollars now, and Buddy never showed.

Bob Corliss took a different path to the flying life than his friend, Robert McCloud. While his buddy was earning his wings in the Marine Corps and flying combat missions in southeast Asia, Bob, who was ten years older, had aged out of the draft and avoided the war altogether.

The Corliss family ran a roofing truss company that Bob's father began during the years following the Second World War. When American soldiers returned home in droves from their service abroad, a boom of babies and home-building swept across the nation. The elder Corliss, enterprising and shrewd, began building trusses by hand in the rural central Florida town of Bartow to sell to local builders. In a matter of weeks, he could no longer keep up with demand, so he began hiring Mexican migrant workers who were there to pick the oranges from the thousands of acres of groves throughout Polk County. By the end of the first year, he was employing a dozen workers and had purchased a parcel of land on US-17, a prominent shipping thoroughfare at the time, and constructed a series of pole barns on it that were the beginnings of what would eventually become a sprawling truss-building factory.

When Bob Corliss took over the business after his father was killed in a car crash in 1970, Central Florida Truss Works employed more than a hundred people and was a multi-million-dollar-a-year operation. It was in the lap of this abundance that Bob, bored with continuing the life's work of his father, took up flying in the 1980s. What he lacked in the natural aptitude of *good stick* pilots like Colonel McCloud, he made up for with meticulous fussiness when it came to flying and the maintenance and upkeep of his aircraft. Bob had grown to affect an aristocratic air befitting a family of older money than his, but even in this self-exultant state, he was smart enough to know that he did not possess enough inherent skill as a pilot to skimp on preparedness, checklists, and the kind of anal retentiveness absent a barnstormer like the Colonel.

Bob's friendship with the Colonel, begun after the Colonel's retirement from a 28-year military career, was an unlikely one. It was the middle 1990s, and Bob had built a house near the George T. Lewis Airport in Cedar Key, settling into an early semi-retirement at age fifty-six while his two sons, Steve and Scott, ran the business unharmoniously together—two diabolically opposed heirs whose offices on opposite ends of the company headquarters meant they seldom, by design, had chance to meet or interact, preferring the relatively new medium of e-mail for their limited communications. The Colonel had just purchased a twenty-year-old stone crab boat and had it repainted and christened the *Miss Melinda*. Despite the different backgrounds and dispositions of the two pilots, their mutual love for flying was enough to forge a friendship that transcended their differences. They spent many weekends together in the Piper Archer that Bob kept in the hangar beneath his sprawling house.

Bob Corliss' Piper Archer was a compromise with his wife, Cedar Key's famously short runway, and his declining skills as a pilot. Bob had purchased a shimmering new King Air 350, fresh off the 1990 production line, and had flown the complex, twin-engine, 8-passenger plane to the Bahamas for leisure and around the country to visit suppliers and customers for the truss business. His meticulous manner was enough to keep him alive during the five years at the helm of the King Air, but just barely. A hard landing that overshot the runway on a breezy, frozen morning at the Chattanooga Metropolitan Airport was enough to convince Bob to downgrade to a less complex aircraft.

The Piper Archer is the Ford Taurus of airplanes—simple, safe, slow, and easy to fly. Bob's brand-new 1995 model was one of only 24 built that year by a company that was clawing its way out of bankruptcy. It had a normal cruising speed of only 118 knots, compared to the King Air's 310, and its fixed landing gear and smaller size made it a perfect Cedar Key plane. Bob had paid the $144,900 full retail price for his Archer—tail number N82083—but by the time he outfitted it with high-end avionics, upgraded leather seats, and a gaudy custom paint job that mimicked fighter planes from the 1940s, he had spent just over $200,000 on what would be his last airplane. The Colonel could scarcely look at the thing with a straight face, but he sure loved flying it. Anytime he landed the plane with Bob on board, touching it down with the gentle pitter-patter of butterfly feet on a spring azalea, he would smirk at his ham-handed friend who could never get the Archer on the ground without a bounce and a thud.

Despite his misgivings about the Archer's garish appearance, the Colonel was nevertheless distraught, on that morning in late March of 1999, when he learned that Isaac Skipjack had smashed in the windows and kicked apart one of the ailerons of his friend's airplane. Few people on the island, the Colonel among them, would ever know the details of why Isaac had done it, but among those that did, most believed Bob Corliss had it coming.

Isaac Skipjack finished his chicken fingers and headed back to Cedar Key. He had spent the meal in the liminal space between the present and the past, so he was thankful that his mind gave him a reprieve from introspection on the thirty-minute drive home. He had thought all the deep thoughts and felt all the big feelings he could handle for one day, and notwithstanding some new appreciation for his father, Buddy Skipjack was still as dead as ever. Garth Brooks came on the radio, and Isaac sang along about having *two pina coladas, one for each hand*, though he had never had a colada of any kind, and realized while belting the twangy chorus he wasn't sure he knew what one even was.

When he approached the intersection of State Road 24 and 5th Street on the island, he made a reflexive decision that would alter the trajectory of his life, and though it would take some years to materialize, imperil the island and everyone on it—he decided to make a stop at the hardware store instead of turning right at 5th and heading home.

The David family had a charge account at Island Hardware, and Isaac was authorized to use it. Just before turning for home, Isaac remembered he would be cutting PVC pipe into clam bag stakes the next morning and wanted to go ahead and pick up the pipe so he wouldn't have to get up as early. Ordinarily, David Sea Farms bought the pipe in bulk from a distributor, but their normal delivery was unexpectedly delayed. The cost per stick was considerably higher on the island, but it was worth the expense to not delay the week's clam planting schedule.

The rack of half-inch thin-walled PVC pipe was in a fenced side yard of the store. They were sold in 20-foot lengths. There is no hard and fast rule for how long a clam bag stake should be, and indeed, there is a wide variation in the lengths preferred by different farmers, but the Davids typically used a 10-inch stake. The math worked out nicely, with each 20-foot pipe making 24 stakes, but since each belt of clams utilized twelve stakes, and he needed to buy enough pipe for 150 belts, it took him a bit to work out that he needed to buy 75 pipes.

Isaac finished his calculations and then began counting how many pipes were in stock when he heard laughing behind him, across the side yard, near the covered racks where the crown molding and baseboard were kept. He didn't think much of it until he heard Bob Corliss, a man he knew only as a rich guy with an airplane, but whose high-pitched voice and faux antebellum affectation was instantly recognizable, say, laughing and smug to another man he didn't recognize, "Well 'ol Buddy sure won't be stealing any more clams."

Years later, more than the actual words from Bob Corliss, who had only heard third-hand accounts about the ordeal and who knew next to nothing about clam farming, Isaac would still fixate on the sequence of events that had to transpire for him to be at the PVC rack at the exact moment to hear what he heard. Certainly, if he had just turned for home at 5th Street, he would not have heard it. If he had ordered the peach cobbler at the Big-T, like he normally did, the time spent eating it would have made him miss his interaction with Bob Corliss. If he hadn't waited the extra two minutes in the truck after arriving at the hardware store to finish singing a George

Strait song, he might not have heard the delicate, over-dressed man further remark, "Mark David made sure of that."

There had been no time for Isaac to contemplate whether or not Bob Corliss was telling the truth. His instant, wild reaction was a process begun in the dentist's chair, nurtured by the memories in the wooden booth, and set loose when he heard his father's name. Isaac was six feet, two inches tall but featherweight, all elbows and kneecaps, but the momentum of a running start propelled him into the laughing man like a bighorn sheep crashing into a rival. Bob Corliss hit the ground, gasping for a breath he could not catch, and Isaac would maybe have beaten him to death if the other man hadn't intervened. He tried to pull Isaac away but could make no headway. Finally, he swung a hard blow into Isaac's mouth, knocking him clear of Bob Corliss and onto the ground, bloody and dazed.

The force of the blow scrambled Isaac's brain out of its wildness and into the realization that he needed to get out of the hardware store immediately. He sped away in his truck, driving around the island to calm down, when he happened by chance upon the road running parallel to the airport runway. Here, another improbable fact asserted itself. The Corliss Archer would normally be tucked away in its hangar, out of sight. On this day, however, it was tied up on the apron at the end of the runway, waiting for the Colonel and Bob Corliss, who had planned to fly it on a hundred-dollar hamburger run later that day.

Isaac did what he did to the Archer, felt the adrenaline rush away at last, then steeled his nerve and headed for the David house.

10

GENERAL QUARTERS

L izzy Fraydel was working in the garden at the house on E Street when the airhorn blast rang out.

In the old world, distracted as she was by the hectic pace of modern life, she had killed everything she ever planted. No matter how diligently she thought she worked at it, her thumbs remained as black as a new moon night. In the year since that terrible morning, when the southern horizon exploded in blinding light and then morphed to haunted, lingering gray, the quiet, long hours of life in the new world focused her attention on the task in a way not possible in the whirl and hum of the digital age. She was now, to her prideful delight, a successful grower of things and a provider for her family and neighbors.

Before the world changed, Lizzy was the *Clam Princess* of Cedar Key, an unofficial title given to her by friends because she had been the prom queen, homecoming queen, and captain of the cheerleading squad at the Cedar Key School—a picture of 1990s poof-hair, preppy chic—before marrying a sturdy Italian kid from the basketball team and building, over time, a powerhouse clam farm operation and a loving all-American family. When cancer came for her husband, wearing him away over five hard-fought years, their son Jack, Jr. moved home from college at Florida State and took his father's place at the helm of the bird dog. The rugged, secretly sensitive son knew the weight of his new responsibility and met it head-on, becoming an impressive waterman that even much older clam farmers grew to admire. Just as some stability began to return to the Fraydel family and their farm, the smokestacks fell, taking the lives they had known with them.

Lizzy had met Thomas in a bucket line during the great fire. Dozens of islanders were lined shoulder to shoulder from the bay to the burning houses on 2nd Street, passing buckets of water one to another to help the single fire truck fight the blaze. When Thomas accepted the first bucket from a woman on his right, he had nearly dropped it, caught as he was in the gravitational pull of her perfect face. He was ashamed of his preoccupation with her at such a moment when the island had already lost so much, so many, and now was burning before them.

And yet, there she was, delicate and pretty, handling the heavy buckets as well as any man among them, defiant in the face of adversity. It would take some time, and a few more awkward interactions over the coming weeks, but from that first bucket on, they were moving always closer together, collapsing into one another like dying stars whose combined fire would burn brighter for as long as the life held out.

When Hurricane Jonah carried her home into the Gulf, Lizzy moved into the house on E Street with Thomas, though she had been staying there most nights already for some time. She plowed the side yard under with a shovel and hoe, cutting out the roots and picking out every rock and piece of debris until it was perfect. The garden gave her purpose, steadying her mind with useful work. While Thomas, Hayes, and Rolf worked to solve the island's ever-expanding list of problems, she planted broccoli, carrots, and potatoes. When they built a navy to defend against invaders from the mainland, she planted tomatoes, sugar snap peas, and turnips. All around the island, folks did the things they could do, measuring their contribution by maximizing their own talents, not against the talents of others.

In the years leading up to the flash, there had been in the Western world a campaign, subtle at first and then overt, to abandon the idea that women and men are generally better at different things, indeed that there was much difference in them at all. The corollary to this way of thinking, thinly hidden as inference, was the notion that women choosing more traditionally feminine roles were somehow ceding their power away to the men. Of course, this concept was largely lost on Southern culture, where the mommas might cook more of the meals but are almost always, quietly, the most powerful force in the family. Lizzy Fraydel was such a woman, tending her garden and yielding to Thomas only because he yielded to her in equal, different measure. She was the person toward which Thomas and her son Jack, Jr. would look for emotional leadership in times of trouble, encouragement for the battles that came, solace in defeat.

But it wasn't all vegetables and feelings; when required, some southern women—Deborah Sampson at the Battle of Yorktown, Almeda Hart at Vicksburg, Lizzy Fraydel when the air horn blew—would hitch up their skirts, grab a rifle, and head into the fight.

Luke Buck raced the Big Skiff Energy through the bay and into the back canal, blasting the air horn as he went. Following the invasion of the island by the Meade clan in the early months after the flash, a variety of emergency alerts were standardized and taught to everyone on the island. The single extended air horn blast now reverberating through town was the general quarters alert for the navy. It was to be used only in extreme circumstances, ordering every boat in the fleet to ready for immediate departure. It was also a call for additional citizens who were able, and not normally assigned to a boat crew, to arm themselves and head to the docks on the 3rd Street canal for temporary assignment to a fighting ship.

Lizzy Fraydel was able. She carried her vegetables into the house, retrieved a lever-action rifle from the safe in the front room, and sprinted for the docks.

Isaac Skipjack believed his father was innocent, as all sons must.

The island was too small for him to avoid the stories; it's true that folks, out of decency, did not discuss the matter in Isaac's presence, but he had heard plenty. Life in a small town is like a Shakespeare play—the secrets are constantly being overheard and misunderstood to tragic effect. For Isaac, it was easier to believe there had been a mistake than to believe his father was a thief. He knew this in his belly until he felt it differently in his mouth.

On the way to confront Mark David, blood ran from Isaac's mouth and onto his white shirt. The blow from the man in the hardware store was the hardest he had ever felt. The shock of it had finally faded along with the adrenaline, but he was left now with a sharp ache in his gums, in his teeth, in his front tooth most of all, and it was then he knew his father had stolen the clams.

Worse, he knew why.

Mark David was tinkering in his shed when Isaac arrived with a faraway look in his eyes and more blood on his shirt than he knew.

"You okay, Skipper? What happened to you?"

"Did you do it?" Isaac asked, ignoring the question.

"Did I do what?" Mark replied.

"You know goddamn well what I mean," Isaac said, moving into the shed and toward the older man.

"Hold up, son. Have you lost your mind? Who do you think you're talking to, boy?"

"I'm not a boy, and I ain't your son."

"Be careful, Isaac," Mark replied calmly. "I don't know what's got into you, but you best take a breath here while you still can."

"Answer the question!" Isaac yelled. He was somewhere out of himself now, but his body had kept walking closer to Mark David such that he was face to-face with him before the last word was finished. Just as it was, Mark grabbed him by the back of the neck and shoved him hard into the wall, holding him against it while Isaac breathed hard and fast.

"Take a minute here, Skipper. This ain't went too far yet, but it's close."

Mark's tone was unexpectedly conciliatory, loving even, despite the disrespect he had been shown and the force with which he held the boy's face against the wall of the shed. It was so out of place for the man that it rang tragically false in Isaac's ears. The chemicals in his brain were misinforming him now, and the stilted enunciation of Bob Corliss' feminine voice played on repeat there:

Mark David made sure of that.
Mark David made sure of that.
Mark David made sure of that.

"I know you killed my dad," Isaac said at last, in a whimper, in defeat.

Mark let go immediately. "Son, no..."

But already Isaac was stumbling backward out of the shed.

Over the many years that followed, Mark David would punish himself, in the quiet hours of the night or when he was working on the water alone, for not chasing after the boy immediately. The worst of his fears had been realized in Isaac's accusation, misguided as it was, and he needed a minute to collect himself.

By then, Isaac was gone.

Mark held out hope that a good night's sleep might clear the boy's head, and they could talk things over in the morning. When Isaac didn't show up for work, Hayes and his father went looking for him. They found his truck on the side of the road, on the Cedar Key side of the Number Four Bridge, with a note on the seat that read:

This doesn't belong to me.

Mark David shook his head and smiled when he realized what Isaac had done, seeing the honor in it and feeling, mingled with the loss, a kind of fatherly pride.

The first several months away from Cedar Key were hard times for Isaac, who bounced between the unstable homes of two of his late father's cousins in Bronson and Williston. He made a little money mowing yards with the lesser drunk of the two, but this was sporadic, and he was working on average for a third of what he made with the Davids. Over time, he had been able to save a few hundred dollars but was otherwise progressing toward nothing in particular.

Since that afternoon at the hardware store when Bob Corliss implicated Mark David, there had been little peace for Isaac. He missed being on the water; having developed real aptitude as a waterman, life on land, behind a mower, left him wanting. Whenever he began to indulge feelings of missing his life in Cedar Key, he thought of the day his father had overheard the kids at the city park call his son *Isaac Skiptooth*, how he had chased after them cursing and fell hard by the swings trying to grab one of them by the neck. He thought of the beating his father endured at the end of his life, almost certainly for a decision made that day in the park. He thought of the ache in his tooth while he smashed the windows of the airplane and the way the rough timber of the shed wall felt against his face. More than anything else, he thought of Mark David's calmness that last day, the guileful kindness in his voice, the guilt masquerading as love, and he knew he could never go back.

One morning near the end of June in 1999, Isaac decided he didn't want to mow anymore, so he packed a bag with a change of clothes and walked the twenty-five miles from Williston to the Greyhound bus station in Gainesville. He was offered a few rides along the way but politely refused them. It was late afternoon by the time he arrived, but he was able to buy a ticket for an 8:00 PM bus to Jacksonville, the closest Coast Guard recruiting station.

The decision to try to enlist was made after seeing a television commercial, with no great forethought or reasoning besides simply missing the water. It took the kindness of an administrator at the Cedar Key School to provide Isaac with a high school diploma so he could meet the basic requirements for enlistment. The algebra class he finished the previous December was the last hard requirement for graduation, but absent a sense of pity for his circumstances, disappearing in the middle of even a pointless last semester would have otherwise caused him trouble. At the recruiter's office, Isaac took the ASVAB— Armed Services Vocational Aptitude Battery—a test to determine what jobs he would qualify to train in. A good score on the test is generally thought to be something around 60. Isaac scored a blistering 94, essentially qualifying him for any of the twenty-two different ratings listed in the brochure he was given.

In the United States Navy and Coast Guard, enlisted servicemembers have a rank and a rating. Ranks begin at Seaman Recruit, then advance to Seaman Apprentice, Seaman, through three classes of Petty Officers, then to Chief, Senior Chief, and Master Chief. There are a few exemplary versions of higher Master Chiefs, but never more than a handful in the entire service at any one time.

Ratings are specific to the training and job roles of the individual sailor or guardsman. The ratings vary somewhat between the two branches, but for both, the Boatswain Mate rating is widely regarded as the backbone of the respective fleets. It dates to its inception in 1775 during the Revolutionary War. Along with Quartermaster, Gunner's Mate, and Master-at-Arms, it was one of the four oldest ratings in the American Navy. When the Coast Guard was founded in 1915, Boatswain Mate was one of its inaugural ratings.

Boatswain Mates, called Boats in daily life aboard ship, are responsible for many of the physical operations duties required to keep a ship running smoothly. They supervise the repair and maintenance of the ship's equipment, train personnel in proper seamanship, stand critical watches, command small boats, barges, and tugs, serve in and lead damage control parties, assist with rescue operations, oversee ship-to-ship transfers of equipment and gear, and participate in navigation duties as the ship's helmsman. They are also responsible for the intricate and varied ropework required for ship operation, mastering the marlinspike, a rope-manipulation tool dating to the 1600s and still used in modern navies around the world.

Finally, the Boatswain Mate has a ceremonial and leadership role, demonstrated in their use of a distinctive brass pipe, called the Boatswain Pipe, to signal various happenings on the ship. The shrill, commanding sound of the pipe befits the stature of the rating, which carries additional weight due to its rich maritime history. In practice, Boats are often among the most rugged, physically imposing men of the ship, their bodies honed by the hard labor of life on deck and their dispositions cleansed of extravagance by a spartan life at sea.

Isaac passed his medical exam, and though he qualified for more desirable ratings with signing bonuses, he signed a contract to train as a Boatswain Mate. After eight weeks of basic training in Cape May, New Jersey, and fourteen more at A-School in Yorktown, Virginia, he was a working waterman again.

Twenty-four years later, Senior Chief Boatswain Mate Isaac Skipjack saw the top of a water tower as the Coast Guard Cutter Sawfish sailed into the Captiva Pass.

"There!" he yelled to the crew tending the sails, then ordered the Sawfish to Cabbage Key.

11

— · —

THE ANGEL OF DEATH

Mark David's abandoned boat was sitting low in the water. The distinctive design of the bird dog features an open stern where water can wash on and off the boat. It is a disorienting sensation being on such a boat for the first time because it doesn't look or feel right for water to be coming in; the purpose of most boats is to keep the water out. The genius of the engineering is the fact that the deck of the boat is a flat, wide, enclosed space, about eight inches high. What looks like an incomplete vessel is actually a water-displacing machine that can hold enormous weight without going under. The only way the boat risks sinking is if water finds its way into the enclosed deck.

When Hayes pulled the Cogency alongside his father's bird dog, he knew immediately that it would soon sink. He didn't care about saving the boat but wanted to see if any clues remained about where his father and uncle might be. Ryland held the two vessels together while Hayes and Thomas jumped onto the crippled boat to look around, and Rolf stood watch, rifle at the ready.

"Here," Thomas said, pointing at three small holes in the fiberglass dry box in the center of the deck, each almost big enough for a pinky finger to fit inside.

"Entry holes," Hayes said as he examined them.

"They're at a downward angle," Thomas said, motioning in a diagonal with his hand.

"How in hell would you know that?" Hayes asked.

"The shape is more elliptical than round."

"What?" Hayes asked skeptically.

"I'm serious," Thomas said. "I used to watch a lot of documentaries on the internet at night before bed. A shot that goes straight in makes a round hole. See how these look like long ovals? The more oblong the hole, the greater the angle of entry."

"Son of a bitch," Hayes replied. "That makes sense. If you're right and the shots came from up high, then..."

"Yep," Thomas interrupted as he opened the lid of the dry box, revealing three additional holes angling down into the deck of the boat.

Hayes said, "They must have gone all the way through, down into the water."

"Explains why she's sitting so low," Thomas said.

Hayes unscrewed the access hatch and stuck his arm down into the enclosed area. "About half full," he said. "There's not enough water in here for this to have happened very long ago."

"Hayes," Thomas said, pointing toward the helm. "Blood."

It didn't look like a television crime scene, but the single crimson streak was nevertheless unnerving on the white fiberglass helm.

Hayes processed the image with trademark David calm. "Let's go; they aren't far ahead of us," he said, jumping back over to the Cogency as Thomas followed.

Hayes took the controls while everyone else crouched low along the gunnels, peering down barrels and feeling certain an ambush was coming. The gasifier belched thin columns of black smoke into the air, and the inefficiency of the wood gas easily tripled the sound coming from the normally quiet Suzuki 4-stroke outboard. There could be no hope of surprising their adversaries by water. When Hayes steered around another bend in the canal, Rolf pointed toward an uncovered dock extending slightly further out from the others.

"We should get out there," Rolf said. "We're easy targets on the water. Coming from land, we might have a chance to get up close before they see us."

"Agreed," Hayes replied as he steered toward the dock.

When the Cogency was tied up, the four men gathered their gear and slipped into the side yard of the singlewide trailer belonging to the dock.

"I'm gonna get out ahead, fast as I can," Rolf said, his eyes narrowing into the grim intensity that always overtook him in a fight. "I'll find a position I can do some good from, near that mast," he said, pointing at the sail above the houses, trailers, and docks.

Hayes nodded his approval. "If everything goes to hell, we meet back here at the boat, deal?"

"Deal," Rolf said, then turned and disappeared into the afternoon sun, a revenant in human form stalking along the canals.

Thomas and Ryland looked toward Hayes for direction.

"I'm better on the water," Hayes said, "But I know Suwannee pretty good. This road will dead-end into the one that runs up to the Salt Creek Restaurant that used to have the good sweet tea."

"I stayed in those yellow condos on that road with some buddies a few years back," Thomas said. "I know where we're at."

"Yeah," Ryland said, "Me, too. There's a little marina there. I don't know what it's called. We always just called it the *other marina* because it wasn't the one my daddy liked."

Hayes said, "They dredge that little inlet there. Good water for a boat with a deep draft. I bet that's where that mast is coming from."

"That's where we're heading then," Thomas replied. "How bout me and Ryland work our way up the backyards on the other side of the road, and you head up this side? We can meet up at the last house on the end and reassess."

"Sounds good," Hayes replied, moving the .223 rifle to his shoulder and heading up his side of the road.

Thomas and Ryland sprinted across the open ground of the narrow paved road and into the backyard of an elevated bungalow. Suwannee existed in a state of perpetual disrepair in the best of times, so it was hard to tell if the periodic damage they encountered was caused by the end of the world or the normal maelstrom of an angry river. Aside from their own footfalls, the only sounds came from a screeching osprey and wind blowing through cabbage palms.

They made their way from house to house until, suddenly, the background noise was interrupted by the sound of movement on an elevated screened porch above them.

"You hear that?" Thomas asked.

Ryland nodded. "There's somebody in there."

"Dammit," Thomas replied. "If we keep moving ahead, there's nothing to keep him from shooting us in the back."

"We're gonna have to go up there," Ryland said.

"And do what?"

"We got guns."

"He probably does, too," Thomas replied. "And we're not just gonna go shoot somebody 'cause we happen to be under their porch."

"Mighty obliged to hear that," came the voice from above.

The men below nearly exited their skins.

"I don't want any trouble. And if you're headin' after the fellas that sailed those boats into town, I promise I'm your friend."

Thomas called up, "We don't mean you any harm. We're up from Cedar Key, looking for two of our own."

"They took 'em," said the voice. "Why don't you come on up so we can talk better out of sight? I'd sure 'preciate you not shooting me."

"You could just shoot us soon as we popped our heads up," Ryland said.

"I'm not armed, God's gospel truth. You're more likely to get hurt on those rickety ass stairs than you are from me."

"Well, there's two of us," Thomas replied. "So if you're lying and looking down a shotgun when we get to the top of the stairs, my money is you only get one of us before the other puts you down."

"Fair enough, then. Come on up."

The trek up the outside stairs to the elevated porch was thankfully uneventful. At the top, Thomas and Ryland met a smiling, rotund man in overalls. He was of indeterminate age but likely somewhere between old and real, real old. Overalls and a long white beard made him a dead ringer for Uncle Jesse from The Dukes of Hazzard, an aesthetic that amused Thomas and was lost on Ryland.

"Come on in, come on in," he said in a fast-twitch drawl as he led them into them into the house. "I'm Percy."

"Nice to meet you, Mr. Percy. I'm Thomas, and this is Ryland. We can only stay a minute. We have to meet our partner shortly at the end of the road."

"You here after the two older fellas in the clam boat?"

"Yes, sir," Ryland replied. "You saw them being taken?"

Percy's hand shook in short bursts, one at a time, and he licked at his lips in an off-putting rhythm as he spoke. "They had a little shoot-out with one of the smaller sailing boats... not sailboats, just regular boats with sails put on 'em."

Thomas said, "We chased them around the fog in Cedar Key but never got a good look at them. Anything you could tell us, we'd be much obliged."

"A pile of boats," Percy said. "Probably nine or ten. Most are just regular center consoles or V-hulls... but they got one giant Coast Guard boat like one of those drug catchers on Miami Vice."

Again, Ryland missed the reference, but he could picture the kind of boat Percy was describing.

"I've only seen one mast since we got here," Thomas replied. "And it didn't look big enough to be the kind of boat you're describing. Any idea where it and the rest of them are?"

Percy grew more animated as he talked about the sailing boats. "The big one has to be at the Suwannee Marina, a little further upriver on the other side of town. I don't know what the draft is on that thing, but no way it can go up the canals. When all the boats first got here, looked like maybe twenty men spread out across town kicking in doors and looting."

"They didn't hit you?" Thomas asked.

A giant smile spread the width of Percy's wide face. "They tried to come up here, but I held 'em off pretty good."

"How?" asked Ryland. "You said you weren't armed."

Percy let out a shaking, whole-body laugh that sounded like an 18-wheeler horn. "First time here, son? I just meant I didn't have anything in my arms at the moment. The housecats are packing heat in Suwannee, young fella. Look around."

The afternoon sun was low in the sky, so Percy's elevated house was fairly dark, but when Ryland and Thomas looked past the fidgety man, they saw cheap glass-front gun cases lined side by side through the living and dining rooms, maybe twenty in all. Long guns of every type hung like museum paintings, ready to leap from display to action. On the coffee table, spread haphazardly about, were a baker's dozen of handguns—Glock 19s, a Springfield 1911, a matching pair of cowboy six-shooter *big irons*, and a 500 magnum revolver that fired .50 caliber rounds. Boxes of shells and cartridges were piled three feet high and ten deep on the kitchen counter.

"Whoa," Ryland said, wide-eyed and envious.

Percy beamed. "There's only a handful of folks still here on this part of the river, and they're spread out around town. These little beauties even the odds for me when trouble comes callin'. The sailing boats ain't the first to come and probably won't be the last. But I don't figure these particular villains will come up my road again."

"Hell yeah, Percy. Good for you," Thomas said. "What you've told us is a big help. At least now we've got some kind of idea what we're up against. We better get to the meeting spot, though, or our partner is gonna come looking. I need you to know something, and hopefully the little trust we've built here will help..."

Percy said, "We're friends now, even if you don't know it yet. So what's shakin', friend? Besides me, of course. Seems I'm always shakin' like a damn Chee-wah-wah."

In fits and starts, Percy shook on.

"We sent somebody back to the island to round up every boat and gun we've got," Thomas replied. "They'll be here within the hour if everything goes right."

"Good," Percy said. "Maybe you can run these outlaws back to where they came from. How can I help?"

Thomas replied, "I just wanted you to know our people were coming so you didn't unleash holy hell on them."

Percy's smile filled the room and he spoke excitedly, "You got it, friend. I don't guess I've talked to another person since everything went off the rails, so this was good for me. Most times I try to make friends, I end up feeling like a housecat at a raccoon orgy. I never was much good at socializing, so I hope I ain't running you off by being weird."

"You gotta be a little weird to live in Cedar Key, Mr. Percy, " Ryland said. "So you fit right in with us. We've just gotta meet our friend so he doesn't think we got ourselves killed already. "

Percy, delighted, replied, "Well I'm right proud to know you, fellas. A year's a long time to only talk to yourself. I'd be much obliged if y'all stopped back by after you find your buddies. I got coffee, piles of it. Come back if you can... your whole outfit's welcome."

Thomas extended a hand, but Percy wrapped him up in a big hug instead. Ryland, too.

"Happy hunting, boys. And if I see you tangled up with the sailing boats, I'll help if I can."

Thomas and Ryland negotiated the treacherous stairs and headed toward the meeting place. Hayes was pacing anxiously below the stilt house at the end of the road when they finally arrived.

"What happened to you?" Hayes asked.

"There was somebody living in one of the houses we went under," Ryland replied.

Thomas said, "He saw them take your Dad and Mr. Mark."

"You sure he said they took them both, right? Not just one?"

"He said both," Ryland replied.

A small wave of relief washed over the mayor. One or the other was at least not at the bottom of the river, shot dead. Thomas relayed everything Percy had told them, and Hayes agreed that the big boat could only either be further upriver or at the Suwannee Marina.

"I still say we head for that closest mast and start there," Hayes said, pointing across the intersection.

"At the other marina," Ryland said. "But there's a canal between us and it. How do we get there from here?"

Hayes replied, "A little further up the road, past the yellow condos you were talking about, is a way around."

Thomas scanned the road ahead with a worried look on his face. "There's no cover," he said. "If they know we're here, it'll be like a shooting gallery at the fair."

"Except we're the little yellow ducks," Ryland said.

Hayes, steady as ever, replied, "Yep. But we're either ducks on the road or ducks back there in the boat."

"Don't guess I've ever seen a duck in a boat," Ryland said, "At least not one I hadn't just shot."

Thomas laughed. "Weird way to get there, Ryland... but it's kinda hard to argue with your logic."

"The road then," Hayes said before turning and sprinting full out toward the condos with Thomas and Ryland close behind.

It was a little over a tenth of a mile from the cover of the house on the corner to the cut-through behind the last condominium building. All three of them were in good shape, honed by years of physical labor on the water, but Ryland benefitted from the additional advantage of youth. By the time they made it a third of the way there, he had already passed the older men and was beginning to open a wide lead when the shots started ringing out—four deafening blasts in quick succession. There had been no time to think before each man picked an instant defense. Ryland kept running, faster now than ever in his life, while Thomas and Hayes dove from the road and into the brown water of the canal on the right, leaving their rifles behind. Before they were even fully submerged, the firing abruptly stopped and quiet rushed back into the afternoon.

Ryland reached the cover of the condo building, crouched down and waited for more fire that never came. Instinctively, Hayes and Thomas held their breaths for as long as they could, using the water as a shield they no longer needed. When their chests tightened and the burning in their lungs became unbearable, they eased above the surface and into a quiet serenity that was as disorienting as the shots had been frightening.

They waited, still as death, in the water for several minutes, expecting a re-engagement at any moment. None came. A scraggly Virginia willow overhung the canal a few yards ahead. Hayes used it to pull himself onto the bank and then pull Thomas up behind him. They found their rifles, then sprinted, wet and slow, toward Ryland. The cover of the back wall of the building allowed the three men a place to catch their breath and regain their bearings.

Thomas lay flat on the ground, breathing fast and labored. Sporadic gray clouds moved fast through his field of view, across the lighter gray of the wider sky, like a movie dream sequence, a wispy glimpse at a monochrome afterlife he had narrowly avoided.

Then, suddenly, the Angel of Death appeared, staring down at him from the condo building roof, a terrifying grin on his half-Cuban face.

"They saw you running," Rolf said. "But I got 'em."

The Colonel poured the last of a bag of rice into the pot. The water had reached its rolling boil over a fire made with wood from a maintenance barn he had been disassembling slowly over the past three months.

Rice and canned goods from the restaurant's dry storage room, augmented by the abundant snook and snapper that congregated under the island's main boat dock, made the physical task of living on Cabbage Key relatively easy. The mental and emotional burden was a different thing altogether. It would have been inconceivable to the Colonel, on that first night in the inn, full of pickled eggs and plans for getting home, that he would still be here three months later. There were only two obstacles standing between himself and Melinda Beth, whom he pined for at least as much as he had over the long months of separation during his service in Vietnam—repairing the holes in the Archer's fuel tanks and finding fuel to fill them.

The order of difficulty for these tasks turned out to be the opposite of what would seem intuitive. Repairing the bullet holes in the fuel tanks without the help of a welder or machinist would have been a tall order for most regular people, but not for an older Marine with an interest in history. Before all the fuel had even streamed out of the holes in the Archer, the Colonel's thoughts had turned to the Marines at the Battle of Chosin Reservoir, a two-week bloodbath during the Korean War.

The Marine 1st Division was dug into frozen, mountainous terrain near the Chosin Reservoir, where they faced relentless attack from a vastly larger Chinese force. During this engagement, the Marines ran out of 60-millimeter mortars and radioed for an airdrop to replenish their supply, using the code word for the mortars, *Tootsie Roll*. The Air Force operator who received the request didn't have the code sheets, so he sent an aircraft to parachute multiple pallets of actual Tootsie Rolls to the besieged Marines who, befuddled, nonetheless thawed them in the warmth of their armpits and ate them for energy during the prolonged battle. The real benefit of the abundant candy revealed itself, however, when the Marines used chewed-up Tootsie Rolls to plug holes in the gas tanks and radiators of their shot up vehicles. The temporary repair was surprisingly effective and relatively long-lived.

On his second day on Cabbage Key, the Colonel discovered the large candy jar at the check-in desk of the inn, finding seventeen small Tootsie Rolls total in the jar. A few days later, he found three boxes of assorted candy in a storage closet from which the candy jar had presumably been refilled when the inn was operational. He didn't physically count all the Tootsie Rolls in the clear plastic bags inside the boxes, but by his rough estimate, there were enough to build a whole airplane out of chewy brown candy if needed. There would be considerable unease flying a plane whose fuel was held in by such a substance, but it was a risk the Colonel would have no problem taking.

Small airplanes like the Piper Archer typically run on a fuel called 100 Low-Lead, which is a 100-octane gasoline made from hydrocarbons, additives, and tetraethyl lead. This mixture resisted excessive detonation in high-compression engines like the Lycoming-360 that powered the Archer. In a pinch, small planes can fly on regular gasoline, though less safely. Degraded engine performance and rougher running would be a likely result, and over time, the risk of complete engine failure would be a concern, but for the hour and a half flight from Cayo Costa to Cedar Key, the Archer should be able to fly on regular gas.

In the old world, when gasoline powered so much of modern life, it could be found anywhere. Indeed, even in the weeks after the flash, it was easy to siphon from abandoned cars. Because Cabbage Key was only accessible by boat and had no roads, there were simply no cars on the island. The tractor in the maintenance barn ran on diesel, and the two four-wheelers stored with it had less than 3 gallons of gas total between them. At an estimated fuel burn of 9 gallons per hour, a little worse than the 8.5 gallons that could be expected using 100 LL, the Colonel would need at least 14 gallons of gas to make it home and closer to twenty to feel good about the trip, even if none leaked from the Tootsie Roll repairs.

On Cabbage Key, twenty gallons may as well have been two hundred. Three times during the first month on the island, the Colonel tried to strike out to the mainland or nearby islands in search of gasoline, each time being thwarted, to the ruination of his self-esteem, by the limitations of his age and strength to make the voyage. On the third such trip, a strong current and a frigid storm had almost stranded him at sea. Having fought several hours just to get back to Cabbage Key, the Colonel collapsed on the rocky bank of the island's leeward shore, coughing and unwell. For three weeks after, he battled a fever and then pneumonia that came close to killing him.

On the day the Colonel finally began to regain his strength, while fishing for his supper, he saw a twinkling on the horizon near the south end of Cayo Costa. The twinkling morphed into steady movement and seemed to be growing closer. The Colonel began to slowly climb to the top of the water tower to get a better look. In his diminished state, it took some time to get to the top, but from the elevated vantage, the baleful object came clearly into view.

The cutter Sawfish was sailing fast through Captiva Pass, bearing down on Cabbage Key.

12

STRAIGHTENING THE CURVES

In his late forties, Allen Mikes pulled off one of the rarest of achievements in the world of men: He changed for the better. In his youth, he was tempestuous, quick to anger, and always ready to fight. Throughout much of his adult life as a blue crabber and mullet fisherman, folks gave him a wide berth. He was handsome, tall, and built like an Abrams Tank. The cool quiet of his voice served only to enhance his intimidating demeanor.

When Allen heard that Buddy Skipjack had died in Chief Vernon's police car, he felt strangely numb to the news. His family had been hit especially hard by the net ban, and by that spring of 1998, the new venture of clam farming was just beginning to pay the bills, and only barely. When clams began to go missing, there had been no doubt in his mind about the moral imperative to stop a thief that was stealing from those struggling so mightily to make up for what the state had already taken from them. Allen's disposition had always been a throwback to a prior age, a relic from a time when calling the police for help with anything would feel like cowardice. Nothing about his actions on the boat that dark night with Mark David, when Buddy Skipjack was discovered in a boat filled with Hodge Hals' clams, could have ever felt anything other than necessary and right to him.

And yet, as he went about his life on the water, especially after Buddy's son began to work alongside his friend Mark David, Allen thought often of his actions that night on the water. He went so far as to ask Chief Vernon privately if he thought the beating had contributed to Buddy's death. The Chief, decent as always, reiterated that Buddy had been fine on the way to the jail, cheerful even and that the coroner made no mention of any contributing factors to the death beyond the official cause of heart failure. Allen knew the Chief was being kind, but he took comfort in the exchange all the same.

After some renewed interest in the affair following Isaac Skipjack's pummeling of Bob Corliss and the damage he inflicted on his aircraft—damage Mark David paid for in exchange for no charges being pressed against the boy—time began to slip by, quicker each year, until no one really talked about the Skipjacks anymore.

Mark David never ended his private, mournful vigil that began the day he found Isaac's truck at Number Four Bridge. Allen Mikes slowly drifted away from his quarrelsome past and into a spiritual, if not religious, reformation. His sprightly, beautiful wife Linda had loved him as a bruiser and found she loved him even more in his requiescence. He took a two-night-a-week gig at the Island Hotel's Trident lounge, playing his full-bodied Guild guitar and singing cowboy love songs, dulcet and warm, to clam farmers, retirees, and tourists at the bar.

Isaac Skipjack was holding pressure on the wound in Allen Mikes' shoulder when five shots rang out from the other side of the small town of Suwannee.

When he left Cedar Key at eighteen years old, he was six feet, two inches tall, and a hundred and sixty pounds of mostly bone, skin, and hair. Two decades and a full military career later, the forty-two-year-old had transformed his body into an imposing, lean-muscled machine.

"Seaman Weaver, go find out what that's about," Isaac ordered the younger man. "See if it came from one of ours and report back here as quick as you can."

"Aye, Aye, Senior Chief."

"And send HS Morgan in here on your way out. The bleeding's started again."

"I'm fine," Allen said in a weak voice.

Mark David fumed from across the pilot house of the cutter Sawfish. "He's not fine, Skipper. Untie me, goddamn it, so I can help you."

"Don't call me that," Isaac replied sharply.

Mark David bristled. "I sure as shit ain't gonna call you Senior Chief, you can count on that."

"That's fine," Isaac replied cooly. "I told the crew we could drop all that. But with everything that's changed in the past year, they wanted to keep something from how it used to be so I let them keep up the formality. How's Miss Bette?"

"Don't talk to me like we're friends when you just tried to kill us."

Isaac made a show of steadiness, answering in a moderated tone, "Things got out of hand in the canal. They didn't know who you were… and they said you shot at them first."

Allen Mikes labored to turn his head toward Isaac to say, "I did," before slumping over.

"Let me help him, Isaac, for Christ's sake."

Isaac replied matter-of-factly, "You've turned into an old man, Mr. Mark. But I'm not stupid. Sit tight. Help's coming."

Finally, the Health Service Technician arrived with his med kit.

"His color looks terrible, Senior Chief."

"He was doing better," Isaac replied. "I've been holding pressure like you said."

"In the movies, getting shot in the shoulder is never a big deal, but in real life, all kinds of bad things can happen," HT Morgan explained. "Do we know who shot him?"

"Houseman," Isaac replied.

"So one of the rifles from the ship, then. Those 5.56 rounds don't always go straight through. They're famous for tumbling when they hit stuff. I think what happened here is the bullet hit bone and tumbled around inside his shoulder and arm, tearing everything all to hell."

"What can we do about it?" Isaac asked.

"If the brachial artery was severed, there's not much we can do," the HT replied. "Without surgery, he'll die, probably today."

Mark David was indignant. "So we just sit here and wait to see?"

HT Morgan continued, "The immediate concern is the amount of blood he's lost. Assuming the artery's intact, he still might not make it. Do you know his blood type?"

"O positive, same as mine," Mark replied. "We tried to give blood together at the school one time, and he passed out, and I never let him hear the end of it. I remember us talking about how we had the same type."

"I've never actually done it," HT Morgan said. "But it's called a walking blood bank or buddy transfusion. We learned about it in A-school. It seems pretty straightforward, and the risks are much lower than leaving him in this condition. His pulse is weak, and he just looks like shit."

Mark David said without hesitancy, "Do it."

"Senior Chief?" HT Morgan asked.

"Of course. Help him if you can," Isaac replied.

The immediacy of Isaac's compassion was unsettling to Mark David, but his concern for Allen outweighed his desire to push the issue. HT Morgan left to gather supplies from below deck for the transfusion, leaving Isaac and Mark to sit with two decades of things unsaid. The tension quickly made the silence unbearable.

"She's fine, by the way," Mark said at last.

"Who's fine?" Isaac asked.

"My wife. You asked about her."

"Oh, yes. Great," Isaac said, fumbling and feeling, despite half a life now of leading men, like it was the first day on Mark David's bird dog, planting clams instead of returning to class. "I'm glad to hear it."

"She got the flu pretty bad about a month after everything went to hell. She was as sick as I've ever seen her, but right when it seemed we were about to lose her, she just got better... stubborn and tough as ever."

"That sounds like her," Isaac said.

"You should have taken the truck."

"What?" Isaac replied.

"When you left," Mark said. "We gave you that truck because you'd earned it. It was yours, and you should have taken it. You were stupid to walk all that way."

Isaac had let his guard down too much already, and the thought of the truck was a step too far.

"Nice catching up, Mr. Mark, but that's enough," Isaac said gruffly. "I didn't come all this way for a reunion."

Mark David, implacable as the march of time, pressed, "Why did you come? Still think I had something to do with your daddy... 'cause some uppity asshole told you so?"

"You're not in a position to ask me anything," Isaac replied, icy with regained composure.

"Well, what then, Senior Chief?" Mark asked, emphasizing Isaac's rank with a scornful flourish of tone. "Does it take a whole navy just to settle up with me, or you planning to take it out on the whole island?

"I don't want to hurt anyone," Isaac snapped.

"Tell that to Geoff McCloud."

Isaac steamed, "I don't know who that is, but we're done talking."

"Then do something!" Mark David exploded with hurt badly concealed as rage, "Instead of pussy-dragging around asking about my wife."

Both men were thankful to hear HT Morgan returning to the pilot house. He worked quickly, sterilizing Mark David's arm and inserting the 16-gauge needle into a vein. Dark blood flowed free and easy. Besides periodic instructions for Mark to squeeze the rubber ball he had been given, the fifteen minutes it took to draw the needed blood passed in uncomfortable silence. Allen Mikes had opened his eyes again but they were glassy and dull inside a head he was too weak to move.

"This should be enough," HT Morgan said.

It took another few minutes to prepare the patient to receive the transfusion. As he worked, HT Morgan explained a list of possible complications, the most serious of which was the risk of anaphylaxis if Allen's immune system had an adverse reaction to an allergen in Mark's blood.

"In the hospital, a blood transfusion can take 3 or 4 hours." HT Morgan explained. "But I don't think this patient has that long. We need to push it much faster."

The needle went into Allen's arm, and the blood began to flow. The HT listened to Allen's heart and took his vitals while Isaac continued to hold pressure on the wound in his shoulder. A few minutes into the procedure, Seaman Weaver burst into the pilot house, flush from a hard run.

"Bullard and Henley are dead, Senior Chief. On the deck of the Atlas, shot to hell. There's another body in the water that's gotta be Houseman."

"What?" Isaac said, releasing his hold on the towel he had pressed into Allen Mikes' shoulder. "Who did this?"

"I didn't see anyone. But I didn't look much either. I just turned and ran here as fast as I could, like you said. A bunch of our guys are already heading toward the shots, and the crews on the boats in the canal up by the main road are probably inbound as well."

"Round up everybody else get them armed and ready to move... everybody!" Isaac yelled.

"Aye, Aye, Senior Chief.."

"What do you know about this?" Isaac demanded of Mark David.

"Nothing."

"We'll see," Isaac said, dropping the towel to the floor and racing out of the pilot house.

Blood began to slowly run free from the wound.

"Untie me," Mark said to HT Morgan. "So I can hold the pressure."

There was no time for the Health Services Technician to contemplate the wisdom of such a move. His patient was dying, and he was determined to stop it.

He cut the rope from Mark David's hands, and the two men worked together, one pushing the blood in, the other fighting to keep it from rushing out.

Rolf climbed down from the roof of the condo building using the storm gutter. His eyes and skin were nitid with surging dopamine and adrenaline. In everyday life he was often placid to the point of malaise, but in the prosecution of violence a rush of energetic zeal would nearly levitate him off the ground.

"I didn't shoot 'em in the back or anything," Rolf said. "As soon as you got out in the open, they had rifles on you. The first shot was one of them. Looks like he missed. The next three were mine. I didn't miss."

Thomas, seldom at a loss for words, stared quietly ahead.

"Damn," Ryland said, at last, ending the hard silence spreading among them.

"Glad you were up there, bud," Hayes said. "I swear I heard that first round zip right past my ear."

"Can you imagine?" Thomas asked, breaking free of his trance. "What are the odds of getting two ears shot off in one lifetime?"

Rolf at least tried not to laugh, but Ryland and Thomas made no such effort, leaning into the gallows humor. During Cedar Key's first invasion by the Meade clan in the early months after the flash, Hayes jumped off a roof onto Leon Meade, cousin of the head outlaw in Sumner, and got his ear shot off on the way down. A centimeter's difference in the flight of the bullet would have left his brains spread across the Timucuan middens where invader and defender had become entangled. Instead, a brief, intimate struggle left Leon cut open from belly to chest and the blood of both men running in comingled streams down the gentle slope of the bank and into the estuary.

"All right, yuck it up, gents," Hayes said. "But get yourselves squared away so we can get moving."

Rolf said, "You probably couldn't see it while you were running, but the boat below that mast is some kind of trawler. It's just big enough that your dad and Mr. Mark could be in there. Let's head there next to rule it out."

Hayes replied, "Agreed. If they're not there, we'll head north to the Suwannee Marina."

"Deep water there," Rolf replied. "Deep enough to hold the big boat that rammed me and Geoff."

"Percy said he saw it heading that way," Thomas added.

"Who's Percy?" Rolf asked.

Thomas and Ryland shot each other a grin.

"Some moonshiner-looking guy in overalls and a scraggly Santa Claus beard," Ryland replied.

"Like Uncle Jesse?" Hayes inquired.

"I think it *is* him," Thomas replied with a grin. "Sure wish we had them Duke boys and the General Lee with us."

"Just a good ol' boys," Rolf sang, just above his breath, as the four men walked toward the other marina, scanning the way ahead with military precision.

"Never meanin' no harm," Hayes whisper-sang in response.

In compulsory unison, the three older men sang together the anthem of all little southern boys in the 1980s:

> *Beats all you never saw*
> *Been in trouble with the law*
> *Since the day they was born.*

Hayes, Thomas, and Rolf, buoyed as always by the cultivated adolescence of their close friendship—their unlikely but treasured brotherhood—enjoyed the moment of silliness before the bad business that lay ahead.

There were two sailors on the deck of the 25-foot trawler, supine and still. A third floated face down in the dredged inlet leading to the docks, the cool breeze pushing him slowly toward the river. The Suwannee had been in a flood stage for much of the winter, and while its levels were falling daily toward the norm, it was still high enough that a fast current remained. Once the body reached the river, it would begin a swift journey to the Gulf; in a few days' time, the fallen sailor could be anywhere from Yankeetown to Tampa.

"That's an Atlas," Hayes said.

"What?" Rolf replied.

"Company out of Cape Coral. They make these little pocket trawlers right here in Florida. They're small, but they're built to handle pretty big water. People like 'em cause you can trailer them. Bet that one makes 20 knots, easy."

Thomas had become accustomed to his friend's encyclopedic knowledge of boats, especially ones made in Florida, so it didn't strike him as out of place at all that Hayes would fixate on the trawler and not the bodies strewn about its deck.

"Cover me while I go aboard," Hayes said.

Rolf took a position near the dock while Ryland and Thomas posted up on opposite sides of the boat, rifles shouldered.

Hayes jumped aboard the trawler, calling out, "Dad! Uncle Allen!"

There was no reply.

"Anything?" Ryland asked.

"Nothing here," Hayes called back as he finished his search.

In the half second between the moment Hayes' feet left the gunnel of the trawler and when they landed back on the dock, the eerie tranquility of the past several minutes ended in a burst of crackling sound as a sustained volley of rifle fire enfiladed the trawler and the dock. Hayes was hit immediately. He collapsed hard onto the dock, the momentum of the fall carrying him over the edge and into the tannic water. Rolf took cover behind the gas pump at the end of the dock as rounds peppered into it, puncturing the hose and shattering the glass that covered the old-style gauge of rolling numbers. Thomas and Ryland tried to return fire, but they were shooting at nothing and were withering in the barrage. In desperation, they ran for the cover of the metal *Gateway Marina* building, somehow managing to get inside unscathed as rounds hit all around them.

Time observed the peril of the scene, curled about itself, and lingered. Rolf was pinned down, Hayes had not resurfaced in the water, and men were emerging from the trees.

13

—·—

ISAAC'S CREW

If he had been younger, the Colonel thought often in the months to come, he might have made a different decision upon seeing the Sawfish heading his way. If he hadn't been weakened by illness to the brink of death, he might have concealed himself in the shadows of the island and mounted a one-man guerilla fight against the people who had shot him down and were presently making landfall on Cabbage Key. The version of himself that had rescued the besieged Army soldiers outside the ancient Vietnamese city of Huey during the Tet Offensive, providing cover fire with one hand while holding the controls of his Sea Knight helicopter with the other, would certainly have lived up to the nickname he earned that day—Captain McCool—and met this new enemy with steadfast resolve.

The Colonel was no longer that man, and he knew it.

Melinda Beth and his son Geoff were suffering in his absence; indeed, his home island might be facing all manner of difficulties that required all hands to overcome. For as long as he remained separated from the people he loved, from the only place on Earth that had ever mattered to him, his purpose in the world was at an end. Whatever momentary boost his ego might receive from reckless action against the Sawfish and its crew was overrun by the practical concerns of his mission to get home again.

For all the detriments of age, here its wisdom won the day as the Colonel waved his arms for all he was worth, jumping up and down in calculated exuberance, to welcome the Sawfish to Cabbage Key. In response, the Coast Guard cutter rang the ship's bell eight times, the storied *8 bells and all is well* signal, and the Colonel began the slow process of climbing down from the tower to meet the people that had tried to kill him.

His plan was almost ended in its earliest moments. When the Sawfish was safely secured to the outside dock, the one normally occupied by the multi-million-dollar pleasure craft of the island's wealthy old-world clientele, a gangplank was lowered, and the obvious commander of the vessel strode across it wearing the Coast Guard's operation blue working uniform with a Sig Sauer P229 sidearm holstered on his hip. When he introduced himself as Senior Chief Skipjack, the Colonel froze awkwardly, his mind racing at the sound of the distinctive name, trying uselessly to convince himself that it was a coincidence. Several seconds of silence passed as his brain connected the dots between the name and the stories from home, to the specific story of the Skipjack boy who had tried to destroy Bob Corliss' Archer, the same Archer—with its instantly recognizable, tacky paint job—that this commander had shot out of the sky minutes after seeing it.

"Welcome, Senior Chief. My name's Robert," the Colonel said at last, immediately lamenting that he had given his real name. He hadn't been retired from the Marines long before Buddy Skipjack died, and he had never actually met his son. It was plausible, even likely, that the Skipjack boy, if he was, in fact, the hulking man standing before him now, had never heard of him.

"Nice to meet you, Robert," the commander said, "And please, call me Isaac. As far as I can tell, we might be the last of the Coast Guard, or the American military for that matter, so no need for formality."

"Welcome, Isaac," the Colonel said. "You're the first people I've seen since the sky exploded. I'm the caretaker here. The owners wanted to close the place down while we waited to see if everything would blow over. I was here wrapping all that up when… well… when it didn't blow over. I figured somebody would eventually come to get me, but no one ever did."

"What all do you know about what happened?" Isaac asked.

"Only what I could see from here," the Colonel replied. "A flash, then fires and smoke. Everything was gray the first few months."

Isaac put his hand on the older man's shoulder. "No one's coming, Robert. From what we've seen, there's almost nobody left. You're the first person we've seen as well."

"Oh God," the Colonel replied, doing his best to look surprised by the knowledge he had already seen firsthand beneath the wings of the Archer. "I was holding out hope that it wasn't as bad as it seemed, but I knew it had to be."

Isaac then volunteered a piece of information that was strangely reassuring to the Colonel as he continued to play a role he hoped would help get him home.

"There was a plane, though," Isaac said. "We hadn't seen or heard anything for weeks… then suddenly a little single-engine plane was buzzing our boat, back and forth, getting lower every pass. We finally had to engage it, but it slipped into the fog, and we lost sight. Since then, quiet. Absolutely nothing until you."

The Colonel felt as though his stomach might fall right out of his body. Was this story an attempt to smoke him out, or had Isaac simply shared it to illustrate his point about the level of destruction away from the island? Certainly, his tone had been sincere, comforting even.

The Colonel played along.

"Well, I'm sure glad you're here, Senior Chief... sorry... Isaac. How many are with you?"

"Twenty-seven, including me."

"Between the rooms at the inn and the rental houses, there's plenty of room for everyone. Truth is, I'm mighty glad to have the company. You boys are welcome here as long as you'd like to stay."

"We'd be much obliged," Isaac replied. "But it's not just boys. We've got six women in the crew."

"All the better," the Colonel replied.

"This boat normally has a crew of ten, but we picked up extra survivors from Coast Guard Station Fort Myers Beach on the day everything went down. We've been crammed together for a while now, stopping where we could, so your island is looking like paradise at the moment."

The Colonel affected a whole body, convincing smile. "Well, come on then, let me show you around."

Isaac released his crew, putting Petty Officer Morgan, his Health Services Technician and most senior subordinate, in charge. Excited, they spread out across Cabbage Key. There was a bed for everyone and a feeling of general elation among the new arrivals to be off the crowded boat. Isaac stuck close to the Colonel during a tour of the island, showing an intense interest in everything the Colonel showed him.

"I assume you get your water from the tower," Isaac said.

"Yes sir," the Colonel replied.

"Please don't call me sir," Isaac chided good-naturedly. "I'm enlisted, so I work for a living."

The Colonel, a commissioned officer—though this was information he would not share—was familiar with the popular enlisted man's jab and chuckled at it. "I didn't mean sir like *military* sir. I just meant sir like my daddy said I should call men I don't know."

Isaac smiled. "We know each other now, Robert."

"Fair enough," the Colonel replied. "For the first week, when I thought I wasn't going to be here long, I used the water to flush the toilet and take showers. When I started to worry that no one would be coming or that even if they did, there might not be anywhere to go, it dawned on me that without power, I couldn't run the pump to fill the tower back up with water. So I closed the main valve that runs to the inn and all the rental houses. There's a smaller outflow valve just before the main water line that I use to get water for drinking."

"How much do you think is left?" Isaac asked.

"Hard to say, but I couldn't have used that much."

Isaac furrowed his brow in contemplation as they walked on. Roseate Spoonbills flew overhead in a ragged formation, and a school of bait fish scattered in the small cove adjacent to the walking path, exploding the still water into a scattershot of ripples as they tried to outrun redfish on the hunt. The June air had a nip in it that was out of place and season for this part of the state. A little more every day, sunshine was beginning to find its way through the interminable gray that had lingered after the flash, but the disruption of the bombs had been so severe to the atmosphere and to the land and waters that southwest Florida was still learning how to Florida again.

"I'll just level with you, Robert. It's been a hard four months for us," Isaac said, feeling glad to be talking to someone other than the younger people in his charge. "Petty Officer Morgan is the oldest in my crew. He just turned twenty-seven. I can count on him for just about anything. He's decent and competent and I think I even like him... but he's still just a kid. They're all just kids. They try hard most of the time and they do what I tell them, but every day they're looking to me to figure it all out."

"I can't imagine all of you on that boat this whole time," the Colonel replied.

Isaac nodded. "We ran nearly all the diesel out of the boat, looking for a place we could all go. From the Coast Guard Station at Fort Myers Beach to Key West and back... it's bad all over. We're only here because Petty Officer Bennett is from a sailing family. There's a little marina on the back side of Marco Island. The island's barely even there anymore but there were all these sailboats piled up on top of each other like toys. We spent a week there trying to figure out a way to get one or a few of them seaworthy, just to have some more space. We never could, but we salvaged every sail we could get our hands on. It took another two weeks, but we got the big boat rigged up like you see it now."

For a moment, the Colonel forgot the circumstances underlying his interaction with Isaac and marveled at the story he had just heard. "I was a stone crabber in a former life, so I know a little about boats, but sailing always seemed like witchcraft to me. Is it hard to operate a boat that big with the sails?"

Isaac laughed. "It's still witchcraft to me, too. Without Petty Officer Bennett, we'd just go in circles. It doesn't seem all that hard to him, but I'd be in trouble without him. Luckily, he's training some of the others. I worked on a clam boat when I was younger. They were weird ass boats, but at least there was a motor on them."

The Colonel risked a further question, to which he already knew the answer, "I thought they just dug clams out of the mud... what kind of boat do you need for that?"

"That's how they do it up north," Isaac replied. "I worked for a clam farmer here in Florida. They plant millions of them in bags on the bottom of the Gulf. They use a boat called a bird dog. The motor's upfront, sticking down through a cut-out in the hull."

"No shit," the Colonel said as they walked on.

"So about the water," Isaac began again cautiously.

"Yeah?"

"Well, it's a finite resource, and it'd last a hell of a lot longer if you were the only one drinking it," Isaac said flatly.

"I see," the Colonel replied, finally understanding the full intent of Isaac's questions. Of course, a crew of armed military personnel didn't need to ask about the water or anything else on the island. They could take whatever they wanted and the Colonel could no more resist them than a single leaf could push back the army of the wind.

"I got into the Coast Guard because I missed working on the water," Isaac said. "That was it. It never occurred to me to want to command anything. I trained to be a Boatswain Mate because they take care of the ship. I didn't know when I signed up that Boatswain Mate is the only enlisted rating that can command a boat. It was fine when it was just a boat and a crew, and there was this entire military framework in place that meant I wasn't actually in charge of much at all. But now... "

"I get where you're going with this, Isaac, and I understand," the Colonel replied.

"Well, let me just say it out loud so you know the position I'm in," Isaac said, a hint of meekness in his voice that had heretofore been absent.

"Sure. I'd like to hear it," the Colonel replied, feeling intuitively that this conversation would make or upend their relationship going forward.

"That boat out there, the Sawfish... it's a marine protector class. What's unique about this boat is that it's normally commanded by a junior officer and a senior enlisted, non-commissioned officer like me. And by junior, I mean a wet behind the ears 23-year-old O-2 lieutenant, fresh out of college or the academy and generally useless. That's why they pair them up with a gray hair like me."

The Colonel laughed, genuine and warm. "Settle down, young fella… you ain't seen gray yet."

"You get the idea, though," Isaac said, smiling. "Well my particular O-2, Lieutenant Dupont—"

"You're making that up," the Colonel interrupted.

"I'm not," Isaac replied. "Not that kind of Dupont, but a rich kid from Cape Cod all the same."

"People are actually from Cape Cod?"

"Apparently," Isaac replied. "And he was exactly what you'd expect… entitled, arrogant, and worst of all for a leader, timid. Even in training exercises, when push came to shove on a decision of consequence, he either waited for more instructions from the higher-ups or asked me to make the call. He was the kind of guy that gets people killed when the shit hits the fan. So anyway, on the day everything went to shit with the world, we had the Sawfish docked at the new Coast Guard base in Fort Myers Beach. It wasn't set to officially open until later that year, but we were there on a stopover—Dupont, me, and eight enlisted crew—when the first big bombs fell on what had to be MacDill in Tampa. I tell the lieutenant we have to shove off and get as far into the Gulf as possible, but he refuses. He says his orders were for us to be at the station for the next three days. I tell him we have to go, and he digs in and reminds me that he's the officer and I'm the non-com. And by now, the crew and another dozen or so inside the station are running for the boat, and Dupont blocks the gangplank and again says no."

"I take it Dupont's not here on Cabbage Key with us now?" the Colonel asked with a grin.

"I gave him a last chance to change his mind, and he stood there talking about the Uniform Code of Military Justice until I kicked him in the stomach out of the way and fired up the Sawfish. We were maybe ten miles out when the next round of bombs fell. Two of my crew that were looking back toward the base were blinded, just for a few days, but Dupont and the new base and everything else was just...." Isaac made a gesture with his hands, extending his fingers out quickly in all directions, pantomiming the explosion. "Gone."

The Colonel knew why Isaac had told this story. He appreciated it even, in that Southern way of gilding harshness with allegory or parable.

With a knowing glance, the Colonel replied, "We can start collecting the rainwater."

"Very good," Isaac said with relief in his voice as the two men walked back to the inn.

The understanding between them was unsaid but clear.

In a breath, another month passed by. The Colonel assumed an unofficial position in the chain of command, something akin to an executive officer alongside Petty Officer Morgan. Isaac quickly grew to rely on the older man's wisdom and his knowledge of the island as everyone worked to make Cabbage Key a place where twenty-eight people could live indefinitely. There could be no doubt that Isaac was in charge. He undertook the care of his crew in the paternalistic manner of Robert E. Lee and their discipline with the rigid intransigence of George S. Patton. In short, they loved and feared the Senior Chief, and he loved them back.

The Colonel had not been aboard the Sawfish on the day of the flash and had not witnessed or benefitted from Isaac's heroism with the negligent Lieutenant Dupont. He did not owe his life to the Senior Chief and could not—while staying capable of all treacheries that might be required to get home again—ever love him. He did find daily cause, however, to admire the young leader and found him easy to like.

On a Thursday afternoon in the sixth week since the Sawfish arrived on Cabbage Key, a bright pink kayak washed into the mangroves near the southern end of the island where Seaman Apprentice Jensen was throwing a cast net in knee-deep water. She was tall and stout with a dainty face unsuited to the heartiness of her frame. The interplay of the two had a disarming effect on men that was intimidating or enthralling depending on the moment and the man. Seaman Apprentice Jensen only noticed the kayak when it broke free of a nearby mangrove and collided gently with the back of her thigh. It startled her to the extent that she jumped, lost her balance, and fell back onto the kayak, somehow landing atop it without falling ass over tea kettle into the water.

By the next day, the Colonel had outfitted the kayak with an improvised paddle, and different members of the crew began paddling it to the nearby barrier islands whose surrounding waters were too shallow for the Sawfish's 7-foot draft. They adventured in search of any supplies that might enhance life on Cabbage Key. On the fourth such day of exploration, just as the sun was beginning to set, a familiar sound crept slowly across the island, gaining in volume and clarity as it drew closer.

"Do you hear that?" Isaac asked the Colonel as they cleaned fish together on the main dock.

"It can't be," the Colonel replied.

Isaac's ears perked toward the sound, and his face began to brighten. "It is… and by the way it's purring, I think it's a 4-stroke."

Rounding into the deep water near the Sawfish came an unbelievable sight: Petty Officer Henley was at the helm of a 25-foot fiberglass trawler. The pink kayak was on its deck, and a 200-horsepower Honda outboard was pushing it smoothly through the aquamarine water.

Isaac's crew scurried to the dock, whooping and hollering with excitement. The Senior Chief, too, gave into the revelry. They would delight to the story of the boat's discovery—a second vessel for a fleet they could all now dream of building—and be brought to frenzy at the news of at least three more that might be salvageable.

The Colonel's excitement was measured but unmistakable. All he could think about was the gas in the trawler's tanks.

14

LETTERS TO MELINDA BETH

The late afternoon was beginning to slip away as Mark David held pressure on his friend's wound in the low light of the Sawfish's pilot house. Allen Mikes had closed his eyes again. HT Morgan, struggling to keep the blood bag elevated and monitor his patient's vital signs, improvised by hanging the bag from a communications cable running along the ceiling. This freed his hands to operate a stethoscope and perform a variety of manual tests a single machine would have handled effortlessly in the old world.

"How will we know if it's working?" Mark David asked.

"He won't die," HT Morgan replied, distracted by the workload of care and intending none of the callousness his remark conveyed.

Mark David had never been the kind of man to fill silence with idle words. He could be as affable and social as anyone else, but talking as a defense against the quiet was out of character for him. Yet as he watched Allen lay still as a broken promise—sensing even then that they were drifting away from one another—Mark began to tell the Health Services Technician about his friend.

"He married my sister, Linda, which means he isn't blood, but my son Hayes and my daughter Lida Maria call him Uncle Allen. We spilled enough blood together working on crab boats that some of it had to have mixed by now. You've heard that old saying..." Mark asked the HT, "About blood being thicker than water?"

"I have," HT Morgan replied.

"There's another version of it that goes back just as far as the one you know. It says *the blood of the covenant is thicker than the water of the womb.*"

"I don't guess I've heard it that way."

Mark took the measure of his languid friend and said, "I like it better. I've had some blood kin that wasn't worth a drink of water to me or anybody else... but this fella and me have sure been through it. On the crab boats, we had to fight the Gulf, other crabbers, even the damn crabs. The clams we farmed didn't bite back, but it was a fight not to starve to death when we first started growing them together. I reckon I'm pretty tough, but he was always tougher. He'd fight the whole wide world and smile about it. Ain't no way a shot in the shoulder can take out a man like this."

HT Morgan worked at a faster pace than before, checking one thing after another as his face moved slowly from focus to resignation. The towel held against Allen's shoulder had finally soaked through. From the elevated bag to a brachial artery severed threefold by a tumbling bullet, the blood was mixed now, in symbol and in fact, between the two friends—one who continued holding pressure and unavailing faith while the other slipped gently away.

The medic worked on, but Allen Mikes was gone.

It was well past midnight before the excitement died down, and Isaac's crew finally turned in for the night. For them, the trawler represented more than just another boat. It opened the shallower waters of the Intracoastal to exploration. Isaac seemed fixated on the idea of Cabbage Key as a permanent home, but even then, just six weeks in, the boundaries of the island were pushing in on many of the crew. The Colonel cared only about the fuel in the trawler's tanks. As he slipped out of the boat house carrying multiple five-gallon gas cans, he took deep breaths and moderated his expectations, remembering the misplaced hope of his first night on the island.

The trawler was tied up alongside the Sawfish in the wide open of the cove, where anyone looking out from any window on the island could see it clearly. The Colonel knew that if he were discovered, there would be no talking his way out of it, but the thought of Melinda Beth, as always, strengthened his resolve. Because the fuel tanks are below the deck of the trawler, and given that the boat was in the water and not sitting up on a trailer, he would not be able to use gravity to start a siphon. He could not get his gas cans lower than the trawler's tanks without them being underwater. Luckily, the trawler was powered by an outboard motor whose fuel line had a primer bulb. It would be tedious, long work, as each squeeze of the bulb only produced about a third of a cup of fuel, but so long as the crew slept snugly in their beds, the Colonel had time.

Using the end of a vintage letter opener that he found alongside the stationary in the dresser drawer of his room in the inn, the Colonel loosened the clamp that held the fuel line onto the inlet nipple of the 4-stroke Honda outboard, then fed the end of the freed fuel line into a 5-gallon can. He didn't know the numbers, so as he began pumping the bulb, he couldn't distract himself with the same kind of calculations he made with the candles in the restaurant—sixteen cups in a gallon, three pumps per cup, 48 pumps per gallon. Seventeen gallons were needed, to go along with the three he salvaged from the four-wheelers, so a total of 816 pumps separated the Colonel from a plausible way home. If he had been to see a doctor anytime in the previous several years, he would have known the aching in his fingers, from even the lightest of work with them, was caused by rheumatoid arthritis, a thing his father had also borne unwittingly and without protest in the twilight of his own life.

Whatever the cost in pain and tedium, the Colonel was prepared to pay, so when, on pump 192 with just a shade over four gallons in the first can, the fuel line spit and wheezed, the Colonel hung his head and sighed in disgust. He repositioned the line time and again, pumping fast and steady until only air came from the end. He reattached the line to the motor, using the letter opener to retighten the clamp that held it on. He collected his cans, swallowed his disappointment, and slipped away with four more gallons than he had the day before.

The next morning, Isaac and four other crewmembers loaded onto the trawler, intending to visit the island where the additional boats had been found. Seaman Weaver turned the key in the ignition, spinning the starter and the outboard's flywheel. Over and over, they spun, the motor choking and lurching but never firing up.

"It's not getting fuel," Isaac said. "What's the gauge say?"

"That's it," Seaman Weaver said, "Flat empty."

Isaac called to the bow of the trawler, "What did the gauge say yesterday, Henley?"

"I was so excited when I turned the key, and it started, that I don't guess I ever looked," Henley replied.

"Lucky there was enough for you to make it here," Isaac said. "Somebody get Bennett down here, and let's start the work to fit it with a sail.

The pink kayak continued its daily departures in tandem with a lacquered wooden canoe that washed ashore in an afternoon thunderstorm. Over the next month, three more boats came motoring into the cove, but Isaac ordered their fuel pumped out immediately and stored in the large above-ground tank behind the inn. A gas-powered generator had been located in the storage room of a rental house, and Isaac had plans to try to use it to power the island's well pump that could replenish the water tower. Petty Officer Houseman was an Electrician's Mate with five years of experience in the rating, so Isaac charged him with the task of utilizing the underpowered generator to run the pump. When, a few days later, the pump roared back to life, filling the water tower over several labored hours while the little generator whined and shook, the Colonel knew that gasoline would henceforth be such a treasured commodity that squirreling away any for the Archer would be exponentially more difficult.

Eight more boats, including a 14-foot skiff, a v-hull cuddy cabin, two pontoon boats, and four center consoles of varying lengths, made their way to Cabbage Key over the next few months, their fuel guarded as closely as the crown jewels. The process of fitting sails to each new boat began as soon as the fuel was offloaded. The Colonel conceived of many different plans for getting fuel out of the storage tank, but no matter their complexity or shrewdness, they were always thwarted by the military manner in which Isaac managed the 24-hour guarding of the precious resource. As he did from his earliest days on the island, Isaac worried most about water. Without fuel to operate the generator that ran the well pump, and given the inefficiency of catching rainwater, he knew the island could not support his crew for long.

Life continued, and the seasons changed on Cabbage Key. Months elapsed with no additional boat discoveries or action of much consequence. The Colonel's biggest fear, that the Archer would be discovered, improbably never materialized. Cayo Costa was so desolate that the kayak and the wooden canoe always set out in the opposite direction from it, toward the islands closer to the mainland. That summer, cooler than any in a hundred years, was followed by a surprisingly temperate autumn. By then, the gray was mostly gone from the sky. Fishing was easy and bountiful. Crabs were reliably caught in relatively large numbers. A lone tangerine tree produced thirty-seven tangerines that were divided equally among everyone on the island, their electric sweetness overwhelming palates deprived of modern allotments of sugar. Winter dug in, bitter and unforgiving, but still the kayak and canoe made near daily foraging trips and every member of the crew spent time learning sailing techniques from Petty Officer Bennett. By the end of January, the fuel in the tank behind the inn was almost at an end. Twice the generator had stopped working, but twice it had been brought back to life, each time a little weaker than it was before.

On the fourteenth of February, a 24-foot Morgan bay boat, twin to Hayes Davids' Cogency, rounded the north side of the island just as darkness was falling. As Seaman Bartholomew steered the vessel toward the dock, her smile could be seen a hundred yards out, even in the low light, along with a flood of raven hair blowing crazy in the wind. Isaac had called an all-hands crew meeting to deal with what he described as a matter of some severity, so the Morgan's fuel pumping, critical as it was, would wait until the next morning. The Colonel was also summoned to the meeting, but despite the gravity of a proceeding in which he would likely be asked to deliberate, his thoughts were preoccupied with plans for a late-night pilfering of the Morgan's fuel.

As he contemplated the sleek black vessel tied to the dock, the Colonel decided that no matter the amount of fuel he pulled from it, he would make an attempt with it to leave Cabbage Key, reasoning that any distance north was at least progress toward home.

The instant this decision was made, the Colonel felt lighter on his feet.

When he arrived at the Dollar Bill Bar, tables and chairs had been arranged into a kind of makeshift courtroom with Isaac in a chair at a table facing the gallery of crew. Isaac motioned for the Colonel to take the other chair at the table beside him. To his left sat Seaman Recruit Butler, a ruddy-faced 20-year-old from Massachusetts, who had only been out of Coast Guard boot camp for two months when the bombs fell. He was diminutive but well built, with a head half-again too large for the thin neck and narrow shoulders on which it sat. Blood ran from his nose, and one of his eyes was swollen shut. On his cheeks and down the length of both arms ran deep, jagged scratches.

To Isaac's right sat Seaman Apprentice Jensen, her long auburn hair tousled and dirty and her clothes caked in wet mud. Aside from these untidy aesthetics, she appeared to be physically unharmed.

"This is exactly what it looks like," Isaac announced to the assembled crew. "Seaman Recruit Butler was observed by three other crew members in the act of assaulting Seaman Apprentice Jensen. We're here to figure out what to do about it."

There were whispers and gasps throughout the bar.

Isaac asked sternly, "What do you have to say for yourself, Seaman Recruit Butler?"

"She attacked me," SR Butler replied belligerently.

Isaac was unpersuaded. "Petty Officers Morgan, Henley, and Bennett, on your feet."

The three crew members stood and snapped to attention, though no such order was given.

"Is Seaman Recruit Butler telling the truth, as you saw it happen?"

Petty Officer Morgan replied, "He was on top of her, Senior Chief, pulling at her pants."

"That's right," Petty Officer Henley said. "There wasn't any way to mistake what Butler was trying to do."

"I agree," Petty Officer Bennett replied, eyes forward and formal.

Isaac asked, "Did you try to assist your crew member who was in distress?"

"The three of us ran toward them," Petty Officer Morgan replied. "But by the time we reached them, Seaman Apprentice Jensen had taken control of the situation."

Isaac turned to the accused. "How did you get those injuries, Seaman Recruit Butler?"

SR Butler looked away in humiliation, refusing to answer.

The Senior Chief did not relent. "Your participation in this proceeding is not optional. Did you receive these injuries from Seaman Apprentice Jensen?"

SR Butler turned his good eye toward the Senior Chief, staring defiantly at him in silence.

"Very well, Seaman Recruit Butler. You have been given the opportunity to face your accuser and defend yourself. You have refused to do so. I find that there is sufficient evidence to judge you guilty of this crime. Stand to hear your sentence."

Something about the finality of the Senior Chief's pronouncement pushed the Seaman Recruit into timid compliance. He stood to his feet, looking away from his fellow crew members.

The Senior Chief stood as well.

"It's been an eventful day. It's unfortunate that we have a threat living here among us, when we've got our hands full doing everything we can to take care of each other. It's too hard to face the difficulties of this new world if we're working against ourselves. For this reason, Seaman Recruit Butler is hereby removed from our crew and to the extent that the Coast Guard exists anymore and I have anything to say about it, he is also discharged from it. There was no honor in his attack on a fellow crew member and, sadly, I believe no possibility of his serving with us honorably in the future."

Seaman Recruit Butler's timidity shifted to panic. "What does that mean? You're just gonna send me away? Where would I go?"

Isaac replied, "No, Butler, you'll be staying here."

These words sent a confused charge through the room.

"What?" Seaman Apprentice Jensen asked loudly.

"That's the other purpose of this gathering," Isaac began. "We found another boat today, three-quarters full of fuel, and congrats to Bartholomew on the effort, but our Electrician's Mate tells me the generator has run for the last time. He's kept it operating longer than anyone else could have, but the strain of running the well pump has worn it out beyond our ability to fix it with the materials on hand."

"So no more water?" a crew member yelled from the back.

"There's a good amount in the tower now, enough to fill every container we can get our hands on before we set sail."

"Where are we sailing to?" Seaman Weaver asked.

"Tell them, Robert," Isaac said, catching the Colonel off guard.

"I'm sorry, I don't understand."

"I think you do," Isaac replied, cooly, as he produced a stack of papers from his bag and sat them on the table.

The Colonel looked calmly toward Isaac, who smiled blankly back at him. At the top of each paper, printed in elegant green calligraphy, were the words *Cabbage Key Inn*. The Colonel's handwriting filled page after page. He had begun writing the letters to Melinda Beth almost immediately after he and his big white cooler made landfall on the island. They were a way of passing the time, documenting his struggles, and keeping hope that he would one day be able to deliver them to his wife. It was a sentimental undertaking while stranded alone but utterly reckless to continue after the Sawfish arrived and the Colonel settled into the prolonged ruse of his false identity.

One early decision, however, befitting a military officer with combat experience in an enemy land, would serve to keep his hopes alive of returning home. The fear of the Archer being discovered so terrified the Colonel that even in his letters to a wife he might never see, he always referenced the Archer as crashed and sunk in the Gulf. Every mention of working to get home again was described in generality, in longing, leaving out details about things like stealing gas or hoarding Tootsie Rolls.

The net effect was a kind of betrayal that Isaac would be unable to accept, but not one that was likely to lead to the destruction of his aircraft. The letters were filled, though, with talk of home. The Colonel mused at length about Hayes David and the town council, hand pumps on backyard wells, thieves from Sumner, the Number Four Bridge, the chickens in the cemetery, and the clams on the leases. The detail was sufficient to focus Isaac's attention squarely on the home he had left so long ago, on scores unsettled, and most calamitously, on resources that Cabbage Key could no longer provide.

"Well, Robert... don't keep the crew waiting. Tell them where we're heading just as soon as we can get the new boat fitted with a sail."

"Another island," the Colonel began shakily, playing along as ever but lacking the naivete to imagine he would be included in the passage, "A bigger island north of here that escaped the worst of the blasts."

The Colonel looked again toward the expressionless Senior Chief and took a deep breath.

"You'll be sailing to Cedar Key."

15

— · —

THE SERPENT

Luke Buck persuaded his new wife Kinsey to stay behind under the auspices of helping Miss Bette and others defend the island while the navy was away. He had no such luck with Lizzy, who brushed aside his admonition with a wave of her hand and a sharp sideways glance as she began loading more wood for the gasifier onto the skiff.

There was a maturity in the manner of Luke's leadership on the docks of the canal that day as he ran from boat to boat, relaying Hayes' orders for a splitting of the fleet between Raulerson Creek and Alligator Pass and encouraging everyone to keep the preparations for departure moving as quickly as possible. His calm authority was so conspicuous that the older captains peppered him with questions about the mission ahead. He made such an impression that the Colonel, without a regular boat crew of his own, headed straight for the Big Skiff Energy. Officer Biscuit, right-hand man to Police Chief Jank Edwins, followed the Colonel onto the little skiff as well.

For a general quarters alert—the airhorn blast that had summoned the entire navy and many non-navy citizens to immediate duty—it was decided that Police Chief Edwins and Fire Chief Roberts would stay behind to keep the island operating, prepare for its defense, and ready Nurse Toni's clinic to accept any wounded that might return on the boats. The two Chiefs were exceedingly different men, one a by-the-book contrarian whose firehouse was a model of regulation and efficiency, the other a charismatic Wild West throwback with a sharp mind and a wide smile. In a crisis, though, they were both leaders on whom the island could rely. With so many of the fighting men and women leaving on the boats, the Chiefs began immediate efforts to mobilize their own auxiliary force to guard the home front.

The fires were started, and one by one, the gasifiers began to produce the wood gas that powered each boat's outboard motor. Joey Bannon marshaled his half of the fleet for a run to Raulerson Creek while Luke and the others set out for Alligator Pass. The sun was beginning its late afternoon slide toward the horizon as Luke Buck led the navy out of the canal and into the Waccasassa Bay. It would be a race to beat the darkness to Suwannee, so every captain ran wide open as soon as they reached deeper water.

Rolf was trapped behind a gas pump, Thomas and Ryland were taking fire inside the Gateway Marina, and Hayes was still missing in the water. Their situation grew more dire by the minute, but the Cedar Key Navy was coming.

Isaac seemed pleased with the Colonel's performance. It wasn't lost on him why the Colonel had chosen to deceive him. The Sawfish had, in fact, attacked the Archer, and if the roles were reversed, he could imagine himself making the same self-preserving decision as the Colonel. In their months together on Cabbage Key, the two men had worked well together, always, as far as could be known, for the betterment of everyone on the island. Still, charged as he was with the well-being of so many, Isaac knew the Colonel could no more be trusted now than Seaman Recruit Butler, despite his personal inclination to respect and even like the older man.

"Get a good night's rest," Isaac announced to the crew. "We'll muster at dawn to start a hard day of preparations. Petty Officers Palmer and Bullard, please escort Seaman Recruit Butler to his room and keep him confined there until we sail. Rotate however you'd like, but keep a guard on the door at all times."

As the two burliest men in the crew moved toward him, Seaman Recruit Butler finally realized the gravity of his sentence, and he panicked. He jumped from his chair and scrambled toward the back door of the bar. What followed was an extraordinary series of calculations that happened nearly instantaneously in both the Colonel's and the Senior Chief's brains. The moment Seamen Recruit Butler sprang from his chair, both men assessed the options available to the would-be fugitive, noting their location on a tiny island, and concluded, correctly, that he was heading for the Morgan tied up at the dock. For Isaac, the Morgan would comfortably round out his new sailing fleet; for the Colonel, the fuel in its tanks was his last hope of getting the Archer airborne again.

Seaman Recruit Butler managed two steps toward the door before the Colonel slid quickly off his wooden chair and hurled it into the fleeing man's face. Seaman Recruit Butler crumpled in a heap, and Isaac was upon him before he had an opportunity to recover. The mix of fear, adrenaline, and pain enveloped the smaller man who, thoroughly beaten with no hope of escape, chose the worst of all possible next moves, grabbing for the Sig Sauer sidearm holstered always on the Senior Chief's hip.

If Isaac had wanted to offset the moral cost of what followed, he could have easily done so. Any rookie cop in any small town in America would attest that the moment a perpetrator reaches for a weapon, the use of all available force is justified. Isaac would neither seek nor desire justification. Insofar as possible in that frenetic half-second, he assessed the wisdom of continued leniency—as Seaman Recruit Butler pulled at the strap of the holster—and judged it lacking. Petty Officers Palmer and Bullard were running toward them as the sharp unsnapping of the leather strap rang out. Isaac allowed the condemned man to touch the weapon, lingering in the discordant slow-motion of the hurried moment. When Seaman Recruit Butler began to pull it free of the holster, Isaac snatched it from him, spun the barrel hard into his chest, and fired twice.

The younger man slumped, coughed once, and died.

Isaac stood, gathered the letters from the table, and turned calmly to the Colonel.

"Come with me, Robert."

The remaining crew members in the bar were frozen in place by what they had witnessed. The air in the room was so heavy it labored the breathing of the watchers as Isaac and the Colonel worked their way through them toward the hallway that led to the rooms in the inn.

As they turned to leave, Isaac looked back and said to everyone and no one in particular, "An attack on any of us is an attack on all of us. If we don't take care of each other, we're dead already."

The Colonel followed as Isaac walked on. Shortly, they arrived at the Colonel's room. Isaac opened the door and motioned for him to go in.

"Have a seat," Isaac said, sitting himself in one of the two straight-back chairs near the window.

The Colonel complied, disoriented by the graciousness in Isaac's manner, especially in light of the events of the past several minutes.

"You've been a help to me and my crew," Isaac began. "I know we could have just taken what we needed here, but you never made it seem like we had to."

"We did some good together," the Colonel replied.

"You could have chosen to be honest with me," Isaac said, his tone sharpening a little.

"Well, you did shoot me out of the sky. Or as you described it... *finally had to engage* me."

Isaac nodded at the Colonel's probity, stopping a wry smile short. "Fair enough."

"That stupid paint job on the Archer," the Colonel said with a chuckle. "Just the worst."

"I hated that son of a bitch Bob Corliss. Even his name bothered me," Isaac said.

"He had the same effect on me at first," the Colonel replied. "But I warmed up to him over time. It was just nice to have someone to fly with after I got out of the service."

"It was a failure on my part," Isaac said contemplatively. "I saw you shaking the wings. I knew you were trying to communicate. Of course, I thought it was Corliss, but after everything we had seen and been through, I guess I was offended more than anything else... that somehow that rich piece of shit was flying around in that stupid plane when almost everybody else was gone. I gave the order to engage you. I made the crew think you were a threat. I'll own that."

"Fair enough," the Colonel said, echoing Isaac from before.

Isaac leafed through the Colonel's letters, finding the one he wanted, and read from it:

When I think of the odds of meeting the Skipjack kid like I did, way down here where there doesn't seem to be many people left, I have to imagine some bigger purpose in it. How could a thing like this be a coincidence? He knew where the Archer came from when he shot at it. No way he could have forgotten that plane. I'm worried he'll take his crew to Cedar Key when this island runs out of everything they need. These seem to be good people, and they're being led by a good man, but these are hard times, Melinda Beth. If he had to, I know Isaac would take what we have if it would save his crew. I don't know that I could even blame him for trying... cause I would snap my fingers and make every one of these good people disappear from the Earth if it brought me a mile closer to you. If it comes to it, I'll do what I can to stop them. Until then, I'll keep trying to find a way home.

I remain, affectionately yours, Robert.

The Colonel took a deep breath, exhaling it slowly as he looked away. "For what it's worth, I'm not ashamed of anything I said there."

"You shouldn't be," Isaac said with surprising warmth. "And all of it's true. Of course I knew that goddamn plane the minute I saw it. I just didn't know it was you in it."

"Would it have changed anything if you had?"

"Hard to say," Isaac replied. "The reason why you and I have gotten on so well these many months is because we are practical men. Writing these letters is the first impractical thing I've seen from you, but I understand why you needed to do it. You just should have hidden them better."

The Colonel smiled. "I should have."

"Of course, you understand why I can't risk you coming with us?"

The Colonel shook his head in acknowledgment. "Honestly, I don't understand why I'm still alive."

Isaac felt a strange sadness at the Colonel's remark. "Because of what you just saw in the bar? Butler was a dirtbag from the beginning. He took more than he contributed, he half-assed every job I ever gave him, and he was stupid to boot. He got the beating he needed from Jensen, and I could have left it at just leaving him behind if he hadn't lost his damn mind. He got what he deserved. You don't deserve to be left here, Robert."

"I don't guess I could persuade you to deliver these letters?"

Both men knew how impossible such a thing would be, and they laughed briefly together about it.

"You better hang onto them," Isaac said, standing and offering his hand.

The Colonel stood and shook it warmly. "Whatever hard feelings you have for Cedar Key... give them a chance when you get there."

Isaac did not reply. He turned to leave, then paused to say, "There will be a guard outside the door until we leave tomorrow. Save us both the trouble and don't try to leave this room until then."

"Roger that, Senior Chief."

"I'll leave some water for you in the tower."

The Colonel had been careless with the letters, but he had fortunately been more careful with an important item from his rucksack—the .38 caliber revolver he had hidden in the wall space behind a loosened wood panel. Marine helicopter pilots in Vietnam had some latitude in selecting their sidearms. Most preferred the standard military issue Model 1911 .45-caliber, but many, like the Colonel, preferred the simplicity of the revolver. The Model 1911 was a fairly reliable semi-automatic handgun, but they did occasionally jam. Misfires with revolvers were exceedingly rare. When he left the service, the Colonel purchased a copy of his trusted service weapon, hoping to never again have reason to fire it in hostility. It took some finagling, but he was able to work the wall panel free to retrieve the revolver, then verified his stash of Tootsie Rolls was undisturbed on the shelf in the wardrobe across the room.

Darkness had fallen over the island, but people were still moving about. For the next several hours, the Colonel had only to wait and look out the window often to verify the Morgan was still at the dock. At half past three in the morning, when the quiet stillness had been set in for hours, the Colonel could wait no longer. He had rehearsed every possible scenario for how things might go when he turned the doorknob and opened the door of his room. In every mental model he could conceive, there would be a make-or-break interaction with the guard on the other side of the door, and thereafter, no better than even odds he would make it off the island.

As he walked toward the door with the rucksack strapped to his back and the revolver in his hand, the Colonel made peace with the fact that the next few minutes might be his last. With Seaman Recruit Butler gone, he could think of no one on the other side of the door that he could bear hurting. He would bear it, of course, because whomever he encountered in the hall would be standing between himself and Melinda Beth. That immutable fact would make them enemies. He had his favorites, but with few exceptions, he found the Coasties in Isaac's crew to be worth every ounce of effort the Senior Chief put into their care.

The Colonel turned his head from side to side, limbering the muscles in his neck and working up his nerve, then turned the knob smooth and easy. Quiet remained on the other side. He pushed the door forward, gentle as a whisper, and was met with a sight that momentarily froze his ambition to continue. Maybe it was a generational blind spot or the patriarchal conditioning of a Southern upbringing, but none of the Colonel's plans had considered the possibility that a young woman would be his guard. Certainly, given the tough night she had already endured, it was impossible for Seaman Apprentice Jensen to be the one in the chair facing the door.

And yet, there she was, pretty and peaceful as she indulged in a guilty nap, every bit the Colonel's match in physical prowess, but a woman—a young girl to his eyes—all the same.

Suddenly, the cocked revolver felt like a serpent in the old man's hand. He kept it pointed at her all the same, taking quiet half steps into the hall and believing, momentarily, that he might simply tiptoe away from her and avoid the awfulness altogether. There were few good breaks to be had in this new world, and neither the Colonel nor the Seaman Apprentice would receive one in the small hours of that frigid February morning.

A cautious next step inevitably creaked a wooden floorboard, cliché as a low-budget slasher film, and Jensen's delicate face sprang to life. She raised her sidearm in a snap response, its barrel nearly touching that of the Colonel's revolver. She instinctively flexed the muscle in her jaw that began to open her mouth to let out a scream, and fast-twitch muscles in her trigger finger received the signal to pull back, but in that same eternal zeptosecond, the flit of time that would haunt him in every quiet moment of his remaining life, the Colonel flipped his left wrist toward her, plunging the ornate brass letter opener—with the mother of pearl inlaid handle—into the neck of his fetching adversary.

Seaman Apprentice Jensen's finger fell away from the trigger, and the light fell out of her eyes. The Colonel caught her up in his arms to save the sound of a crashing body and to hold her face close to his as he whispered, in crazed agony, the false comfort of a grandfather to a hurting child, "It's okay, honey... it's okay, it's okay."

When she was gone, the Colonel slipped quietly down the hall and into the night.

16

MAGNETOS

"I'm sorry," HT Morgan said as he finally stopped his work on Allen Mikes.

Mark David released the pressure from his friend's shoulder and sat on the deck of the pilot house, bereft. The Health Services Technician was exhausted from this frantic work, so he sat down as well. A long stretch of silence grew between the two men. There was sufficient time in the quiet for both to work out the difficult logistics that were likely to follow. Mark David had been a captive, bound and harmless, but now his friend was dead, and he was free.

"I appreciate what you tried to do for him," Mark said.

"It's my job," HT Morgan replied flatly.

"You did it well… and whatever happens next, I'll be grateful to you for it."

The HT nodded. Mark David leaned his head back against the bulkhead and closed his eyes for a few moments. Allen Mikes had been the better brawler of the two, but Mark was often in the fray alongside his friend, never backing away from a fight that needed fighting.

"I don't guess we could just talk this out?" HT Morgan asked.

"I don't figure we can," Mark replied with sadness in his voice.

The younger man was every bit as stout as Mark David, but his twenty-seven years had been spent in the relative ease of a suburban childhood and as an adult caring for others in hospitals and shipboard clinics. His resolve, like so many in Isaac's crew, was admirable, but compared to the coarse waterman sitting across from him, the lack of violence in his life was an impediment.

There could be no doubt now about what must transpire between them, but Mark David was content to let the interim linger along with his dead friend's spirit that still filled the pilot house and his heart.

"It didn't surprise me to learn Isaac was in command of your... whatever it is you all are. He was seventeen when he came to work on my clam boat. I knew the first day he'd be a skipper of something before it was all over with. He just knew his way around the boat from the start. My boy Hayes is the same way. Everybody thinks he gets it from me, but truth is I had to work at it harder than most. If Isaac hadn't left for the Coast Guard, I had it all figured that him and my boy would run the whole island together before it was all over with. Did he tell you I was a Boat as well?"

"He never talks about his life before the service," HT Morgan replied. "Come to think of it, I mean literally never. I like to think he and I are something like friends, and I had never heard about Cedar Key until we sailed toward it."

"Well, that's too bad," Mark replied. "I guess I hoped he wanted to be a Boatswain Mate 'cause I was one... but maybe we never even talked about it."

"For what it's worth," the HT began, "I've seen a lot of Boats in my time and not one that was better at the job than the Senior Chief."

"Very good," Mark David replied, flexing his fingers and stretching his back as he slowly made his way up off the floor.

"Alright," HT Morgan replied, rising quickly to his feet.

"You're between me and that door, Petty Officer. I'm gonna give you a chance not to be."

"Sorry, Boat."

Mark David smiled, elevated by his proximity to the raw courage of the younger man, the adherence to duty—fatalistic as it was—so lacking in the wider world, such that the following ninety seconds would hurt him thereafter the rest of his life.

When it was finished, Mark David limped out of the pilot house, considered for five foolhardy seconds an attempt to work the sails of the Sawfish, then made his way off the boat and toward a canoe on a rack by the marina's entrance.

The Colonel was a raw nerve in the night.

Jensen's face, frozen in surprise and fear, clouded his thinking as he pushed against the adrenaline haze and sprinted toward the boat house near the dock. The seven gallons of gas that had taken him ten months to stockpile were hidden in the half-attic scuttle space above the toilet in the women's bathroom of the boathouse. The plan up to this point had been to load what gas he needed into the canoe and paddle quietly to Cayo Costa, but the sight of the Morgan at the dock, its keys in the ignition, shimmering in the light of a half-moon filtering through sporadic clouds, and the building fear in his belly of being discovered, changed the plan. He would load the fuel cans into the Morgan and race it to the Archer.

The sound of the outboard firing up and the boat motoring away would almost certainly sound the alarm, and Isaac's crew would come running. The Colonel was banking that Isaac would not have time to reach him in a sailing boat before he could get to the Archer, chew up the Tootsie Rolls, use them to repair the holes in the tanks, pour what fuel he had into those tanks, pump the primer bulb another several hundred times for the rest of the needed fuel, pour that into the tanks, then start the aircraft and manage a soft-field takeoff in the low light of the small hours. As he thought it all out in detail, the odds of success grew longer in his mind, but they remained better, by his estimation, than being able to pump enough fuel from the Morgan where it sat and then paddle away with it before Seaman Apprentice Jensen's relief arrived and found her as they would find her. The one advantage the Colonel would have rested with the fact the Morgan would make maybe 30 knots as it sped away from Cabbage Key, and this speed might be enough to help obscure its heading from the pursuers.

The Colonel made it to the bathroom and managed to get the first five-gallon gas can down from the attic, but as he carried it along the dock leading to the Morgan, candlelight appeared in the hallway windows of the inn. The light moved steadily through the hallway in the direction of his room, where, inevitably, it illuminated the fallen girl. Yelling and sounds of panicked commotion filled the air. The Colonel sprinted as best he could the rest of the way to the Morgan, lifted the gas can into it, and began to untie the lines mooring it to the dock. By the time he finished and boarded the boat, three crew members had emerged from the front double doors of the inn. The Colonel could see them almost clearly enough to make out their faces, and they could see the movement on the Morgan.

Here, finally, a break—the motor started immediately despite batteries weakened from months of disuse. The Colonel spun the Morgan hard around and throttled it full. As soon as the vessel cleared the obstruction of the boathouse, rifle rounds from the front yard of the inn began to riddle its fiberglass hull. One entered the Colonel's rucksack and tore through a half dozen Tootsie Rolls before exiting out the other side. Rounds buzzed by the Colonel's ears in a flurry like the tymbals of a thousand cicadas. He pushed the Morgan hard ahead, ducking his head down low and steering by memory in the general direction of the channel. Shortly, he was far enough away from Cabbage Key that the rounds no longer hit the boat.

Even with the sporadic moonlight, the Colonel was lucky not to hit a channel marker or run aground on the many shoals and sandbars between Cabbage Key and the windward shore of Cayo Costa. Twice, the Morgan had drifted just feet out of the channel, dragging the outboard's skeg through the sandy bottom and throwing the Colonel hard into the steering wheel as the boat rapidly decelerated. Only a quick course correction kept the boat from being stranded and ending the Colonel's chances of getting home.

Cayo Costa's beach was long and non-descript, a quality that had made it a good landing strip for the disabled Archer, but in the low light of 4 AM, these features made it impossible for the Colonel to find his camouflaged aircraft from the water. He made his best approximation of where along the beach he might have landed, then shut off the outboard motor and anchored the Morgan in waist-deep water a few yards offshore. When he hopped overboard to wade to the shore and look for his airplane, the gelid water shocked his senses and quickened his breath. On land, the gentle breeze cut through him in the 38-degree air.

It took a half hour of searching for the Colonel to locate the Archer, a half mile away from the Morgan. Seeing the aircraft again after so many months spent dreaming about it, even as his teeth chattered and his lips blued, invigorated the Colonel. He placed his rucksack near the shore to mark the Archer's position, then jogged back to the Morgan, pushing his body hard to warm it up while looking often in the direction of Cabbage Key, expecting to see sails at any moment.

The Colonel's good fortune thus far in the mission ended abruptly when he reached the Morgan, climbed aboard, and turned the key in the ignition—click click click click click. On the sixth click, the motor surged to the tip edge of firing up, then fell back into a steady chorus of further clicking. The boat's batteries had lasted longer than they should have over the many months since the flash, but the alternator had not. The battery's remaining power had been expended with Seaman Bartholomew's first turn of the ignition and the Colonel's last on the dock. The half-mile was too far for the Colonel to carry fuel multiple times from the boat to the plane. Even if his strength held out, he likely did not have the amount of time it would take before Isaac and his crew found him on the beach.

The Colonel tried to use the bow line to drag the Morgan parallel to the shore ithe direction of the Archer as he walked along the beach, but the water near the shore was too shallow, and the boat ran aground every few feet. His only remaining option would push his body to its absolute limits; he had to wade out to waist-deep water and push the boat by hand. In Cedar Key, clam farmers would sometimes have to push their boats through the shallow waters between the ramp and the clam leases, especially on a winter blow-out tide, and the Colonel had many times pushed his stone crab boat back into a missed channel. The Morgan pushed easily enough, but the distance that had to be traversed meant prolonged exposure to the frigid water.

By the time the Colonel finished the first third of the half-mile, the cold had morphed from painful to numbing. Halfway to the Archer, he began to experience symptoms of hypothermia—intense shivering, a slowed heart rate, and mild disorientation. The basic motor skills required to keep his hands on the boat and push as he walked became increasingly more difficult. By the time he neared the rucksack marking the location of his aircraft, the Colonel was shivering so violently that his muscles ached from the exertion of it, and he felt an overwhelming drowsiness that would otherwise have been impossible in the heightened atmosphere of his attempted escape. Somehow, he was able to throw the anchor and make his way out of the water.

He dragged the rucksack through the sand on the way to the Archer, and after considerable difficulty was able to strip out of his wet clothes and crawl inside it. He had no immediate energy for putting on the one change of clothes from his rucksack but was able to spread them partially over himself as his body slowly warmed inside the plane. Over the course of another half hour, the shivering slowed, and the fog began to lift from his mind as he chewed Tootsie Rolls from the rucksack. The Colonel summoned all of his remaining strength, put on the dry clothes, and exited the plane. Using his Ferro rod, he dared to light a single tea light candle, weighing the risk of it giving away his position against the need to see the bullet holes in the wings of the Archer.

A twenty-five-gallon thin aluminum fuel bladder was built seamlessly into both wings of the Archer, giving it a 50-gallon total capacity with 48 gallons of useable fuel. The left wing's bladder had been hit with a single round, and the right wing's bladder had taken three hits. Even though twenty gallons would comfortably get him back to Cedar Key, the Colonel intended to repair both tanks, reasoning that if a repair failed in one of the tanks, he would have the second one for a backup. Since the Sawfish had been firing at the Archer from below it, the exit holes were generally in the top of the fuel tanks. The Colonel would do his best to fill these holes as well, but they were less critical than the ones in the bottom of the tanks.

He chewed several Tootsie Rolls at once, but the process was painstakingly slow, with the candies hardened as they were by the cold.

Once he had a mouthful chewed to a workable consistency, warmed by the heat of his mouth, the Colonel pressed the soft brown substance into the first bullet hole. Using his thumbs and aided occasionally by the letter opener that was still stained with Seaman Apprentice Jensen's blood, he was able to plug the hole in a way that looked reasonably secure. He repeated this process multiple times until his jaws ached and all the holes were filled. By the time he finished filling the last hole, the cold air had already hardened the Tootsie Rolls from the first few holes like epoxy. When the remaining holes had hardened, the Colonel poured the five gallons from the gas can into one of the fuel tanks and watched the holes intently for leaks, nervously running his fingers over the hardened brown patches to feel for dampness. For several agonizing minutes he waited, knowing his mission, and likely his life, depended on globs of chewed-up candy. After a final, thorough inspection, the Colonel nodded to his Marine brothers from generations past and judged the repair to be working.

The Colonel saw no sails in any direction as he carried the empty can and the letter opener to the Morgan to begin the tedious process of pumping fuel from its tanks. It took twenty minutes to fill the five-gallon can the first time because the Colonel had to take frequent breaks to change hands as the joints in his fingers began to burn and stiffen. After he carried the can to the plane and poured it into one of the tanks, he ran his fingers along the filled holes again, finding no leaks and feeling the first stirrings of optimism that he might actually get the Archer back into the air. Ten gallons on board, ten to go. The next round of pumping consumed a half hour despite the Colonel's best efforts to push through the pain and cold. With fifteen gallons now in the Archer and the candy repair holding, the Colonel headed back to the Morgan to fill the can a final time. Halfway back to the boat, the awful visage of a sailing mast finally appeared, small but distinct, near the far end of Cayo Costa.

The Colonel dropped the empty gas can and ran back to his airplane. Fifteen gallons was theoretically enough fuel to get him home if none leaked out and there were no serious headwinds along the way. The soft breeze near the water would slow the sailing boat's progress toward the Archer if they had even spotted it yet, but there remained a significant obstacle for the Colonel to overcome before he could attempt a takeoff on the beach. The 24-volt battery required to power the Archer was totally dead, which the Colonel had expected. While warming inside the cockpit, he turned the ignition key for confirmation and found the battery lacked the juice to even produce a click. Fortunately, the ignition system of a small airplane differs from that of an automobile or outboard motor. Planes like the Piper Archer don't utilize the electrical current produced by the battery to spark ignition. Rather, they utilize magnetos, which are, as the name implies, magnets that spin in close proximity to a coil of wire. As the magnet spins, it creates a strong and growing magnetic current. When the current reaches its maximum capacity, a breaker point switch is thrown, sending high voltage into two spark plugs that create a tiny spark sufficient to ignite the fuel in the engine's cylinders. This system needs only a mechanism to spin the magneto magnets, and the airplane can be started.

Luckily for the Colonel, as the sails grew larger and the terrible outline of the Sawfish began to emerge, airplanes have a spinning mechanism built into their design—the propeller, or prop. Hand-starting a piston motor is a technology that's older than airplanes. It was the procedure utilized by tractors, motorcycles, and automobiles for many years until the electric starter was invented in 1911. Wilber and Orville Wright hand-propped the motor of the Wright Flyer for the first sustained, powered flight in 1903 in Kittyhawk, North Carolina. Hand-propping works like it sounds: a person spins the prop of the airplane by hand. This, in turn, spins the magnetos that send a spark to the spark plugs, igniting the fuel in the cylinders and starting the engine.

In the Colonel's weakened condition, there was a real possibility that he would simply lack the strength to spin the prop with enough force to start the engine. He had never been an overtly religious or even spiritual man, but as he gripped the propeller and made the first stroke of the prop, the Colonel felt what he would later describe as a supernatural source of power emanating from within himself. Three times, he spun the prop with the strength of many men as the engine chugged out of its hibernation. On the fourth spin, it roared to life as the Colonel flexed his muscles and screamed like the first man to make a fire.

There was no time to reflect on the achievement; the Sawfish was bearing down on his position.

The Colonel climbed into the Archer, pushed the throttle slowly forward, and used the rudder pedals to carefully maneuver the plane from its hiding place in the seagrass and toward the more compacted sand near the water. The seagrass indicated the wind was coming from the direction of the Sawfish, but the Colonel decided a downwind takeoff was less dangerous than one in the direction of the military vessel that had shot him down ten months before. When the Archer was turned fully away from the enemy boat, toward Captiva Pass, he pushed the throttle full, holding full back pressure on the yoke to rotate off the soft field as soon as possible, then quickly began building speed in the reduced drag of the ground effect. In a few seconds more, the Archer pitched up and began an aggressive climb away from Cayo Costa and the fearsome Sawfish.

At long last, the Colonel was flying again.

17

—·—

You can't fly home again

Mark David pulled a rental canoe and paddle off an outdoor rack near the back door of the Suwannee Marina. In his fight to get past HT Morgan to the door of the Sawfish's pilot house, both men had fallen hard together. His ankle bent back awkwardly, causing an instant sprain and a hairline fracture to his talus, the bone connecting the foot to the leg. This injury hobbled him some, but the adrenaline of the fight prevented him from feeling the severe pain that often accompanied such an injury. He had formulated no real plan except to get away from any boat with a sail. If needed, he thought, he would paddle all the way back to Cedar Key.

With considerable effort, he was eventually able to drag the canoe to the edge of the dock and into the water. Just as he negotiated his way into the canoe, an avalanche of sound rang out from across town. Rapid, prolonged gunfire punctuated the quiet twilight, and he instinctively ducked down low as he paddled down the narrow but deep inlet leading from the marina to the open river. Mark David had no way of knowing that his son and friends were on the receiving end of that gunfire or, indeed, that they were even in Suwannee. He thought now mostly of his wife Bette and what he believed was the need to get back to the island as quickly as possible to share the deadly lessons learned in Suwannee.

When he reached the open river, the current from the elevated water levels quickly accelerated the canoe such that he only had to use the paddle as a steering rudder. The further downriver the canoe traveled, the louder the gunfire became. After passing several houses along a stretch of river, Mark approached the inlet to the Gateway Marina. He stared intently at the scene there, trying to process the information streaming into his eyes—Rolf Alverez emerging from behind the gas pump on the dock and sprinting toward the front door of the marina as bullets hit the ground all around him like the special effects sequences from an episode of *The A-Team.*

The river was moving so fast that he only had a few seconds to see down the inlet before he would be pulled away, and have his view obscured by more houses and trailers. In that narrow window of time, his heart leaped when he saw Rolf run the impossible gauntlet into the front door of the marina, then sank suddenly when a figure emerged from the underside of the dock and into the same line of withering fire.

Mark paddled backward for all he was worth in a futile, desperate push against the heavy water.

The figure was his son.

Isaac had indeed spotted the Archer, and he ordered his mounted 50-calibers to engage it while he and several others fired rifles at it as well. This time, however, there would be no further dramatics with the Sawfish. Despite an improbable series of small triumphs and setbacks, providence and mischance over the better part of a year on Cabbage Key, at the end, the Colonel was simply five good minutes ahead of his pursuers. By the time the Archer turned north toward home, it was too far away to be a realistic target. The Colonel would not be shot down, but there were yet challenges to overcome on the flight ahead.

While an airplane's magnetos provide the current the spark plugs need, without a working battery none of the electrical instruments or systems can operate. The Colonel would have to rely on the old school navigation skills that were taught more stringently during his time as a young pilot than they were in the age of GPS and glass panel avionics.

The first order of business for the Colonel was to point the aircraft on a northerly heading. The low light of the half-moon was darkening as dawn approached, so the first half hour of the flight was an exercise in faith and compass following. Older vacuum-powered attitude indicators needed no electricity to operate, but the Archer's was the modern variety and thus inoperable. Without it or reliable visual markers for orientation, care would have to be taken to prevent a stall of the wings. A wing stall occurs when the air flowing over the wings is disrupted by a too-steep angle of attack during a climb. When this happens, an airplane shifts from an aerodynamic, elegant flying machine to a tumbling, spinning hunk of metal whose sole desire is to fall clumsily out of the sky. The darkness and the patchy clouds demanded the Colonel's full attention, but his lifetime of pilot-in-command experience proved equal to the task.

As the Archer approached the edge of where Sarasota used to be, the sun peeked above the eastern horizon, shimmering and serene, casting ethereal light over an endless field of loss, of human avarice and stupidity, of a land remembered for a wild splendor lost generations before the bombs finally fell.

Eventually, everyone breaks. Even in a time of plenty, the daily hardships of life wear them away in minute measures until, eventually, the accumulation of untended psychic wounds overwhelms them. The Colonel had dispensed and avoided death in Vietnamese jungles, watched his friends and fellow watermen die en masse from the haunted wind on the bay, and felt the last breath of the beautiful Seaman Apprentice Jensen against his cheek; through these unbearable moments, he was borne up by the sense of duty that animated his adult life. There had simply been no time or opportunity for frailty. Now, as the soft light of dawn pushed away the darkness and softened the edges of the lost world beneath the wings of his aircraft, the Colonel took in the discrepant images—the peacefulness and beauty of the dead land—and for the first time since the day the smokestacks fell, he broke.

He was confused by the tears running fast and free from both eyes, startled by the sobs he tried but failed to hold back. In every moment since the Archer landed on Cayo Costa, no matter the task or intrigue that occupied his immediate attention, the dream of flight lived always in the back of his mind; now, he was flying again, and still his heart despaired. He had left those months ago to see what remained of the wider world, to see what place Cedar Key might have in it. As he flew the long-delayed return leg of that mission, he resented the tranquil light for illuminating all the places that no longer were. Gone now was the ungovernable and fantastic Florida that had always so captivated him, that held him in lusty rapture for three-quarters of a century, that pined for him while he was away at war and welcomed him home in peace.

Tampa Bay was below him then, and he thought of the missing Sunshine Skyway Bridge and how Melinda Beth had never stopped being terrified of crossing it, how he would roll the windows down and howl at its giant steel cables as they drove over it to get a panicked reaction from her. He felt a moment of satisfaction when he realized that no one would ever have to drive on the miserable Interstate-4 again, then returned to his doleful nostalgia imagining where Ybor City used to be, his mouth watering at the thought of a Cuban sandwich or ropa vieja from the Columbia Restaurant. Off his right wing, he thought he could just make out Lake Hollingsworth in Lakeland, on whose banks used to sit Florida Southern College and the largest collection of Frank Lloyd Wright architecture in the world. The Colonel was an architecture enthusiast with a special interest in the American master whose work featured so strangely in the tiny college of a hardscrabble phosphate and citrus town.

Up ahead, the peerless white sand of Clearwater Beach remained as striking as ever, even more so against the backdrop of the burned-out areas just beyond it. A third of its iconic pier somehow remained, the isolated section standing alone in the Gulf, cut off from the shore. The Archer was leveled out at 3,000 feet, its Lycoming engine purring despite the months of sitting still in the sand. Tarpon Springs drew near as the morning spread out against the sky. Here and there, a few sponge docks remained, vestiges of a once-thriving Greek culture.

Just as the Colonel began to see the landscape change from urban destruction to intermittent verdancy, the Archer's engine spit hard and began to choke. In most single-engine planes, the pilot has to manually switch from one fuel tank to the other. The Colonel was still several minutes away from his first planned switching, but the fuel in the right wing, with its multiple patched holes, was clearly at an end. Two of the three had begun slowly leaking just minutes into the flight, sending a fine mist of fuel behind the Archer that the Colonel had been unable to see.

He switched to the left tank, and the motor quickly returned to smooth performance. Because there had been a three times greater likelihood of a failure in the right tank, the Colonel had put less fuel in it, but a failure was nonetheless a grave concern. Frantically, he began to run the math in his head. Even without a failure, there was precious little extra gas for the trip home. Based on the ease with which the engine was keeping up a good cruising speed, the Colonel concluded the Archer was enjoying a healthy tailwind. If it held, there was still a small chance he would make it back to Cedar Key, or at least close enough to walk the remaining distance if he could get the plane on the ground safely when the fuel ran out.

The Colonel continued flying the aircraft, and Florida passed like a grade school filmstrip beneath him. When he reached Weeki Wachee Springs, he began to feel for the first time that he might actually make it home. The mermaids were no longer singing each to each, but the waterslide was still there, bright blue and garish. Even from the elevated vantage, the piercing aquamarine water in the spring stood out. Florida has the largest collection of freshwater springs on planet Earth, more than 700 total, and the Colonel had always delighted in them. From the labyrinthine cave system of Little River Springs to the incredible depths of Wakulla and the wonderment of Devil's Den, he indulged the memories of his favorites and felt encouraged; the cities had fallen, but the cold, clear water of the springs continued to flow.

A stretch of green extended for a few minutes more, and then Crystal River came into view. The expanse of land that had once contained the smokestacks was gray upon gray and lifeless as the moon. The fallen smokestacks had come to represent the fall of man to the residents of Cedar Key. Their place on the horizon had been fixed for so long that their sudden absence served as a constant reminder of the day the world changed.

The field of destruction continued into what had been a Duke Energy solar panel farm. Here and there, a pristine section of panels would be standing among a sea of twisted metal and burned-out scrap, like news reports from the old world showing neighborhoods flattened by a hurricane, save for a random house standing weirdly undamaged in the rubble. Just beyond the remnants of the sprawling solar farm lay the first section of the great boondoggle, the Cross Florida Barge Canal, an ambitious, preposterous project to cut a 12-foot-deep ditch across much of the peninsula, connecting the Atlantic to the Gulf. Begun in 1935 as part of Franklin Delano Roosevelt's New Deal, the canal was promoted first as a jobs creator and economic engine, then later as a way of hardening the national defense while the world was at war for the second time in a quarter century. Cost overruns, engineering failures, and a growing understanding of the environmental calamity of the project led to its eventual failure. From the Colonel's perspective, the eight-and-a-half mile unnaturally straight line of water running from the Withlacoochee Bay to Lake Rousseau looked like an incision from a surgeon's scalpel, its gruesomeness somehow amplified by the precision.

The Withlacoochee River was next, meandering 141 miles in total from the bay to its headwaters in the Green Swamp in Polk County, passing the destroyed Yankeetown Coast Guard Station along the way. Whenever Cedar Key had an emergency on the water, this was the station from which the Coast Guard would deploy its assets to help. In the days after the flash across the bay, when no boats or cutters or aircraft appeared from the west, as they always would when trouble came, the islanders knew that more than the smokestacks had fallen.

With only a compass for navigation, the Colonel had thus far in the trip simply flown up Florida's western coastline; now, the *Big Bend* of the state's geography presented him with a decision point. From his present position, a direct route to Cedar Key was only around 23 miles, but all of it would be over open, often turbulent, waters. The safer route, but one the Colonel felt sure he did not have the fuel to complete, was more than double the distance in a long L-shape up US Highway 19 and then left at State Road 24 near the town of Otter Creek. Running out of fuel on the longer route would mean a low-stress landing on a highway with no oncoming cars. Running out of gas on the shorter route might not kill him straight away, but the Gulf almost certainly would sometime thereafter.

Here, the Archer's dead battery bared its teeth once more as the lack of electric power meant the fuel gauges were useless. Even if the candy patch job on the single hole in the left tank had leaked no additional fuel from the plane, the Colonel's most optimistic estimates had him running out sometime soon. As he began to do the math in his head another time, leaning toward the prudent choice but needing hard numbers to seal the deal, his left hand moved of its own volition, ignoring the brain's call for caution, and banked the Archer hard to the left, out over the water, toward home. The move surprised him because he had not yet known which option he would pick. There is an old saying about picking between two choices by flipping a coin: *as soon as the coin is in the air, you know which one you want to win.* As soon as the Archer began its bank, the Colonel's brain knew it wanted the same thing as his hand. Melinda Beth and Cedar Key were due west, and no part of him could abide anything but a direct course to them.

Off his right wing, the Colonel saw the tiny island of Porpoise Point in Lows Bay, a marshy estuary of the Waccasassa Bay Preserve State Park, and thought of an ordeal that occurred there in the year leading up to the flash. Two sixteen-year-old girls were spending their spring break in Cedar Key and made the unfortunate decision—as decisions from teenagers are wont to be—to go paddleboarding on a day when the winds were gusting above 30 knots. They managed to paddle the short distance from the main island to the barrier key of Atsena Otie, where they enjoyed time playing on the sandbar and walking on the beach. When they began to paddle back, the heavy winds overwhelmed the paddleboards and pushed the girls farther and farther east of Cedar Key.

By the time it was discovered the girls were missing, more than an hour had passed. Thomas Buck led a large-scale civilian search and rescue operation to find the girls. In a short period of time, more than thirty Cedar Key boats had joined the community-led search. FWC and Coast Guard vessels arrived an hour later, and when the girls were still not located by nightfall, helicopters from Coast Guard Station Yankeetown joined the effort. The search continued through the frigid night and into the early morning before the girls were found fifteen miles away on Porpoise Point, freezing and cut up from oyster shells but alive and otherwise well. When dawn had broken that morning, most volunteers believed they were searching for bodies and not live teenagers, so when news of their safe rescue made its way to the boats in the water and the workers on the dock, joyful shouts and prayers of thanks rang out. The Colonel often thought of the girls' parents, nearly catatonic with fear and dread as that cold night dragged on, how the community had taken them in at their hour of need, how beautiful and quintessentially Cedar Key it had been. Seeing the tiny island again, he was comforted by the knowledge that Melinda Beth would have been similarly cared for when her husband failed to return from the sky.

Aside from a building cloud bank over Cedar Key, the next dozen miles passed so quickly and smoothly that the Colonel began to believe his math was wrong and he might actually fly straight on to the airport. He was disavowed of this notion a few miles later when the Archer's engine began its familiar cough-surge-sputter routine, the one that had forced the landing on Cayo Costa nearly a year before. The Colonel switched back and forth between the two tanks, hoping to find any extra drop of fuel. The engine sputtered to a rough idle, not quite dead but not alive enough to provide any real lift. At 3,000 feet of altitude, the Archer's glide ratio would give it another five and a half miles or so before it hit the water. Without his navigation instruments, the Colonel could only estimate the distance remaining to the airport; the actual distance turned out to be fractionally more than the Archer had ratio to glide.

So it was that on the 15th of February in the second year of the new world, a battered Piper Archer burst through low-hanging clouds, sputtering and wild, missing the water tower by a nose hair and plunging, more or less uncontrolled, into the Daughtry Bayou a hundred yards short and wide of the George T. Lewis Airport runway.

An old man emerged from the wreckage, laughing, and began the short swim for home.

18

—·—

SEMPER PARATUS

The pain in Hayes David's right foot was remarkably intense. When Leon Meade shot his right ear off behind the old David fish house during the first invasion of the island two months into the new world, Hayes felt almost nothing at all. When bits of the ear began to fall away in small pieces after the initial blast, Hayes picked at the bloody spot, mystified by the lack of feeling. Now, as he emerged from under the dock and tried to make his way out of the water, every step produced a searing pain emanating from the place where his little toe used to be. It raced through his foot, up his leg, and all throughout the neural pathways of his body. It was so distractingly intense that he scarcely noticed Rolf diving safely into the Gateway Marina or that the rifles previously trained on his soldierly friend were swinging in his direction.

A full two seconds of silence elapsed before the sound of gunfire began again, but this time from a different direction. Hayes continued to work his way out of the water as quickly as his injured foot would allow. He had already made peace with the low odds of making it to safety before one of the rounds eventually put him down, but he knew he could not stay hidden under the dock forever. With every additional step, he grew more confused at the lack of fire coming his way. As he quickened his pace, settling into a half shuffle that kept his weight away from the far side of his right foot, he saw a man in overalls on the opposite bank of the canal he and Thomas had dove into earlier. His unkempt white beard was blowing wild about his round face, and his smile was as pure an expression of joy as a kid with a new bike on Christmas morning. Steady flashes of light and color pulsed from the end of an enormous M60 machine gun that the bearish older man was miraculously deploying from his hip before dropping into a more protected prone position with one end of the heavy weapon resting on its barrel-mounted tripod.

The Hughes Amendment to the Firearms Protection Act of 1986 made it illegal to manufacture or possess fully automatic machine guns made after the date the law went into effect. Any such weapons made before that date could still be acquired and possessed after a lengthy and expensive licensing and registration process. Overnight, a bustling market developed for pre-1986 machine guns like the refurbished 1968 General Dynamics M60 that Percy Walters was now using to lay down devastating cover fire on the riflemen in the tree line near the marina. The year and legality of Percy's M60 were a moot point. He had not acquired it in a manner consistent with the Hughes Amendment or any other law, and to the extent that laws ever mattered much in Suwannee, they were even less relevant now. Five hundred non-government-approved rounds per minute were blanketing the tree line as Hayes David climbed out of the water and limped his way into the Gateway Marina.

After the initial shock and awe of Percy's counterattack from the west, an attack that left Petty Officer Palmer gut-shot and dying and Seaman Bartholomew grazed twice in one arm as she tried in vain to care for him, Isaac's crew regrouped and concentrated their fire on the older man as he struggled to change out an overheated barrel on the M60. Undeterred, Percy completed the changeout and recommenced firing, but he was pinned down now and in real trouble.

"Is everybody okay?" Hayes asked as he slid behind the overturned desk his friends were using as a shield against rounds that made their way into the marina.

"We're good," Ryland said.

"You're bleeding," Hayes said to Rolf, who had not known until being told.

"Where?"

"Your palm," Thomas said, grabbing Rolf's wrist to get a closer look.

A section of his palm, about the size of a nickel, was missing from the right side of his left hand. It was clear that blood had been pouring from the wound and running down into the sleeve of Rolf's shirt as his left arm was elevated to support the barrel of his rifle, but the bleeding had mostly stopped by then. He had felt no pain as he danced for his life behind the gas pump or now as he fixated on the door where he expected the enemy to be pouring in at any moment.

"I'll be fine," Rolf said. "How did you make it in here?"

"They saw me in the water after you got away," Hayes said. "I'm shot in the foot and moving slow, so I thought for sure I'd be dead in two seconds, but somebody laid into 'em from across the channel. Sounded like a whole army, but I only saw one guy."

"That wasn't a regular gun," Rolf added. "It was full auto, big rounds."

"Was it a big fella? White beard?" Ryland asked.

"Actually, yeah... I think so." Hayes said.

"Hell yeah. Attaboy, Percy," Ryland said, gritting his teeth as the automatic fire continued outside the marina in long, deafening bursts, accompanied by the comparatively benign-sounding popping of individual rifles from the other direction.

A barrage of sound and flying metal pushed through the twilight as rounds hit all around the machine gunner. When one finally found its target, a glancing blow from an obtuse angle that tore away a part of his cheekbone, Percy reacted in a crazy way, rising to his feet and continuing to spray fresh hell toward the trees.

Rounds began to hit him almost immediately, but still Percy Walters stood, magnificent as Stonewall Jackson at Manassas, delivering what judgment he could to invaders that would soon kill him, smiling brightly as a guileless child when they did.

From the river, Mark David marveled at the rampaging gunner, knowing the stranger had saved his son's life, and felt instantly bereaved when Percy fell at last. Mark had given up the futile effort to paddle upstream and was focusing on steering his canoe toward the shore, but the current had already pushed him well past the marina and halfway to Alligator Pass when the Big Skiff Energy came speeding around the bend. Luke Buck had his skiff running wide open and nearly hit the canoe, zipping past it and only recognizing his neighbor and friend as he raced by. Luke pulled back on the throttle and spun quickly back around.

"Mr. Mark!"

"What in the hell are you doing here?" Mark yelled back.

"Looking for you and Mr. Allen," Luke replied.

"Come pick me up. Hurry!"

When the B.S.E. was alongside the canoe, Officer Biscuit and the Colonel grabbed Mark by the shoulders and pulled him onto the skiff, allowing the canoe to be carried away by the current.

"They've got Hayes and Rolf pinned down at the Gateway Marina," Mark said sternly. "We've got to get to them."

"What about Thomas?" Lizzy asked.

"I only saw Rolf and my son," Mark replied. "But he might be inside the marina, too."

The Colonel said, "If you know where Isaac is, I can try to talk to him."

"I tried that already," Mark replied. "It got Allen killed."

The news of Allen Mikes' death landed heavily on the skiff, on Luke especially, who had admired the older man's musicianship and polished voice, making an effort whenever possible to hear him play at the Island Hotel. He would lean into the feelings about it all another time when his dad and friends weren't taking fire.

"If we go head to head with 'em," the Colonel began, "Maybe we win or maybe we don't... but they won't go easy. That crew will fight like hell for Isaac."

"They're doing it now," Mark said, frustrated, "And if we don't stop talking and go help, they're gonna overrun our boys."

Just then, the slower boats in Luke's formation began to arrive from Alligator Pass.

With a hint of pride in his voice, Officer Biscuit said, "We brought everybody."

"All hands, all hands," Luke announced over the radio. "Relay this message to any boat without comms. Mr. Joey, when you hit the river, take your formation downstream to the marina."

"The second one," Mark said.

"The second one," Luke repeated on the radio. "Be prepared to take fire. They've got Mr. Hayes and the others pinned down there. We're coming up from the other direction."

"Roger," Joey replied.

The handful of other boats with generators and radios acknowledged the plan.

Luke waved his hand over his head, signaling the boats in his group to follow, and the Cedar Key Navy descended on the Gateway Marina from two directions as night began to fall.

During the Civil War, the Union had a vastly superior navy compared to that of the Confederacy. Its warships were generally larger, faster, and better armed. Most critically, there were a lot more of them. A major part of their mission was to enforce a naval blockade of the southern states, preventing them from shipping goods and troops by water.

Confederate blockade runners were tasked with evading the ships that enforced the blockade, and they found a good amount of success using smaller boats to operate in inland waterways like the Suwannee. Cotton, munitions, and other dry goods were moved along the Suwannee, making the river strategically important. Historian John E. Clark described the Confederate blockade runners as, "The aquatic equivalent of the Ho Chi Minh Trail," because they allowed the Confederates, like the North Vietnamese, to continue moving supplies and men despite a superior force's efforts to stop them.

On 20 December 1863, just down from where Luke's crew pulled Mark David into the Big Skiff Energy, the Confederate steamer *Little Lilly* ran aground on a sandbar near the mouth of the river. The Union steamer, *USS Fox*, encountered it and opened fire with its single gun, a 12-pounder rifled howitzer. The crew of the unarmed Little Lilly had no choice but to abandon ship and flee as an armed Union boarding party bore down on them. The Union sailors had intended to take the Confederate steamer as a prize and press it into Union service, but they were unable to figure out how to operate its engine. Frustrated, they set fire to the Lilly and burned it to the waterline.

Elsewhere on the Suwannee, local blockade runners met similar fates. The 120-foot steamship *The Madison* was built in 1854 and operated by its owner, Captain James M. Tucker, as a floating general store and mail carrier, servicing communities all along the river. When northern forces invaded Florida, Captain Tucker joined the Confederacy, and the Madison was commissioned as a warship, though one with no guns or armor. Its shallow hull made it capable of moving upriver faster than its contemporaries, a critical feature for a blockade runner. A few years into the Madison's service, the tide of the war had turned sharply against the South, and Federal forces were closing in. In order to keep his prized ship out of the hands of the enemy, Captain Tucker steamed it into the clear water of Troy Springs, near the town of Branford, and sank it. Most historians believe Captain Tucker intended to raise the ship after the war, but by the time hostilities ended, the Madison had been picked clean of its equipment and fittings, rendering it useless and relegating it to the bottom. There it continues to sit, partially intact in the cold, clear water.

Luke and the other local boats pushed forward against the tide of history, greater in number but weaker in firepower than the invaders that had come by sail.

As Isaac watched the Archer lift off the Caya Costa sand, he knew there could be no welcome for him on Cedar Key. Any leanings he may have had toward diplomacy were erased as the plane disappeared into the scattered clouds. The rage caused by Seaman Apprentice Jensen's death metastasized in the morning sun into grim determination. The loss of the generator meant Cabbage Key could no longer support his crew. He canceled plans to outfit the Morgan and ordered preparations for immediate departure. Robert would beat him to Cedar Key, but Isaac was determined to give the island as little time as possible to prepare. Finding Robert's letters had triggered the same feelings of betrayal he had for Mark David and an entire island he blamed for his father's death, but the details in them had given him cause for hope—wells operating on hand pumps, vegetable gardens, clams. As he considered his crew's hardships in the first month after the flash, finding little in the way of resources and being pushed to the brink of thirst and hunger, Isaac's decision became clear. Cedar Key was the last best hope for their survival.

In less than an hour, the Sawfish sailed through Captiva Pass with nine other heavily armed boats, riding a hard wind into the Gulf and racing north. Prevailing winds for Florida are typically out of the north in the winter, from the panhandle down to the Orlando area, with more variability in the southern part of the state. The sustained southerly winds pushing his fleet at such a fast clip were an anomaly that Isaac interpreted as a sign he was doing the right thing. From the earliest days of life in the new world, as it became clear the normal order of things was gone forever, Isaac wrestled with his moral obligations. He spent more than two decades in a service whose primary aim was protection, but now his allegiance had shifted from the nation at large to the twenty-four younger Coasties left in his charge. He knew his young crew viewed him in a fatherly role, and he also knew that any television pop psychologist could diagnose him as wholly unfit for such an obligation, beleaguered as he continued to be by daddy issues as cliché as they were tragic.

Aboard the cutter *Yamacraw* in Savanna, Georgia, in 1922, Captain Francis Saltus Van Boskerck wrote the words to what would become the official Coast Guard Marching Song, *Semper Paratus*. The Latin phrase translated to *Always Prepared* and grew over time into the Coast Guard's motto. Men whose fathers die young spend the rest of their lives looking to recover a thing that is unrecoverable, seeking a replacement for the foundation of identity that even negligent fathers provide for their boys. Isaac had grasped and foolishly let go of it with Mark David, then blended himself into the artificial kindred of the Coast Guard, trading family tradition for military bearing and Latin mottos. By necessity, he internalized the high-minded ideals of the Semper Paratus chorus:

> *We're always ready for the call,*
> *We place our trust in Thee.*
> *Through surf and storm and howling gale,*
> *High shall our purpose be.*
> *Semper Paratus is our guide,*
> *Our fame, our glory too.*
> *To fight to save or fight and die,*
> *Aye! Coast Guard we are for you!*

The high purpose of Isaac's life now, even if it came at the cost of everyone on Cedar Key, was vested in the young crew following behind the Sawfish in the blustery, counternatural winds pushing them impossibly fast toward a new home.

They would fight to save themselves from a world gone crazy. They would fight and die for each other.

19

THE YOUNG CAPTAIN

Sierra Solaro took up the work in the garden on E Street while Lizzy was away with the navy. Most of the island's soil was so sandy that growing anything in it was a challenge. Luke and Ryland had begun digging richer soil from across the channel and bringing it to the island on the back of a bird dog to supplement the island's gardens. It was a strenuous, boring job, like so much of the work in the new world, but the return was paid in tangible currency—rich, red tomatoes, field snaps, peppers, squash, and okra. These sparks of color were essential ingredients to happiness because they broke up the monotony of mullet, crabs, and clams, followed by more mullet, crabs, and clams—clams eternal and drab when the last of the hot sauce and crackers ran out.

Sierra was Rapunzel-haired and beautiful, with sad, soulful eyes set in an otherwise cheerful face. She and Lizzy's son, Jack Fraydel, Jr., had fallen in love while the world was falling apart. He heated water in pots on a charcoal grill to fill a jacuzzi tub for their first romantic night together. On that same night, not certainly but likely the night Sierra and Jack, Jr.'s union was sealed by conception, Lizzy fled the house to give the young lovers privacy and found her way by bicycle to Thomas' porch. Hours later, by the petrichor and percussion of a Florida thunderstorm, they, too, had fallen in love.

Even well into the last trimester of her pregnancy, Sierra moved about the garden with grace and youthful ease, pulling weeds and tending each plant with the earliest stirrings of motherly instinct. The other women on the island made a fuss over her at every opportunity. Hers would be the first new world baby in Cedar Key, the symbolism was lost on no one. When Lizzy first heard the news that she was going to be a grandmother for the first time, she was overjoyed in the way that all parents are at such news, but she felt a deep contentment for the island as well.

"Nothing makes things matter like a baby," Lizzy had remarked when told of the pregnancy, accidentally evoking the secret of civilization, the magic that separated humankind from the beasts of the field and monkeys in the jungle: The only reason to care about anything for long is so the little ones can inherit a better world.

As Sierra bent over to pull a crawling thing from a new tomato plant, a sharp pain in her belly doubled her over and into the dirt. From inside the house, Kinsey, the newest member of the Buck family, heard Sierra calling for help. When she reached the garden, Sierra was on the ground writhing. The scrunchy white socks Sierra had pilfered from Lizzy's closet were drenched in water and blood, and the fear in her eyes sent Kinsey into a panic.

"Oh my God, oh my God," Kinsey said.

"Help me," Sierra pleaded.

"I'll get Miss Bette," Kinsey replied. "Stay right here."

Kinsey ran for all she was worth. The David house was just a block and a half away, but in the terror of the moment it felt like miles as she ran. She found Miss Bette, predictably, in her own garden while her daughter Lida Maria sat on a bucket in the backyard, hand sewing a fishing net.

"There's something wrong with Sierra," Kinsey relayed in a panic. "The baby might be coming."

"It's too soon," Miss Bette said, dropping her tools and rising to her feet. "Where is she?"

"In the garden at Thomas' house."

"Lida Maria!" Miss Bette yelled across the yard. "Get some towels from the house, quick. Kinsey, run get Nurse Toni and tell her to meet us at Thomas' house as fast as possible. Tell her Sierra's in labor."

Kinsey sprinted out of the yard, heading toward the clinic. Lida Maria returned with the towels, and she and Miss Bette ran down E Street toward Sierra. They found her flat on her back in the tomato patch, breathing heavily and scared.

"It's okay, honey," Miss Bette said. "Kinsey is on her way to get Nurse Toni. Just hang on."

"Why is this happening?" Sierra pleaded.

"It might be nothing," Lida Maria ventured, trying to be encouraging but immediately realizing that she had missed the mark.

"It's definitely something," Sierra moaned. "What do I do, what do I do, Miss Bette?"

"Just hold on, Nurse Toni's coming."

"I don't think I can," Sierra said, then screamed like she had never screamed before.

It happened so quickly after that that none of the three women had time to think about what they should do or how it should be done. Lida Maria held Sierra's hand and assured her everything was going to be okay while Miss Bette received the tiny child in a cradle of bath towels. The little boy required no help to begin spontaneous breathing. He cried out strong and loud while Miss Bette cleared away his mouth and nose.

Nurse Toni arrived with a medical bag and got right to work checking all the things that needed to be checked, but her demeanor was so relaxed and non-hurried that everyone involved felt assured that the danger had passed. Sierra would have no way of knowing that she had been a few weeks further along than estimated, but this precious extra time had made all the difference for her son. A child born prematurely in the opulence of old-world medical care would not be cause for significant alarm. In the tomato patch, without access to comprehensive diagnostic testing and modern drugs, the odds of survival were certainly decreased, but there was such a defiant vigor in the boy that the odds felt immaterial.

While his father captained a boat heading into the building night, into the teeth of a fight on the river, Jack Fraydel, III, named for a grandfather gone too soon from the world, fought his way into the light of life—life in a broken world but life indeed, hopeful and new.

Two months later, Lara Budd would carry her baby to full term, feeling healthy and assured throughout the pregnancy. The labor began uneventfully and then stalled. Hours later, Lara began bleeding, and despite Nurse Toni's best efforts, she didn't stop until she and her baby were dead. Without modern equipment in a hospital setting, the *Placenta Previa* condition that caused the bleeding would go undiagnosed.

Since the flash across the bay, dying was the easiest thing in the world.

Night fell as quickly and finally as Percy on the bank of the canal. Isaac had worked his way from the Sawfish at the Suwannee Marina to the firefight at the Gateway Marina just as the last light was fading. The two properties were only a third of a mile from each other as the crow flies, but a series of canals made it impossible to take a direct route. By the time

Isaac arrived, there was little left to see. A cloudy night and a new moon blended enemy and friend together in the darkness. The faint orange glow of the gasifiers dimly lit wispy columns of smoke that tangled together as they rose, but the net effect was an ambiguation of the fleet rather than the illumination of potential targets.

Now, as in the time of Alexander or Napolean or U.S. Grant, fighting in a dark night was simply not practicable. The rifles in the trees were as likely to hit each other as they were an enemy, and the two sections of the Cedar Key Navy had their hands full forming around the inlet to the marina and dropping their anchors before being pulled away by the river's current.

To Isaac's credit, he did not let the emotion of the moment overwhelm his judgment. The sight of the injured Seaman Bartholomew, only then accepting that Petty Officer Palmer was gone and crying quietly over him, could have swayed a lesser leader to reckless action. It took unusual resolve not to be overcome by simple math. Butler and Jensen on Cabbage Key, Dennison and Nelson on Deer Island, Bullard, Henley, and Houseman on the Atlas, and now Palmer in the trees made eight crew members that Isaac could not protect. When the Sawfish first sailed away from Coast Guard Station Fort Myers Beach and the insane pedantry of Lieutenant Dupont, Isaac had twenty-six Coasties in his charge; only eighteen remained. His crew had thus far been reduced by thirty-one percent, a casualty rate rivaling Normandy or Okinawa. It would have been easy, even forgivable, to let the anger and the blood spill over into a Pickett's Charge instead of the Dunkirk that was required.

In the river, Joey Bannon anchored his boat near the Big Skiff Energy, seeking instruction from the younger captain. To Luke Buck's credit, he did not let the largeness of the moment or the impediment of his age shrink his nerve.

"The shooting's stopped," Luke said. "I expect it'll start again at first light. The way I see it, we've got to figure a way to get them out of the marina tonight."

"Then what?" Joey asked. "We're here, and we finally know where they are. Seems like we ought to take the fight to them while we can."

"Maybe that's exactly what we do," Luke replied. "But we're doing nothing until we get my dad and the rest of them back."

"The boy's right," Mark David said. "We get our people back and then figure out how to end this thing for good."

In the trees, Isaac assigned two of his crew members to keep an armed watch on the marina and the inlet leading to it, one to lay down fire if necessary and another to run back to report any movements from the island navy. He then gathered the remainder of his crew and quietly led them back toward the Sawfish to plan for the fight that was almost certainly coming at dawn. Two of the larger men carried Petty Officer Palmer's body, somber and slow.

There are few examples in the history of war where a strategic retreat is accompanied by high morale, and here, the precedent held. They were no closer to a permanent home, and their numbers were shrinking. Worse, they could point to no meaningful victories to justify the costs they were paying in lives and struggle. The light had been low when the Cedar Key Navy began assembling in the river, but this partial concealment served only to amplify their projection of force to Isaac and his crew. From their perspective in the trees, the boats blurred together in the night and seemed to go on forever.

On the boats, the mood was similarly less than jubilant. Mark David had witnessed the full extent of the firepower in the trees, and though the shots were tapering off by the time the navy assembled, the sound of the barrage barreled along the water such that both formations had heard it long before they reached the stretch of river near the Gateway Marina. Isaac and his crew had fallen back quietly and carefully, so the islanders had every reason to believe the trees were still populated with rifles trained on them and the building in which their people were barricaded.

Lizzy paced in small circles on the bow of the skiff while the Colonel and Officer Biscuit kept a military-style watch, rifles at the ready.

"What now?" Lizzy asked Luke. "Surely we aren't just gonna sit here till morning? We have to go get them."

Luke replied, "I've got an idea, but I'll need some help."

"Just tell me what you need, and I'll do it," Lizzy said anxiously.

Luke smiled. "I know you would."

He had a deep affection for Lizzy. She was easy to like, to be sure, but Luke loved her for the way she so unfailingly loved his father. For all of Thomas' success in the world—his plays and books that found a wide audience around the country, the phenomenon of the Cedar Key Shark Swim he conceived and organized, the clam farm he grew from nothing to bountiful despite no training or inherent aptitude for the waterman life, and the close bond he built and maintained with his son—he had always been ashamed of the three failed marriages he fought losingly and shamelessly to keep. In Lizzy, Luke saw, at long last, the reward he felt his father deserved in the world.

Lizzy pressed, "I can do more than garden. And I'm a better shot than you'd think."

"I'm sure that's true," Luke said. "But for this plan, I'm gonna need Uncle Jud."

Jud Bollins wasn't Luke's uncle, but he had married Lizzy's sister Jonya which made him uncle to Jack, Jr. The fact that half the island called him Uncle Jud was because he was good at the things Southern uncles are supposed to teach their nephews—shooting, cussing, fishing, telling dirty jokes, and fixing trucks. He was also funny, kind, and whip-smart.

It was Jud's skill at holding his breath that Luke was interested in now, one Jud had learned in his youth working on Greek sponge-diving boats. Luke and his dad had been freediving Florida's springs all of Luke's life, challenging each other to go ever farther into them and back on a single breath. In the years leading up to the flash, Thomas always looked forward to the spiny lobster mini-season in July, when he and Jud would freedive the rocks and grass ledges offshore from Key West in a two-day, hyper-competitive race to catch more *bugs* than the other man. Long after Lizzy, Jonya, and the kids had settled into repose and the eating of snacks on the boat, Jud and Thomas would keep up the hunt until the sun sat low on the horizon.

Luke called over the radio, "Uncle Jud, Uncle Jud, you got your ears on? Over."

Even in the smothering tension, or maybe specifically because of it, Jud called back in a stilted trucker drawl, "Ten-four good buddy, come back."

"What's your twenty?" Luke asked.

"Ol' Uncle Jud's right where you saw him last, bout a hundred feet down river in the crab boat named after my old lady."

"Copy that, good buddy... the Big Skiff Energy will head on over."

Officer Biscuit couldn't contain his laughter. "Y'all ain't right."

Luke pulled the anchor on the B.S.E and let it drift toward the Isabella, a bay boat captained by Randal Solaro, clam farmer and compulsive winker, then pulled the skiff around it by hand. Drifting from boat to boat in this way, he eventually pulled alongside the Miss Jonya.

"I've got a plan, Uncle Jud."

"Let's hear it."

"Our best bet to get to them in the marina is during the night."

Jud nodded. "I agree. They probably don't even know we're here."

"The good news is that it's dark as hell out," Luke said. "But if we just run a boat up that inlet, they're gonna open up on us with all those guns, and we'll be sitting ducks."

Jud said, "I'm worried if we don't get to them soon, they're gonna eventually try to come out of there. Even if they get away without getting hit, they won't know where to go. If they disappear somewhere in the town, we're right back where we started."

"Absolutely," Luke said. "How're your lungs feeling?"

"Like I could blow a piggy's house down," Jud replied.

"Perfect."

Luke filled Uncle Jud in on the details of the plan. The two of them would slip over the side of the skiff at the mouth of the inlet to the marina and swim as far as they could on a breath. The distance from the main river to the dock under which Hayes had hidden was more than six hundred feet, so they would not be able to make it on a single breath. Still, the hope was that a few quick, quiet breaths at the surface along the way would go unnoticed in the darkness.

At the point of making it to the dock, the plan began to lose focus. They figured they would figure it out when they got there, hoping that even a mad dash from the water to the door of the marina could be accomplished before the rifles in the trees could hope to fire an accurate shot at them in the dark. If they maintained the element of surprise about the moment they would emerge from the water, both men believed in at least even odds that one of them would make it through. Mark David, Lizzy and the Colonel offloaded onto the larger Miss Jonya, which Mark would now captain, and Jud joined Luke and Officer Biscuit on the skiff. Working together, they slowly pulled it upriver to the start of the inlet.

"I'll anchor the skiff here and keep watch as best I can," Officer Biscuit said. "That way if you run into any trouble I can get in there quick to pick you up."

"Thanks, Biscuit," Jud said as he set down on the gunnel.

Luke nodded to Uncle Jud, and then both men filled their lungs and slipped into the tea-colored water.

Isaac made his way into the pilot house of the Sawfish, fumbled in the darkness to find the box of tea-light candles he brought from the restaurant on Cabbage Key, and after some difficulty, managed to get one lit. The feeble light pushed against the heavy weight of the moonless night, moving slower than it should toward the far wall, ambitious but overmatched by the dark, failing, at last, to reach even halfway there. At the tip edge of its reach, a wisp of light drifted down to the floor and onto the face of HT Morgan. The Petty Officer shook now and then, meekly, as ragged breaths rattled in and out of a collapsed lung in asynchronous meter, the light of life and the lighter touch of death casting lots over him.

Isaac was undone.

20

DANGEROUS, DEEP WATERS

Thomas Buck and Jac Johnston met in the middle school band in the sleepy central Florida town of Bartow, the county seat of Polk County. Lakeland was by far the largest city in the county, but Bartow held the power because it held the old money of the citrus and cattle families before the citrus moved to South America and the cows had their pastures plowed under for ticky-tacky subdivisions with names like Oak Preserve, despite zero of the oaks being preserved when the dozers came.

Jac's father was the Episcopal priest in town, and his mother, the authority in the house, was a childhood development researcher. The family lived in the parsonage on the church property, a few blocks from Bartow Senior High School, home of the fightin' Yellow Jackets. By all accounts, their life was the picture of middle-America splendor. Jac was athletic but not overly so, enjoying a middling high school swimming career and playing the saxophone in the marching band. He was active in the church youth group and seldom got in trouble, despite the efforts of his best friend Thomas to lead him astray. Thomas was poor but smart, oblivious to the limitations of poverty and class, skipping through life on the nimble feet of a blithe charisma that made people like him for no particular reason. He lived with his single mother in a doublewide trailer in a withering orange grove near a tributary creek of the Peace River in Connersville, a hamlet six miles outside of town on Highway 60.

Connersville was prime phosphate country, containing dozens of enormous pits that were the remnants of strip mines dug with hulking dragline machines. When the mining companies reclaimed the land, they left behind the pits that had filled with water, some with clay cliffs and overhanging trees that were impossible for kids to stay away from. As teenagers, Thomas, Jac, and their buddies, along with whatever girls they could fast-talk, would sneak away as often as possible to swim in the pit off Gandy Cemetery Road. On weekends, with the parents of each boy believing they were having a sleepover at the other's house, Thomas and Jac would hold court over as many as thirty kids camping in cheap Walmart tents or sleeping on the ground beside the pit, around a fire summoning spirits on the phosphate waters, night swimming with the moccasins, alligators, and good girls who were the first to take their clothes off. A kid named Georgie Pilsner always brought a guitar, and despite the myriad sins that necessarily and wonderfully accompanied those nights, the sacred reverie of church camp music was as fundamental to the procession as the cheap beer and fumbling sex.

Half-drunk and immortal, they would sing:

> *Friends are friends forever, if the lord's the lord of them...*
> and
> *Thy word is a lamp unto my feet, and a light unto my path...*
> and
> *Some glad morning when this life is over, I'll fly away...*

It was *Stand by Me, Dead Poet's Society,* and *The Neverending Story* in real life, the *Kyrie Eleison* of friendships that could never end until they did. One by one, the ancillary players from those nights drifted away after graduation. A few passed suddenly; most died slowly from the inside out, never again finding the kind of sublime connection that was so free and easy in the dangerous, deep waters of the phosphate pit.

This was not the case for Thomas Buck, Jac Johnston, James Bryan, Georgie Pilsner, Arthur Droz, and Drew Warren, who found in their adventures and each other a blueprint for living and realized, with wisdom beyond their teenage years, that the treasure of a best friend—especially five of them—was a thing worth keeping a lifetime.

On the eve of Jac's departure for the Air Force Academy and Arthur's enlistment in the Navy, the six friends met in an upstairs Sunday School classroom of the church building for an overwrought ceremony with candles, clunky prose, and individual affirmations of lifetime devotion to each other. It was a weird thing for heterosexual boys in a rural Florida backwater to even think of, but something in the years of shared communion wine, or the phosphate accidentally swallowed when jumping off the high clay cliffs, had infected all of them in equal measure.

They would, without exception, keep their promises in the old world and the new.

The fantastic nature of Thomas' present predicament, pinned down inside a marina in a lawless river town at the end of the world with slow time to pass for reflection, naturally turned his thoughts to the phosphate pits and those dear friends for whom he held out little hope for survival.

On the day of the flash, Jac was a freshly retired Air Force Lieutenant Colonel reaping the spoils of a cushy defense contractor job in Colorado Springs—something to do with rockets or satellites or some other important thing above the pay grade or clearance of his Florida friends. His home was in close enough proximity to the US Space Command at Peterson Space Force Base and surrounding facilities at Cheyenne Mountain,

Shriever, and the Academy that innumerable bombs were almost certainly dropped in his backyard. Of all the boys in the candle ceremony those years ago at the church, Jac was the one likely to have suffered the least, vaporized as quickly and gently as a passing thought of a warm spring day.

James Bryant was a tech executive living in metropolitan Orlando, a place described by the Colonel on his return to the island as having: *not much left besides that stupid Epcot ball.*

Drew Warren moved back to Bartow after law school, becoming a partner at a prestigious local firm, where his family's long history in the citrus business granted him access to the monied clients of the area. If he had actually been in Bartow on the day of the flash and not in D.C. preparing for the American Association for Justice's winter convention that year, Thomas' clarinet-playing, sharp-witted, contrarian friend might still live.

Arthur Droz also lived in their hometown but drove three days a week to Tampa to manage a sleep clinic, parlaying his time as a hospital corpsman in the Navy into a better job than he ever had cause to dream of behind the borrowed tuba in the back line of the Yellow Jacket marching band. On the day of the flash, Arthur was sitting in a dimly lit clinic a half mile from the US Central Command at MacDill Air Force Base, watching an obese Realtor gasp and snore while hooked to a tangle of wires and diodes.

Georgie Pilsner lived in Harrisonburg, Virginia, twenty-nine miles from the National Security Agency's Sugar Grove Station, responsible for intercepting all international communications for the eastern United States. A bomb for Crystal River's civilian power plant meant at least one for Sugar Grove and dire straits for the Pilsner clan. Of all his friends, though, Thomas believed most of all that Georgie would miraculously appear on the island again one day, imperial and magnificent as the day of his storied dead-last finish in the inaugural Cedar Key Shark Swim.

These men, the boys who taught Thomas to love, were mostly, if not totally, gone from the world now and Thomas felt the loss sharply as he sat against the prefinished metal back wall of the Gateway Marina building, waiting for death to come for him as well.

If it did, he would face it with Hayes David and Rolf Alverez, III, his last remaining best friends in the world.

The Suwannee River Water Management District has documented more than 300 freshwater springs along the river, outflowing 567 million gallons of 70-degree water per day into it. The moderating effect of this incredible volume of warmer water makes the river as much as ten degrees warmer in the winter months than the Gulf into which it flows. Luke Buck and Jud Bollins were thankful for warmer water on a frigid February night as they slipped over the side of the Big Skiff Energy and into the six-hundred-foot-long inlet leading to the marina.

Luke swam in front, his sinewy frame gliding through the dark water like drifting through outer space, steadily moving forward with nothing to orient himself and no way to even roughly estimate the distance traveled. Uncle Jud, still a powerful swimmer despite the less than aquadynamic shape his middle-aged body had assumed in the loving embrace of Jonya's cooking, plowed through the water like a wrecking ball. He occasionally bumped into Luke's feet as they went along, and this brief contact was a steadying influence on them both as they made slow progress through the inlet.

The swimmers had a system—whenever one needed to surface for air, they would do so and remain at the surface until the other also appeared. As long as they agreed to never resubmerge unless they did so together, they could stay reasonably close to one another despite the impenetrable darkness of the night and water. Luke's chest began to burn from the lack of oxygen, but still he pushed on, farther than he had ever swum on a single breath before, beyond what seemed to him the farthest reach of human possibility, before quietly surfacing. He was surprised not to see his partner waiting for him. Five excruciating seconds passed in molasses time, then five more. Finally, Jud emerged an impossible distance ahead of Luke, having somehow missed touching him on the way by. Luke swam quietly to his partner.

"You decide to stop for lunch?" Jud whispered mockingly.

"How'd you do that?" Luke asked in a low voice, genuinely shocked.

"Never underestimate the old guy, young buck. He'll clean your clock before you can spit."

"I don't even own a clock," Luke said. "But maybe you should be in front from here on in."

"No, let's keep it like we have it. I'll try to stay close."

They swam on.

In the sensory deprivation of the river, Luke thought of his father, concluding incorrectly that this was the first time his dad had ever been in any real distress. To be sure, Thomas had faced all manner of hardships, setbacks, and even peril during their life together, but like all dads worth a damn, he would never dream of letting his boy be troubled with such knowledge. A father's lot is to suffer alone so that his children can sleep easily.

When Luke surfaced the second time, Uncle Jud bumped gently into him and came up as well. By this point, they were out of the inlet and into the small harbor of empty boat slips, less than a hundred feet from the dock where Hayes David had taken shelter from the rifles in the trees. Jud held a finger to his lips to urge silence because they were close enough to the tree line now to be heard, then pointed toward the dock. Luke nodded, and they slipped under once more, swimming close and reaching the dock without difficulty. When they surfaced again, they were reasonably concealed in the eighteen inches of space between the water and the underside of the dock and felt safe to whisper again.

"My plan got us here," Luke said. "But now that we're here, I'm not sure how bright it was."

"It's a good plan," Jud whispered warmly. "The only way to break a stalemate is to bust right through it. At some point, we were always gonna have to charge in. At least from here, we can maybe get all the way to the bank before we do."

"The dark helps," Luke replied, talking himself into the path ahead.

"It does. I think we've got a good shot at making it to that door. If it's locked and we start dodging bullets, run for the back of the building as fast as you can."

Luke nodded. "Well, let's get after it then. Follow me."

Jud grabbed the boy's arm to stop his advance. "Not this time, Luke."

"What do you mean?"

"The real danger here is not the guns in the trees but the ones behind the door."

"I don't understand," Luke said.

"They've gotta be expecting the bad guys to bring the fight to them," Jud replied. "They'd be crazy not to have guns on the doors. I'll go first."

"That doesn't make sense," Luke said. "If they start shooting when somebody goes through the door, they've got a lot better chance of hitting you than me."

Jud took two full seconds to process Luke's quip, then stifled a laugh. "What are you saying, you little shit?"

"I was hoping I didn't have to actually say it," Luke said with the trademark Buck smirk imprinted on him in the nucleotides underpinning his genetic code.

Uncle Jud's quiet chuckle was a recognition of the boy's ascendency to something more than Thomas Buck's son, but his next words reconstituted the order of things between the elder and younger captains.

"I'm not saying you're wrong, Luke... but I am saying you're not going through that door first where your daddy might accidentally shoot his son. You got it?"

"Yes sir," Luke said, without hesitation, giving in to the protection of an uncle, of his and everyone's Uncle Jud.

No more words were said before Jud eased to the end of the dock where it met the bank. He looked back to Luke, who nodded, then both men sprang from the water and sprinted the thirty feet to the front door of the marina. The door was unlocked.

Shots rang out the minute Jud pulled it open.

On the boats, against the stagnant quiet, the gunshots jolted the island navy. Rifles moved instantly to the ready, but the unrelenting night refused to yield any targets.

Officer Biscuit's heart raced as the adrenaline poured in; he was primed for a fight. In the old world, he had worked the night shift. There was so little crime in Cedar Key, beyond the occasional drunk tourist peeing on a sidewalk or a car parked outside the lines on 2nd Street, that the nights were slow and long. A few times a year, something exciting would happen—methed-up fair-weather lesbians beating each other bloody over a man each suspected the other of screwing, a meth head setting a tree on fire to win the affection of a methamphetamine princess, two totally different meth heads in a bumbling knife fight at the Jiffy Store over a scratch-off ticket. When the excitement finally came, Officer Biscuit would charge into the fray, smiling like Percy on the attack, renewed by useful purpose, ready to crack heads for the common good.

After the two shots put everyone on alert, silence returned as quickly as it departed. Tension grew moment by moment as nothing upon nothing happened on the water.

The scene was different at the door of the marina.

"Dad, Dad, Dad!" Luke screamed as he watched his Uncle Jud fall in front of him and crash onto the concrete floor.

The first shot, in the surprise of the large man appearing suddenly before them, missed. Thomas was normally a capable if not exceptional marksman, but he had fired a microsecond before his aim was established, and the bullet missed wide right. Predictably, unfortunately, Rolf did not miss, though his reflexes were quick enough not only to prevent a second shot but to forestall the first from zeroing in on a critical area. When his brain registered the intruder as Jud Bollins, it fired this information to his trigger finger, but the infinitesimal amount of time that elapsed during the transmission was enough to allow the unstoppable first shot to occur thankfully altered.

"Uncle Jud!" Ryland called out as Luke raced to Jud's aid.

"Son of a bitch," Jud said, grabbing at his left foot. "This hurts like hell."

Even as he rolled on the floor grimacing, Uncle Jud's lighthearted intensity shone through such that everyone in the room felt better.

"Which one of you shitbirds just banked an ass-kicking when I can walk again?"

"Not me," Hayes said.

"Not it," Ryland said with a snicker.

"It could have been me," Thomas said worriedly.

"It wasn't," Rolf said chagrined.

Jud looked toward the Angel of Death with a glare that both men knew was performative. "I should have known it'd be the knock-off Rambo to take me out."

"You okay?" Luke asked.

"Hell no, I'm not okay," Jud replied. "I just ain't gonna die. Help me get my boot off so we can see how bad it is… and somebody keep a gun on that door in case they decide to come in after us."

When Jud pulled his left foot out of the boot, the amount of blood that came with it was worrying, but a closer inspection revealed a wound that was already clotting. The grazing bullet had cut a narrow channel into the meat on the side of his heel about half the length of a finger. It was gnarly looking and throbbing like a hornet's sting, but given the circumstances, it was a better outcome than he expected when he pulled open the marina door.

"They got me in the right foot, and Rolf got you in the left," Hayes said in the slow-talking drawl that gave a listener time to change their mind twice about what they were hearing before it was finished being said. "Least there's two good feet between us."

"Matching set of cripples," Jud replied, pulling his boot back on with Luke's help.

"How did y'all make it to the door without getting shot to hell outside?" Ryland asked.

"We swam underwater from the river… up under the dock," Luke replied.

"You did what?" Thomas asked, only then realizing the extent to which his son had risked his life to make it to him in the marina.

For bad or good, Luke Buck had learned to lead.

Thomas would never have allowed his son to undertake such a plan, but neither could his heart help but swell when learning of it, just as it had when he saw the Big Skiff Energy closing distance on the Cogency earlier in the day, knowing the time had come when the boy could no longer be sent away to safety. A father's most fearsome duty, when the fetters of society fall away, is to kill or die for his children without hesitation or lament. Certainly, all good fathers work to cultivate a world that never demands this cost be paid, but since the great failure of humanity on the day the smokestacks fell, even the best fathers were killing and being killed. Worse, their sons were earning, in the ancient way, the blood currency of war that spends with ease but can never satisfy its debt.

"The boy did good," Jud replied.

Hayes asked, "Luke, were you able to get the whole fleet here?"

"The whole fleet and them some... anchored right over there in the river," Luke said, trying to downplay the pride in his voice.

"Good," Hayes said. "Now we just have to figure out how to get back to it."

"Needs to be tonight," Rolf said. "Everything's likely to go to hell at first light, and we'll be caught here between the two sides."

Jud said, "The water and the dark served us good on the way here. No need to complicate this thing. I say we run right through that door and dive in the water and swim like hell. Even if they open up on us, we're as likely to get through as they are to hit us in the dark."

"I agree staying here's not an option," Hayes said. "If there's gonna be a fight out there, we gotta get back in it. Jud, can you and me lean on each other until we make it to the water?"

"I can handle it if you can."

"We got plenty of guns on the boats?" Rolf asked.

"We loaded everything we could get our hands on," Luke replied.

Rolf nodded. "Then I say we leave everything here so we're as light on our feet as possible."

Luke helped his Uncle Jud to his feet and Hayes limped to him as the others dropped their weapons and stripped away any extra gear, even their coats.

On the Big Skiff Energy, Officer Biscuit began the last few minutes of his life with a sudden flood of cortisol from his adrenal glands when he heard the shots Thomas and Rolf had fired at Jud Bollins.

While the rest of the fleet hesitated in the confusion of the night, Officer Biscuit throttled up the skiff and headed into the fight.

21

—·—

GOULD'S INLET

People often conflate the terms *riptide* and *rip current* but they are incredibly different things. Rip currents, themselves often mischaracterized as the separate phenomenon of *undertows*, are frequently dramatized in popular culture because they occur regularly at beaches where lots of people can be in the water. A rip current is an isolated, usually narrow current near the surface that occurs where waves break near the beach. As wind and waves drive water toward the shore, a slight rise in the water level at the shore is created. When the shore redirects the energy of this water, it tends to flow back out to sea along the path of least resistance. When there is an area of deeper water just offshore, such as a gap in an offshore sandbar or reef, the water will flow more quickly toward this feature, initiating a rip current. The effect can create a strong river of water within the water, which is dangerous to swimmers caught in it. Contrary to some beliefs, a rip current cannot pull a person down and hold them under; it can only carry them away from the shore, often with incredible force, until the current reaches beyond the line of breaking waves, where it will quickly dissipate.

Even world-class, Olympic-level swimmers have no chance to swim against a strong rip current for long, but the natural human inclination, when caught up by such a force, is to work against it. The only way for a swimmer to reliably escape the grasp of a rip current before it runs its course is to swim perpendicular to it, often as little as ten feet or less, until they exit the rip out of one of its sides. Despite this oft-counseled advice, many people panic when caught in a rip current, are quickly exhausted, and drown. Globally, more than a thousand people die as a result of rip currents each year. Despite these grim statistics, rip tides are often significantly more powerful than rip currents.

Rip tides occur as the result of tidal movement through inlets, often near estuaries, barrier beaches, and lagoons. As tides move water in and out, areas of constriction, such as an inlet, create pent-up energy that can propel an ebbing or jetting tide to incredible force. This force can extend for much greater distances than rip currents. Shinnecock Inlet off Long Island, New York, has a predictable rip tide that extends nearly a thousand feet offshore. While rip currents kill more people each year, they can be navigated more easily than strong rip tides, which are often as uncontrollable as the sea itself.

The trajectory of young Billy Morgan's life was altered forever by a rip tide off Saint Simon's Island in coastal southern Georgia.

Billy grew up on the north side of Jacksonville, in a modest home on the Trout River, near the Main Street Bridge and the pier where the Trout River and St. Johns River converge. His father, Leonard Morgan, had risen over twenty-five years from laborer to plant superintendent of the JEA power company's Northside Generating Station a few miles downriver from his house. Once, when Leonard's car wouldn't start before work, he jumped in the 20' fishing boat tied to the dock in front of his house and used it for the commute, moving nimbly between the enormous barges and other commercial vessels that worked along the industrial portion of the river leading to its inlet with the Atlantic Ocean. He found a convenient spot in Nichols Creek alongside Heckscher Drive where he could tie the boat up within a short walk of the plant. Often thereafter, Leonard would take the boat to work just because he enjoyed the time on the water.

From his earliest years, Billy Morgan loved nothing so much as the water. By the time he was twelve years old, he was given free rein to use the family boat on the Trout River as long he stayed on the opposite side of the bridge from the larger, more dangerous St. Johns. Using the river and its innumerable tributary creeks, Billy and his best friend Jubal could access a huge swath of the city. They would mow yards in their neighborhood and use the money for the all-you-can-eat ribs at *The Piggie* barbeque restaurant on Lem Turner Drive, which they could access by stashing the boat under the nearby C. Ray Greene Bridge. Both boys saw their first naked boobs when they tried to sneak into the *Honey Pot* gentlemen's club on Trout River Boulevard. They were caught and thrown out almost immediately, but not before their lives were changed forever by the quick glimpse of flesh through a narrow opening in the bright purple curtains that separated the lobby from the lounge. Jubal's first job at age 16 was at *Beckman's Outboard Motors* as a helper and shop cleaner. Billy often dropped him off for work via a creek that ran along I-95.

Theirs was a coming of age in full, a throwback to a time before nervous modern parenting robbed children of the freedom to adventure and fail on their own. For Billy and Jubal, freedom would be associated with the water for the rest of their lives, one long and one lost early to the thing they most loved.

For spring break of their senior year in 2014 at Andrew Jackson High School, Billy, Jubal, and two girls they wished were their girlfriends piled into a Honda Civic and headed for a long weekend on Jekyll and Saint Simon's Islands, just over an hour north from their homes. The shops, restaurants, and nightlife were better on Saint Simon's, but it was the swankier of the two, and staying there was out of the kids' budget. They spent much of their trip on this nicer island but camped at night in tents on Jekyll Island.

On the second day of their trip, a Sunday morning to rival the second coming of Christ in splendor and consequence, the girls sunbathed on the northerly end of East Beach on Saint Simon's Island while Billy and Jubal threw a cast net for bait fish. They could see the even more exclusive Sea Island, home to a variety of professional golfers with aristocratic names, just across a shallow stretch of water called Gould's Inlet. Here, a saltwater creek, the brackish Blackbank River, and the Atlantic Ocean converge in a narrow bottleneck of waist to chest-deep water the boys had waded into chasing a school of finger mullet. Jubal threw the net, and Billy carried a five-gallon bucket into which they would dump their catch after each throw of the net. The sun was bright overhead in a clear sky, and the slack tide imbued the inlet with a stillness broken only by ripples from the moving fish and the splash of the net as it spread across the water in a wide circle.

For the better part of an hour, the boys worked the inlet as the tide began to turn. There was a moderate current as the tide moved out from the creeks and rivers, but nothing the boys couldn't easily walk against. When they had caught enough bait to fish the afternoon, they started across the inlet toward the girls on the beach. About halfway back, they stepped into a shallower section of the inlet, where the water went from just below chest-deep to around thigh-deep. This two-foot change in depth corresponded to a significantly stronger current, one the boys tried to push through carrying the net and bucket of bait fish. They made it three or four steps into the shallower water before being swept hard off their feet and pulled toward the open Atlantic.

The bucket was pulled out of Billy's hand immediately, but Jubal was rolled by the current into the cast net and bounced along the bottom, tangling into the net more as he went. Billy tried to reach out for his friend but found himself struggling in the incredible current, fighting to the point of exhaustion against the inexorable push of the water. Jubal was able to get his head above water from time to time for a breath of air, but shortly, Billy saw him surface less and less often. Luckily, one of the girls on the beach had witnessed the first moments of the boys' distress and called 911 immediately. In a fortunate coincidence that would save Billy Morgan's life, a small Coast Guard vessel was in the area and responded with remarkable speed.

Billy did not see the 25-foot Defender Class Coast Guard boat as it approached him. By then, he would later learn, he had swallowed a large amount of seawater and had stopped breathing. His first memory of the boat was waking up on its deck, spitting water on the Health Services Technician whose administering of CPR had brought him out of the darkness. His next memory was seeing the same work other crew members were doing on Jubal, work that seemed to Billy to go on forever. Eventually, though, the work stopped, and Jubal was gone.

In most lives, it's hard to point to a specific moment when a life's work has begun. Usually, people stumble into their careers or artistic and civic endeavors a little at a time as opportunities become available piece-meal, often by happenstance or the prearrangements of their social class. This was not the case for HT Morgan, who could contemplate his Coast Guard career and pinpoint the exact moment he knew he would become a Coastie.

On the deck of the Defender, beside his dead friend, Billy Morgan found the purpose of his life.

The irony and tragedy of the first minutes after the six islanders burst out of the door of the Gateway Marina is that Seaman Weaver had not intended to fire.

Hayes, Thomas, and the others were convinced the commotion of Jud and Luke's arrival had put innumerable enemy riflemen on high alert. They were certain those rifles would open up on them the minute they emerged from their besieged position. In reality, the shots that Thomas and Rolf fired at Jud Bollins had sent Seaman Recruit Hightower running back to the Sawfish to report as instructed, leaving only a single rifle pointed in their direction. Just as the door of the marina flew open, Officer Biscuit arrived in the Big Skiff Energy, barreling out of the inlet and into the small harbor into which a half dozen islanders were diving.

As though on cue from a theater tech director up in a booth some-where, a flash of moonlight found a hole in the darkness for an eternal two seconds, long enough for Seaman Weaver to be startled by the flash of light and movement, by a boat turning hard toward the trees to keep from hitting people as they were hitting the water. As quickly as it had raced across the scene, the light vanished again, covering everything in darkness that seemed twice as dark as before.

Disoriented first by the light and then the absence of it, Officer Biscuit managed to narrowly avoid running over his friends, but now his boat was out of control. He made the split-second decision to try to steer it back toward the inlet, but in the rush of doing so, never pulled back on the throttle. The Big Skiff Energy, the fastest boat in the Cedar Key Navy by a comfortable margin, even with the limitations imposed by the gasifier, was blowing past 30 miles per hour when it hit the bank and took flight toward the trees. Only then did Seaman Weaver discharge his weapon, mistaking the crashing sounds as enemy fire.

Seaman Weaver had been a Yeoman in the Coast Guard. After boot camp, he spent eight weeks training in Petaluma, California to earn the crossed quills insignia on his uniform, signifying he had mastered the mostly clerical duties of the Yeoman: human resources, record-keeping, accounting, and other office assistant skills. He was technically qualified on the M4 carbine rifle that he was now firing blindly into the night, but he had no real aptitude for it.

The islanders began surfacing, at various intervals, when they could no longer hold their breaths as they swam toward the river, trying to follow Luke's lead but struggling in the dark. Shots from Seaman Weaver continued to ring out, pushing them back under as soon as they could take a quick, frantic breath. The Coast Guard equips their M4s with 30-round magazines, and Seaman Weaver, in his panic, seemed determined to fire all of them at nothing.

On the boats, there had been unexpected restraint shown when the firing first began, but on shot twelve or thirteen, a round flew by Joey Bannon's head so closely he could feel the air moving across his cheek. When the sound of it hitting the water registered in Joey's ear, he fired his bolt-action Winchester in the direction from which he estimated the round had come. Almost immediately, shots began to fire from boats across the fleet until, shortly, a wall of sound and bullets were heading toward the trees.

"Cease fire, cease fire, cease fire!" the Colonel screamed, knowing they could do no good in the darkness and fearing the swimmers in the water would be caught in the crossfire. With no other options, Luke and the others swam on. As soon as the rounds fired from the boats began hitting all around him, Seaman Weaver turned and ran for the Sawfish. By the time the firing slowed and eventually stopped, the swimmers were well into the inlet and home free.

In the trees, the front third of the skiff had been torn away, and the keel was split down the middle on the remaining two-thirds all the way through the center console. The impact of the crash sent chunks of shattered fiberglass across a wide debris field, and the busted gasifier spilled its contents into a patch of pine straw that ignited, burned brightly for a few moments, and then went out.

The Big Skiff Energy was lost.

Officer Biscuit's body would be discovered the next day, gut shot and shot again in the back of his right leg, with no way of determining whether his injuries had come from Seaman Weaver or the boats in the river. The rest of his body was bent unnaturally from the skiff's impact against the trees, so the possibility remained that his life was ended before the rifles from either side could take it from him.

Half-cocked and foolish but no less gallant, Officer Biscuit had rushed in to help his friends because he was a friend worth having, paying for this valor with the last full measure of his devotion.

22

— • —

THE LONG NIGHT

Leadership is often revealed more sharply in adversity than in times of triumph. Already beleaguered by mounting losses and battling the internal guilt and rage that came for him the moment he saw his most senior petty officer, the closest thing he had to a friend in the world, dying on the floor of the Sawfish, Isaac Skipjack would have been forgiven if the news from Petty Officer Hightower, and then, shortly thereafter, Seaman Weaver had pushed him to careless vengeance.

The Senior Chief stayed the difficult course, refusing to allow the night to take any more of his crew. He took stock of his remaining fleet, considering the Atlas trawler lost due to its location in the effectively blockaded harbor of the Gateway Marina and its three crew dead, one of whose body was presently drifting along Seahorse Reef off Cedar Key, bound for points south in the Gulf. The rest of his boats were either moored with the Sawfish at the Suwannee Marina, a third of a mile from the enemy fleet, or in canals that could be traversed with little risk of confrontation. He dispatched the crews of the boats in the canals with orders to bring them into the main river abeam the Suwannee Marina and anchor there, side by side, readying for a head-on confrontation with the Cedar Key Navy he felt sure was coming at dawn whether he wanted it or not.

While he waited for the outlying boats, Isaac did what little he could to help HT Morgan, managing to get the wound above his eye to stop bleeding and cleaning another on his neck. When he reached the limit of his medical training, he used lifejackets to support his Health Service Technician's head and pulled an emergency blanket from the first aid kit over him. Isaac then led the boats at the marina into formation on the river, anchoring the Sawfish in the center with its 50-caliber machine guns pointed downrange toward an enemy fleet concealed in the darkness. It took some time for the rest of his fleet to arrive and set their anchors. Sailing in the narrow canals was nearly impossible, especially in the dark, so the crews generally had to either paddle or walk along the bank, pulling their boats with ropes.

When the formation was finalized, nine boats ranging in size from a 16-foot Carolina Skiff to the imposing 87-foot Coast Guard Cutter Sawfish were anchored across the river, waiting, joyless as Vladimir and Estragon, for death to arrive with the awful first light of morning. The Cedar Key Navy had more than double the number of Isaac's boats, but the Sawfish's firepower helped to even the odds. Whatever advantages or hindrances each side might have, everyone in the river that night knew the coming fight would exact a heavy toll on the winner and loser alike.

With the preparations made, Isaac checked again on HT Morgan, whose labored breathing unsettled him. With each new variation of wheeze or cough, Isaac steadied himself for the death rattle to come next, the haunting, inimitable sound he had experienced twice in his life, once when a neighbor backed over Henry, his coonhound puppy and the other as his mother tried to say some final words to him that were lost to the dying and the phlegm. At the bottom of each painful exhalation from HT Morgan, in that breathless second, slack like a dead winter tide, Isaac would despair, feeling certain no amount of strength could animate his friend again. Then another breath would find its beginning, restarting a tortured cycle Isaac could only stand for a few minutes at a time. He assigned his Yeoman to stay with the injured man at intervals when he had to get away.

Downriver, Luke led the swimmers through the inlet and into the river. Rolf and Ryland climbed aboard the Isabella with Randal Solaro while the others drifted to the Miss Jonya. Lizzy Fraydel was overjoyed to see Thomas. When he began to climb into the stone crab boat, she reached over the gunnel and snatched him out of the water like a doll, pulling him close and squeezing so hard it was painful and perfect to them both.

"I should have known you'd be here. You never listen," Thomas said, his feigned disapproval making them both smile.

"Shut up," Lizzy said, and he did, kissing her for all he was worth.

Luke sprang from the water with youthful ease while the injured Hayes and Jud worked their way to the back of the boat, where they could use the outboard motor's cavitation plate as a step. With Mr. Mark, Luke, Thomas, and Lizzy all pulling from above, Hayes and Jud made it into the boat.

Mark David had never been accused of being an effusive man. His affection was shown more often than spoken, a kind of emotional breviloquence that seemed spartan only to those who didn't know him well. If Mark David loved you, you didn't need to hear it out loud—you just knew. When he saw his boy limping toward him, the elder David met him halfway, ignoring the normal ritual of their too-firm handshake and pulling him close.

"Hey, Dad. I was coming to get you."

"I know, son. Your dang mama was eavesdropping on us in the shed, I guess?"

"Yes, sir."

"That figures."

Before either man could think of what to say next, a suffocating silence bloomed between them.

As much to find the air to breathe again as anything else, Hayes said, "Sorry I didn't make it to you."

The old man smiled.

"You would have, son."

Hayes nodded, then the David men turned to the work at hand.

Throughout the history of human warfare, the first light of dawn has played an outsized strategic and psychological role in deciding conflicts. Strategically, attacking at dawn provided a marked advantage to an attacking force because they could move into close position in the night and then use the morning's first light for a surprise attack on an enemy that was hopefully unprepared or, at a minimum, whose eyes had not yet adjusted to the light and would therefore be less able to make out the advancing enemy. Generals from Alexander at the Battle of Granicus to Napolean at Rivoli have used this tactic to great success.

One of the most famous dawn attacks in the Western world occurred at the Battle of Agincourt in October of 1415, during the *Hundred Years' War* between England and France. The war was waged intermittently over 116 years, with multi-year stretches of peace interspersed throughout. After a long such stretch of relative peace, England resumed hostilities in 1415, but thereafter, the English army began to suffer significant losses to disease. As a result, the French grew to enjoy at least a two-to-one advantage on the battlefield. While trying to withdraw to English-held Calais in northern France, along the Strait of Dover, the English found their path blocked by the superior French forces.

Led by King Henry V himself, the English launched a surprise dawn attack where English archers, positioned in the mud, fired a relentless volley of arrows in the faint morning light that devastated the French ranks and paved the way for the British to win a decisive victory in brutal, muddy, hand-to-hand conflict. More than 6,000 French soldiers were killed. The battle was such a stunning victory that it paved the way for fourteen years of subsequent English dominance before they were defeated again at the Battle of Orleans in 1429.

The surprise dawn attack at the Battle of Agincourt gave rise to King Henry's famous *Saint Crispin's Day Speech*, immortalized by William Shakespeare in his play *Henry V*. This is the speech that coined the term *Band of Brothers* that grew to represent the deep bonds forged between men in battle. As the dawn approached like a tiger in the night, Shakespeare's version of King Henry says:

> *This story shall the good man teach his son*
> *And Crispin Crispian shall ne'er go by,*
> *From this day to the ending of the world*
> *But we in it shall be remember'd*
> *We few, we happy few, we band of brothers.*

The real King Henry did, in fact, give a speech before the battle, but it bore little resemblance to Shakespeare's more elegant account. The sentiment, however, remained the same—as a new day approached, a day that would no doubt bring misery, those soldiers who waited together for the terrible dawn to break would be linked forever in memory, in sacrifice, in sacred honor.

On the Suwannee, as in Agincourt, bands of brothers and sisters waited for death to come in the morning, clinging to the comfort of the night.

"Let's form up close together," Hayes announced over the radio. "Gunnel to gunnel, across the river as far we make it, with the Miss Jonya in the middle. That way, we can step from boat to boat. Pass the word to the boats without radios."

Other captains acknowledged Hayes' directive, and slowly, the fleet began to assemble together.

Hayes added, "Once we're set, let's all muster on the Miss Jonya and the few boats near it so everybody can hear each other. We need to make a plan."

The screeching chirps of mud hens echoed along the river, a natural levity to the eerie whooping of barred owls in the trees and the loud, mournful song of limpkins as they foraged apple snails on the muddy river bank. Individual seconds lingered like a winter cold as the intransient night held everything in its mortal grasp. Women and men in boats on both sides of the neutral water between them bristled in the cold and made idle talk to hold off the enveloping dread of a thing none were sure they could do when the time arrived.

On the Miss Jonya, Hayes David spoke to his navy, evoking FDR as he leaned against the helm to take the pressure off his mangled foot and minimize any sign of his distress.

"Thank you, Luke, for rounding up what looks like most of the island, and thank all y'all for coming. Seems like a bunch of us have had some kind of run-in with the sailing boats by now. Now's a good time to share everything you know, no matter how small the detail. The more we know about 'em, the better we can fight 'em."

The Colonel spoke up first. "Most of their boats are regular boats like ours, just with sails, so we have the advantage in speed and maneuverability. But the big boat is a problem."

"No shit," Rolf said.

The Colonel continued, "There are two 50-caliber machine guns on its bow, and they've got crates of ammo for it. Those things will cut through us like a buzzsaw."

"Seems like they have plenty of rifles, too," Hayes said. "When they opened up on us at the Gateway, it felt like a whole army."

"The guys that shot at us on my bird dog and killed Allen had assault rifles," Mark David added. "I heard their medic say it was a five-five-six round that hit him."

Hayes asked, "Any idea how many total men they have?"

"Percy said he saw about twenty or so going house to house looting," Ryland replied.

The Colonel said, "There were twenty-seven of them when they first got to Cabbage Key, all piled onto the big boat that shot my plane down. They found ten more boats over the several months they were there and got nine outfitted with sails. Before they left to come here, Isaac killed one of his crew, and I—"

"He did what?" Mark David interrupted.

Even then, knowing that his own son had died at the hands of Isaac's crew, that his friends were shot up and Officer Biscuit was almost certainly dead in the trees, knowing full well that he would have been left on Cabbage Key with no prospects for ever getting home again, the Colonel had a strange impulse in his gut to defend Isaac's killing of Seaman Recruit Butler. It was possible the impulse was self-serving—believing in the necessity of Seaman Recruit Butler's death paved the way to justify his own killing of Seaman Apprentice Jensen—but some part of the Colonel still believed in the basic goodness of Isaac Skipjack.

"He had to," the Colonel said flatly. "They lost another one as well, so as far as I know, twenty-five made it here all total."

Hayes said, "Rolf got two on Deer Island and three more on the trawler... so twenty seems about right."

"The old man with the M60 had to have hit somebody," Mark replied.

"So maybe even less than twenty," Hayes said. "What's our count?"

"Sixty-three total on twenty-four boats before the Big Skiff Energy went in the trees," Luke said. "I saw it when I came up for air. I want to lead a team into the woods to try to find Biscuit."

"I saw it too, son," Thomas interjected. "We don't know how many guns are still in those trees, and the odds of him surviving that crash are close to zero, not even considering the fire he was right in the middle of."

Hayes said, "Biscuit would appreciate what you're trying to do, Luke. We all appreciate it, but your dad's right. We can't risk losing anybody else tonight. As soon we figure out what the morning brings... when we know what we're up against... we'll go looking for him if he don't swim into the river before then."

Luke was dissatisfied with the answer because he was young and flooded with emotion, but he knew the older men were right.

"How we looking on guns?" Rolf asked.

Rick Brown, an oysterman with an outlaw reputation that mischaracterized the decent, competent man attached to it, replied, "Sounds like we're not doing that good, compared to .50 cals and twenty military rifles. I've just got my bolt-action deer rifle. Every one of theirs will put eight or ten rounds down range for every one of mine."

"That math is bad for us," replied Cousin Samantha. "I know we have a handful of AR-15s, but not enough, and Joff Sleady brought a bow and arrow."

"That's what I had," Joff protested.

"We've got some extras. We'll get Joff a rifle," Hayes said.

"We're still in a bad spot," Jim Beck said. "Even with three times more of us, we'll be outgunned. I'm a botanist, not a soldier. I've shot my rifle maybe ten times in my whole life. They're gonna be a lot better at this than some of us."

Dale Warble, who ran a golf cart rental company in the old world, pushed back. "But we're fighting for our home. That's gotta count for something."

"This doesn't look like Cedar Key to me," replied Benji Iver, whose coffee shop had been taken by the great fire.

Of course, everyone gathered there on the boats understood the concept of fighting them where they were before they came back to the island, and the Colonel's account of his time on Cabbage Key left little doubt about Isaac's intentions, but the physical reality of the cold night on the water, in a river town that was not their own, was enough to give pause to even the most hawkish among them.

"I don't know how much what we're fighting for matters when it comes to their guns against ours," Hayes said. "We're definitely up against it. But you all came here because it has to be done. If anyone else feels different, now's the time to speak up. There's nothing between you and Cedar Key.

You could back right out of this river, and you'd be home in bed in an hour."

No one spoke up; maybe no one ever could speak up in a situation such as that and maybe wars go on forever because they must.

"No one's backing out of anything," Ryland said. "And Thomas and I can help with the guns."

"We can?" Thomas asked.

"Percy's house," Ryland replied.

The sound of the wild old man's name filled Thomas with bittersweet excitement. He had not witnessed Percy's gallantry on his and his friends' behalf, but everyone had heard the sound of his charge against the rifles in the trees.

"Of course," Thomas said. "Percy said he would help us if he could and now he's doing it double. His arsenal will give us a fighting chance."

"How many guns we talking?" Rick Brown asked.

"Enough that he was definitely on some kind of government list," Ryland said with a smile.

"My kind of guy," Nick replied.

Thomas and Ryland filled everyone in on the details of what they had seen in Percy's house, then formulated a plan to go get the guns. Hayes would stay with the bulk of the fleet while Thomas, Ryland, Nick, and Rolf took Nick's skiff downriver to the canal where the Cogency was left earlier in the day. Between the two boats, there was room to carry more guns and ammo than they could possibly use in the fight ahead, and, to the mayor's delight, he would get his boat back to marshal into the fight.

"Alright, fellas, get that done and get back here as quick as you can," Hayes said. "For everyone else, let's shut down the gasifiers. We don't have enough wood to run all night and tomorrow. Sunrise is just before seven. I'm wearing my granddaddy's watch. It's a wind-up and still working, so

I'll keep an eye on the time. We need to start the fires again no later than six. If in doubt, keep a watch on the Miss Jonya. When you see its gasifier burning, get yours going, too. Take turns standing watch so everyone can get a little sleep."

Upriver on the Sawfish, Isaac had assembled his crew as well. All but the Yeoman and HT Morgan met on the top deck to make their own plans. From their perspective, it was they, not the islanders, who were facing long odds. Earlier, when they pulled back from the trees in dwindling twilight, it had seemed to them that an endless navy was amassing against them in the river. There would be no Saint Crispin's Day speech on either end of the Suwannee that night. Isaac Skipjack was given even less to rhetorical flourish than Hayes David. For the first time since he took the young Coasties into his charge, to save them from the officious lunatic Lieutenant Dupont, Isaac relaxed his hold a little on the reins of authority he had so scrupulously maintained thus far. It had been his duty to be that authority, at the cost of personal isolation, because the young crew needed it. The one subordinate with whom he could occasionally talk openly was dying on the floor of the pilot house, like Snowden in the belly of the plane, and Isaac felt, more than ever before in a mostly friendless life, totally alone.

"The wind and current are against us, but we could try to make a run further upriver," Isaac said. "We'd make it as far north as the State Road 51 bridge near Mayo. It's too low for the Sawfish to sail under, so if they're determined to fight us, we'll have to do it here or do it there."

Seaman Bartholomew, still shaken from watching Petty Officer Palmer die in her arms, said hesitantly, "I don't mean to question you, Senior Chief. I'm thankful for everything you've done for us. Everybody here knows we'd be dead already without you... but are those really the only two options? Fight here or fight there? Against all those boats?"

With a disarming warmth, Isaac said, "It's okay, Sarah. I'm questioning it, too. That's why we're here talking."

In their year together, Isaac had never called any of his crew by their first name, so a response he had meant to be comforting had the opposite effect. In a new world of constant upheaval and change, the Senior Chief's implacability had been a singular source of comfort for them all, but something in the stillness of the slow night, as time malingered to avoid its passing and the nocturnal advance of self-doubt moved against him in rolling waves, in that leaden progression from moment to regretful moment, he no longer believed he could protect his crew on the strength of authority alone, so Isaac made the tactical mistake of telling them the truth.

"I'll just level with you," Isaac said. "We were out of options. We would have run out of water in a few more weeks on Cabbage Key. You all saw the troubles we had that first month trying to find somewhere to go. When I found Robert's letters about Cedar Key, I thought we might have found a place where we could have a real shot at living. I might have gotten you out of harm's way when the bombs were falling, but I'm the reason we're in this trouble now."

"How do you figure?" asked Petty Officer Chamberlain, a ruddy-faced Aviation Maintenance Technician whose once highly-valued training had been of so little use in the new world he often felt like an outsider in the crew.

"The reason I didn't think to sail for Cedar Key before finding Robert's letters is because I grew up on that island. I've got some history there that I've spent the past twenty-four years trying to forget. I ran off to the Coast Guard to get away from it, but somehow, it found me at the end of the world and now you are all in trouble because of it. I should have told you all of this before I asked you to come here with me."

"You didn't have to ask us anything," Seaman Bartholomew said. "You're the Senior Chief. We were gonna go wherever you told us to."

"That's exactly why I should have told you. That navy downriver is here because I made a mistake with Robert," Isaac said. His pained face held sullen eyes that seemed to be looking at everyone and no one as he spoke. "That first hard month convinced me that everyone outside of this crew was a threat, but over time, I believed Robert had grown to be one of us. When I learned about his deception, that he had been the pilot in the little plane I wrongly ordered you to shoot down, I knew that if he made it back to Cedar Key, he would tell them, and we'd never be welcome there. Of course he would, and he'd be right to do it. So I had to treat him like an enemy."

"He was an enemy," Seaman Bartholomew said sharply. "He killed Jensen."

"I killed her," Isaac replied. "When I locked Robert up and told him we were leaving him behind. I hate him for what he did, but I don't blame him."

"What other choice did you have?" Petty Officer Chamberlain asked.

"What other choice did he have?" Isaac replied. "He saw what I was and knew he had to warn his people I was coming, that I would take what they had to save this crew. He was right. I would have. The only duty I have left on this Earth is to all of you, but I failed you the minute I ordered you to fire on that little plane, and I failed Jensen when I put her between Robert and his people. It was bad luck we ran into that stupid pontoon boat in the fog that started all the killing and sent us up this goddamn river... but as soon as Robert took off from the beach, we were always in for a fight by coming to Cedar Key."

"All the same," Petty Officer Hightower replied, "We still had to come."

"We did," Isaac said. "But I let my personal affection for Robert cloud my judgment. If Cedar Key was our last option, a better leader would have put Robert against a wall instead of leaving him in that room to do what he did."

All of it was in the open now, every indefensible action said out loud, and Isaac knew he had failed his crew, not just in deed but in the self-indulgence of admitting the failure, taking away the one thing he had left to offer them: a reason to believe he could lead them still.

Isaac stared blankly across the dark river and despaired. All of this was his fault.

The long night marched on.

23

FIRST LIGHT

The Cogency was still tied to the dock where it was left earlier in the day. Something about the sight of the familiar boat, commissioned as the new flagship after the loss of the Blue Lang in the Number Four Channel months prior, was comforting to Luke.

He had been manning a mounted rifle near the bow of the Blue Lang that foggy morning when a pinhole breach in the gasifier chamber sent pressurized gasses into its firebox, blowing apart the rear third of the enormous vessel and sending it to the bottom of the channel. Thomas Buck had been on the stern of the flagship, absorbing the worst of the explosion but miraculously surviving despite being thrown more than fifty feet away into the water. For several frantic minutes, Luke had searched for his father in the fog and water, calling out for him and screaming to the others for help. When at last his father appeared, blood-soaked but steady, the inciting events that had put the flagship on a war footing—a few homemade flags planted around the island and graffiti scrawled across the water tower—seemed cartoonishly irrelevant. Mobilizing the navy to search for imagined enemies had almost taken his father from him. Luke spent the somber ride home on the rescuing Miss Jonya feeling, more than anything else, ashamed.

Now, Thomas and Ryland led the way to Percy's house, while Rolf, Luke and Nick followed. As before, the outside stairs leading to the elevated house were perilous, even more so in the dark. A handful of treads were cracked or missing altogether, and the handrail had long ago abandoned its post. Feeling reasonably sure their own navy was between themselves and the sailing ships, Thomas risked turning on a rechargeable flashlight, deploying it as stealthily as possible to light their path up to the house. When they stepped inside, Thomas shone the light on the rows of gun cases along the walls and the boxes of ammunition piled high on the kitchen counter.

"Whoa," Nick Brown said, his eyes widening like Augustus Gloop in the chocolate factory.

"I told you," Ryland said.

Luke added, "I don't think Bickett's Weaponry over in Newberry ever had this many guns in their shop at one time."

"I saw some five-gallon buckets under the house," Rolf said. "I'll go get them for us to put the ammo boxes in."

Any dark room illuminated by a flashlight takes on an eerie countenance but heightened as the night was by the building drums of war, the harsh, focused light on the rows of hanging rifles felt like a glimpse into a mausoleum of soldiers waiting to rise again on the eve of battle. The islanders bypassed the bolt-action weapons and began carrying semi-automatic long guns, four or five at a time, to the Cogency. Rolf carried a full bucket of ammunition boxes in each hand on every trip.

In an hour's time, the bulk of Percy's lethal collection, one he had spent a lifetime carefully curating on both sides of the law, was piled onto the decks of the Cogency and Nick Black's skiff. Rather than taking the time to start a fire and wait for the Cogency's gasifier to begin producing the wood gas that powered its motor, Nick tossed a line to the larger boat and slowly towed it back to the assembled fleet.

The sight of the rifles piled high on both boats sent a wave of optimism from one end of the Cedar Key Navy to the other. The instant spike in morale led to cheers and raucous whooping that Hayes had initially thought to quell before deciding to let them continue in hopes they would demoralize their opponents on the boats upriver. There was no risk of giving away a position the enemy already knew they held, and with hours more to go before the dawn, hours that would continue, after this short reprieve, to sow fear and worry in every man and woman on the cold river, Hayes, as much as anyone else, needed a break in the pressure.

In March of 1867, twenty-eight-year-old John Muir, who would become a noted naturalist, conservationist, author, botanist, philosopher, political activist, zoologist, geologist, and eventual founder of the Sierra Club, nearly lost his vision in an industrial accident. Over six weeks of recovery in the darkness, Muir began to see his life in a different light.

Of his convalescence, Muir wrote:

"This affliction has driven me to the sweet fields. God has to nearly kill us sometimes to teach us lessons."

Later that year, influenced by the life's work of the Prussian explorer Alexander von Humboldt, Muir departed Louisville, Kentucky, on a thousand-mile walk to Florida. He had no specific route planned except to travel by *the wildest, leafiest, and least trodden way* he could find. He meandered through Tennessee and North Carolina to Savannah, Georgia, then into northeastern Florida at Fernandina. From there, he cut a fairly straight path to Gainesville, and finally, seven weeks after his walk began, he arrived in Cedar Key in October of 1867, two years after the end of the Civil War.

Muir recorded his observations of the natural and human world he encountered as he walked through the devastated South, writing:

The traces of war are not only apparent on the broken fields, mills, and woods ruthlessly slaughtered, but also on the countenances of the people.

Upon his arrival in Cedar Key, he took a job at the Hodgson Sawmill to earn money for passage on a schooner to Texas, where he planned to catch a ship to Cuba for his next adventure, but Cedar Key often has different plans for its inhabitants than the ones they devise for themselves. The island has a way of swallowing up or spitting people out, with no discernible criteria for its judgment one way or the other. So it was with John Muir; having survived a thousand miles of often inhospitable wilderness on his journey to Cedar Key, he fell into a malaria-induced coma days after his arrival. Only the extraordinary care of Richard and Sara Hodgson, whom Muir described as having *that unconstrained cordiality which is characteristic of the better class of Southern people*, saved his life.

For months, while sick enough for the kind of reflection that digs deep into a man, Muir would stare across the placid bay from Cedar Key, deconstructing the religions of man and pledging fealty to the *immortal truth and immortal beauty of nature*. There, he laid the philosophical groundwork for a dazzling life's work protecting and conserving the natural resources of a world his ancestors, a century and a half on, would incinerate in a flash of human derangement.

Over the next thousand years, perhaps, the lessons John Muir had nearly been killed to learn would have to be taught again.

On the Sawfish and surrounding boats in Isaac's fleet, the cheering from the island navy had its intended effect. Especially among the youngest of the crew, the two Seaman Recruits and four Seaman Apprentices—none of whom were more than twenty-one years old—the revelry downriver was as unnerving as Viking berserkers.

Fortunately, it had the opposite effect on Senior Chief Skipjack. The cheering struck him as obscene and served to instantly transmute his despair into anger. As a younger man, this anger would have quickly and uncontrollably spilled over into the kind of rage that left Bob Corliss in a pummeled heap on the ground outside the hardware store, and his airplane smashed up and kicked half apart. Now, constrained by the natural temperance that comes with age and refined by two decades of military leadership, Isaac's anger was targeted and useful. He sprang from his self-pity, compartmentalizing the failures he had foolishly and selfishly spoken out loud, and shifted his focus to the preparations needed to face the larger enemy navy.

For two hours, Isaac moved almost continuously, directing his young crew in the positioning of ammunition near tactical positions he picked for them to man on each boat. He personally carried ninety green metal ammo cans, the kind ubiquitous in military surplus stores, and piled them around the .50 caliber machine guns. The cans weighed seventy pounds apiece, containing a belt of one hundred of the enormous rounds, each nearly five and a half inches long. The holes these rounds would punch in a fiberglass boat would send water rushing into their hulls like U-boat torpedoes into the Lusitania. The holes they would punch in clam farmers, oystermen, blue-crabbers, and coffee shop owners would sink them even faster than the boats. The cheering downriver had long faded, but Isaac worked on. He positioned the boats in his fleet farther away from each other to make them more difficult targets, fanning them out in a crude arc so their fire could hit the enemy from multiple angles.

In the distance, a soft orange glow danced on the water.

Against the flat black of the water and sky, darker now than it had been even at the witching hour, the spritely little flicker summoned dragons in the minds of Isaac's crew, rattling even the most stoic among them. Until now, dawn was a distant vision, an allegory, a myth carved in archetype to teach a formless lesson, a nostalgia, the fearful worry of a bad beginning, a quality of light seen in dreams or memory but not by human eyes weakened in the dark—footlights along the path to the end.

Another light, then five more, and finally twenty-four frenetic gasifier demons danced in the smoke, exalting in the waning hour of the night, giving flickering form to the island navy, expanding its size in the abstraction of the low firelight, singing confusing up-tempo dirges that grew louder as they traveled upstream across the swift water of the river.

First light was coming.

Isaac could feel his crew's renewed esprit de corps being overwhelmed by the haunting lights because even he was affected by them. As he began to rally them to stay focused on the work at hand, on readying to defend each other against the coming attack, Seaman Weaver emerged from the pilot house.

"Senior Chief, it's Morgan. Come quick!"

Isaac dropped the belt of ammunition he had been feeding into one of the .50 caliber guns, the phallic, depraved machines on which his crew's survival would rest, and raced for the pilot house. Inside, he found HT Morgan no longer flat on the floor but leaning, impossibly, against a side wall. His sallow face and gray eyes gave him a corpselike languor disturbed only by the weak rising and falling of his chest. Ragged breaths somehow continued to move in and out of one good lung, and one collapsed by a fire extinguisher swung hard into him by Mark David escaping captivity.

The sight of him there, in his defeat, peering into the next life but fighting against the bewitchment of its call, was too much, at last, for Isaac to bear.

He sat beside his petty officer, his friend if ever he had such a thing, and wept. The tears that came were from a storehouse long neglected and full. They came for a motherless boy with a skipped tooth. They came, of course, for Buddy Skipjack in the boat of stolen clams, a father struck down in the desperate business of loving a son, and they came, hardest yet, for the surrogate father on the bird dog boat he had loved fearfully and loved still.

When the last of the tears had been shed, Isaac made a command decision.

Downriver, as the first rays of light began to infiltrate the darkness, the island navy was stricken with the same primitive fear the gasifier lights had caused in Isaac's crew. Hayes did what he could to steady his own nerves, but the moment was fast approaching when the terrible light of morning could wait no longer.

"This is it!" Hayes yelled across the row of boats. "Be ready and wait for my order. No one fires until I say so, then give them everything you've got until there's nothing left."

Sixty-three semi-automatic rifles, forty of which had come from Percy's house, raised to the shoulders of men and women who were, save for the Angel of Death, ill-suited for the grim work they were about to undertake.

The light rushed in.

"Steady!" Hayes called out. "Not yet!"

On both ends of the short expanse of water, those who were about to die hung in the suspended animation of dawn, listening for the war to start.

When it seemed another half-second of tension would explode the hearts of every living thing on the river, an inflatable boat appeared from the rear of the Sawfish, drifting innocently as a cloud into the swift current. Isaac Skipjack waved a cut-out section of a white sail above his head in wide, slow movements as he floated toward the island navy, holding HT Morgan across his lap, doing his best to support his head with one arm as he waved the makeshift white flag with the other.

For several seconds, a shocked stagnation overtyped the scene until finally, Hayes called out, "Hold! Hold! Hold! Nobody fire!"

Joey Bannon, rattled and afraid, heard only *fire* and pulled back on the trigger of his rifle. The fact that no chain reaction followed, no torrent of bullets passing each other across the water, was providence or dumb luck or the intervention at last of a negligent God distracted by beauty elsewhere in the universe. However the intercession had come, by happenstance or paralysis or the Blood of Christ, the normally skillful marksman fired three rounds harmlessly into the water before Mark David jumped from the adjacent boat and tackled Joey Bannon hard onto the deck.

"Hold! Hold! Hold!" Hayes screamed again as Issac and HT Morgan arrived at the bow of the Miss Jonya.

Hayes ran across three boats to meet them there, reaching over the gunnel of Jud Bollins' boat and grabbing the side of the inflatable vessel.

"What are you doing, Skipper?" Hayes asked in a frenzy.

"Help him, please," Isaac replied, wild-eyed and shaking. "You can shoot me where I sit, and my crew won't fire another shot, I swear. On my daddy, on Miss Bette, on anything you want, I swear if you'll take my medic back to your clinic and do what you can to save him, we'll stand down for good. Please, Hayes. Mr. Mark, please!"

Mark David did not wait for Hayes to respond, climbing over his son and onto the boat with Isaac.

"Give me a hand and help me get him out of here," Mark said.

There was a moment of hesitation where no one moved, and nothing was said.

"You sure about this? What if it's a trap?" Benji Iver asked.

"Now, goddamn it. Help me!" Mark exploded.

The Colonel reached toward the man who would have left him to die, extending a hand that Isaac grasped for support while he helped Mark David move HT Morgan toward the waiting arms of the crew onboard the Miss Jonya.

When all three men were safely aboard the big stone crab boat, Mark said to his son, "The Cogency is the fastest after Luke's skiff. Pull the anchor and bring it alongside Jud's boat. I did this. I'll take him myself."

"Dad..."

"Now, son."

There would be details to work out, beginning with Isaac's pledge that he would never again sail further south than the Suwannee Sound, but as Mark David turned the Cogency for home, toward the clinic, toward something short of absolution, and pushed the throttle full, Isaac fired a red flare into the dawn's early light and the Coasties in his charge laid down their guns. Neither side had strong cause to trust the other, but neither were they compelled to die that day if they didn't have to.

Wars have been started and ended for more and for less throughout the history of man. There would be time to contemplate the vicious absurdity of the Two-Day War, to heal from injuries external and within, and to pass judgment on all for whom it was warranted.

For now, as suddenly as it was begun, the war was over.

Over six hard months, roughly the same amount of time it took John Muir to recover from malaria on Cedar Key, HT Morgan regained his health.

During this time, especially after the first several weeks when he was still unable to speak, Nurse Toni and HT Morgan struck up a friendship as they compared the different paths each had taken in the medical profession. As they shared their knowledge and training with each other, they naturally grew closer. The forty-nine-year-old Nurse Practitioner began to feel a stirring in her heart for the young Health Services Technician that had lain dormant since she was widowed to the great hurricane the previous year. HT Morgan was powerless against her rare beauty and confident demeanor, but even if he could have mounted a defense against her, he found no cause to resist. In the old world, especially in an island town as small as any in Faulker's Yoknapatawpha County, such a May-December attraction would set the rumor mill alight. In the new world, no one batted a scandalized eyelash.

It had been a good half year, all things considered, since the long night on the river. Sierra Solaro's baby was strong and chubby. Luke and Kinsey were expecting Thomas' first grandson in the autumn—William, if it was a boy. Lizzy Fraydel's garden was bountiful once again. Tabby Lowery's affection for the mayor continued to grow unchecked despite his missing right toe, which she lovingly called the perfect match to the left ear that was shot off in the Second Battle of Cedar Key. She'd take what amount of him she could get, she would say, and Hayes loved her for it. Aided by the love of his doting wife, Jenny, The Angel of Death mellowed in peacetime, and the world was safer for it. Hayes, Thomas, and Rolf continued their unassailable devotion to one another, trading phosphate pits for the Wacassassa Bay.

Concurrent with HT Morgan's journey to health, the David family patriarch began a relatively slow but steady decline. Nurse Toni did what she could to manage a growing list of ailments that slowed the rugged waterman a little more each week. By the time it was decided that HT Morgan had recovered enough to return to his crew in Suwannee, Mark David was spending most days of the week in bed. Occasionally, he would find the strength to amble to the back porch of his nineteenth-century house and sit on the swing there with Miss Bette, the only woman who had ever held his attention, the north star toward which his heart had always pointed. They would canoodle on the swing like they had as teenagers on the bench seat of whatever old truck Mark David was driving, taking breaks here and there to catch their breath and appreciate the slow passing of an island afternoon.

When Hayes and HT Morgan arrived at the Cogency in the back canal off 3rd Street, they found Mark David sitting on the gunnel of the boat with his feet resting on a thick bundle of mullet net, grinning like a bobcat in the scrub.

It was his last day, and he knew it.

When he woke that morning, there was an unnatural spryness in his step, a burst of vitality that a man with less wisdom would mistake as a sign he might yet have more time. Mark David had lived his life in rhythm with the tides and the phases of the moon. He could track a school of mullet by the faintest ripples on the water and knew when big weather was coming by the way the air smelled the day before. A man thus perceptive to the immortal truth and immortal beauty of nature knew his place in it and when his time there was at an end.

"Before you say anything, just don't. I'm coming," Mark David announced.

Hayes was his father's son, intuitive and smart. While he did not share the hard knowledge that had brought Mark David to the boat that day, he knew that days on the water with his dad were numbered, so he was glad to see the old man and the net.

"Sounds good, Dad," Hayes said. "We fishing today?"

"Thought we might bring a few back for your mama to make her smoked mullet dip."

Hayes took the long way to Suwannee to make the time go slower, through the back waters, past Hog Island where his great grandmother Emma raised hogs to sell to passing boats, and finally into the wide, old river through Harden Creek.

When the Cogency pulled into the Suwannee Marina, Hayes was glad to see the Sawfish moored to the dock and Isaac coming out of the pilot house to meet them. He had returned here a handful of times to give Isaac an update on HT Morgan's progress and to quietly assess the state of things with Isaac and his crew, deciding, some months back, that they were no longer a threat. The Suwannee and its springs held all the freshwater the Coasties could ever need, and over time, they made peace with the few locals remaining in the outlaw river town. The life Isaac had been willing to kill for was finally happening all around his crew. HT Morgan was met with enthusiasm and excitement.

"Can you stay for a meal?" Isaac asked.

"We're short on time," Mark David replied. "But I was hoping you might chase a few mullet with us before we had to head back."

"Absolutely," Isaac replied.

There was much to handle between the two men, but nothing that needed to be said.

Hayes steered the Cogency through the river and back into the creeks until his father pointed at the ripples ahead.

Mark David began to let out the familiar old net, the one he refused to let the government take from him, the one that had fed three generations of the David family.

"Grab the other end and help him, Skipper," Hayes said.

The old man looked across the water and took it all in—the mullet were running, the sun was shining on his face, and he was fishing with his sons again.

Acknowledgements

G.M. Palmer introduced me to T.S. Eliot, R.E.M., and, disastrously, single-malt scotch whiskey. He also turned out to be a top-shelf editor and even better friend. This book, and my writing life in general, would not have been possible without our thirty-year collaboration. G.M. Palmer, Jac Coil, Jimmy Weaver, Morgan Droz, Drew Crawford, and myself were the inspiration for the boys in the *Dangerous, Deep Waters* chapter. I hope everyone cultivates that kind of friendship in their lives. It has meant everything to me.

My life in Cedar Key is immeasurably better because of the Davis family, who welcomed a straggler from the mainland into their fold when he needed it most. Thanks, Mr. Mike, Miss Beth, Heath, Ida Marie and Stephanie May. I'm proud to be one of you.

Mills the Dragon, my friend and brother, was savagely taken from this world as I was writing the final pages of this book. His loving, probing, joyful spirit is bounding through the cosmos once again, zipping with frenetic joy and a deep belly laugh from one universe to the next, singing that Johnathan Colton song we both love and finding beautiful connections in the deepest, darkest parts of space like he always did here on Earth with all of us. I love you, Mills.

To the real life Lizzy Fraydel, on whom I rely for so much: You and me, now and always.